NIKOLAI DANTE
THE GREAT

NIKOLAI DANTE CREATE... & SIMON FRASER

THE STORY SO FAR...

IT WAS IN THE YEAR OF THE TSAR 2666 AD WHEN NIKOLAI DANTE FIRST APPEARED IN THE IMPERIAL COURT OF VLADIMIR THE CONQUEROR — on trial as a thief. But in his wisdom the Tsar elected to spare Dante's life, and recruited him into the Imperial Raven Corps, under the direct command of his daughter, Jena Makarov.

Dante's first mission as a Raven had unpredictable results. Tasked to recover a crashed spacecraft belonging to the Romanov family — a powerful and mysterious dynasty, which had long been locked in a powerplay with the Makarovs — he became "bio-bonded" to a sentient device known as a "Weapons Crest".

The effects of this Crest became immediately apparent as Jena and Dante were attacked by two members of the Romanov family; twins Aleksandr and Aleksandra. These Romanovs manifested bizarre powers, including imperviousness to bullets and nano-weaponry produced directly from the body, before melding into a single super-being. Dante, however, countered this with biologically produced blades extruded from his hands, slaying the Romanovs... and in the process he discovered his own heritage as a half-breed Romanov.

Dante typically "researched" his past by marching directly into the Romanov Winter Palace, where a showdown with Dmitri Romanov (head of the dynasty), Jena Makarov, and the Tsar himself led to Dante re-embracing his "family"... and entering their service. He also survived an assassination attempt by the wife of Count Pyre, the Tsar's personal bodyguard, but at the cost of her life — making Pyre an enemy for the rest of his life.

Dante acquitted himself well on his first adventure as a Romanov, ridding the city of Rudinshtein from a vicious band of thugs, addicted to the proscribed drug "Chert". During this mission, Dante encountered several other members of the Romanov family — Arkady, the youngest son, who had been destined to receive the Weapons Crest that Dante intercepted; Konstantin, the eldest, with the power to generate fusion energy; Lulu, creator of all-devouring cybernetic entities; Viktor, whose powers remain unknown; Andreas, who can generate projectile blades; and finally Nastasia, the "Romanov bitch", who can produce lethal poisons and acids. Dante also discovered that he was a child born of Dmitri Romanov and legendary pirate-queen Katarina Dante... but not born out of love.

Perhaps needing relaxation after the strains of Rudinshtein, Dante next made his way to the famed Hotel Yalta, where he appears to have financed a life of extreme pleasure by acting as a mysterious masked thief — however, even here, Dante met his match in the seductive Contessa de Winter, a thief even more able than he.

Returning to Moscow for a lavish party at the Tsar's palace, Dante was again embroiled in an assassination plot, this time leading to the death of Jena's fencing master, and again hardening her heart against Dante, who by now was clearly falling for her.

During his second mission for the Romanov family, Dante travelled to the gulag-world of Samovar, as a bodyguard to the Lady Khara. It soon transpired that Khara was more than she seemed — in fact, she was from another race and planet entirely. Khara's people were vastly more technologically advanced than humanity, but had split into pro- and anti-human factions. Khara's faction, on the side of humanity, had made a deal with the Romanovs — the Weapons Crest technology for a steady supply of human genetic material, delivered to them via the gulag. During this mission, Dante successfully killed a "White Army Reiver", a high-tech soldier allied to the anti-human alien faction; in recognition of this (and a night together), Khara gave Dante the Huntsman 5000, an immensely powerful and unerringly accurate genetically encoded rifle. When Khara returned to her own people, Dante made his way back to the Romanov Palace...

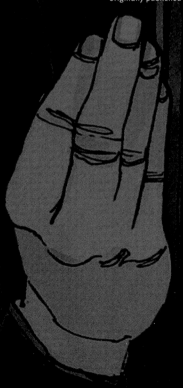

THE TROUBLE WITH ARBATOVS

Script: Robbie Morrison
Art: Simon Fraser
Colours: Alison Kirkpatrick
Letters: Annie Parkhouse

Originally published in *2000 AD* Prog 1083

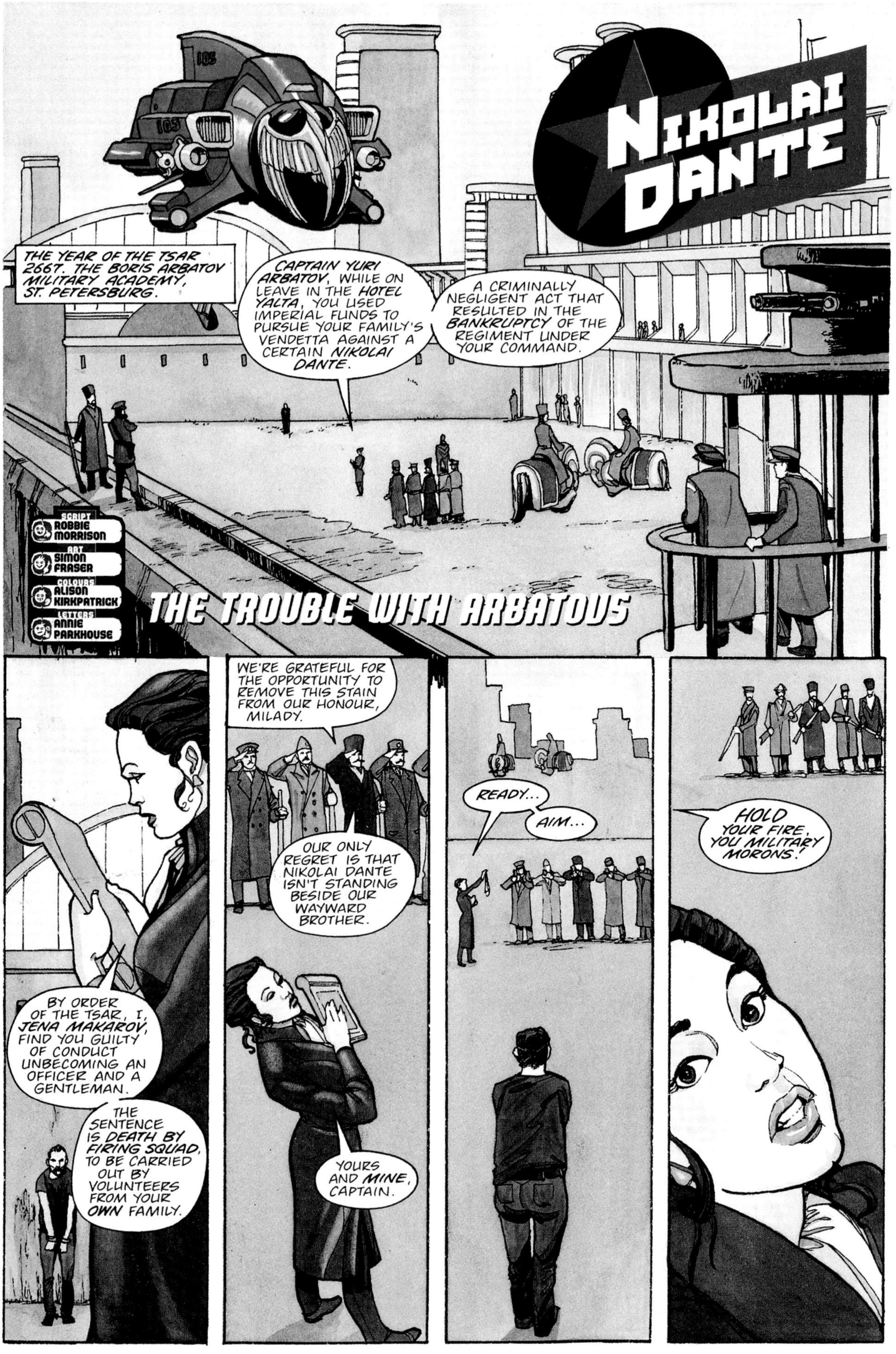
NIKOLAI DANTE
THE YEAR OF THE TSAR 2667. THE BORIS ARBATOV MILITARY ACADEMY, ST. PETERSBURG.
CAPTAIN YURI ARBATOV, WHILE ON LEAVE IN THE HOTEL YALTA, YOU USED IMPERIAL FUNDS TO PURSUE YOUR FAMILY'S VENDETTA AGAINST A CERTAIN NIKOLAI DANTE.
A CRIMINALLY NEGLIGENT ACT THAT RESULTED IN THE BANKRUPTCY OF THE REGIMENT UNDER YOUR COMMAND.
SCRIPT ROBBIE MORRISON
ART SIMON FRASER
COLOURS ALISON KIRKPATRICK
LETTERS ANNIE PARKHOUSE
THE TROUBLE WITH ARBATOVS
BY ORDER OF THE TSAR, I, JENA MAKAROV, FIND YOU GUILTY OF CONDUCT UNBECOMING AN OFFICER AND A GENTLEMAN.
THE SENTENCE IS DEATH BY FIRING SQUAD, TO BE CARRIED OUT BY VOLUNTEERS FROM YOUR OWN FAMILY.
WE'RE GRATEFUL FOR THE OPPORTUNITY TO REMOVE THIS STAIN FROM OUR HONOUR, MILADY.
OUR ONLY REGRET IS THAT NIKOLAI DANTE ISN'T STANDING BESIDE OUR WAYWARD BROTHER.
YOURS AND MINE, CAPTAIN.
READY...
AIM...
HOLD YOUR FIRE, YOU MILITARY MORONS!

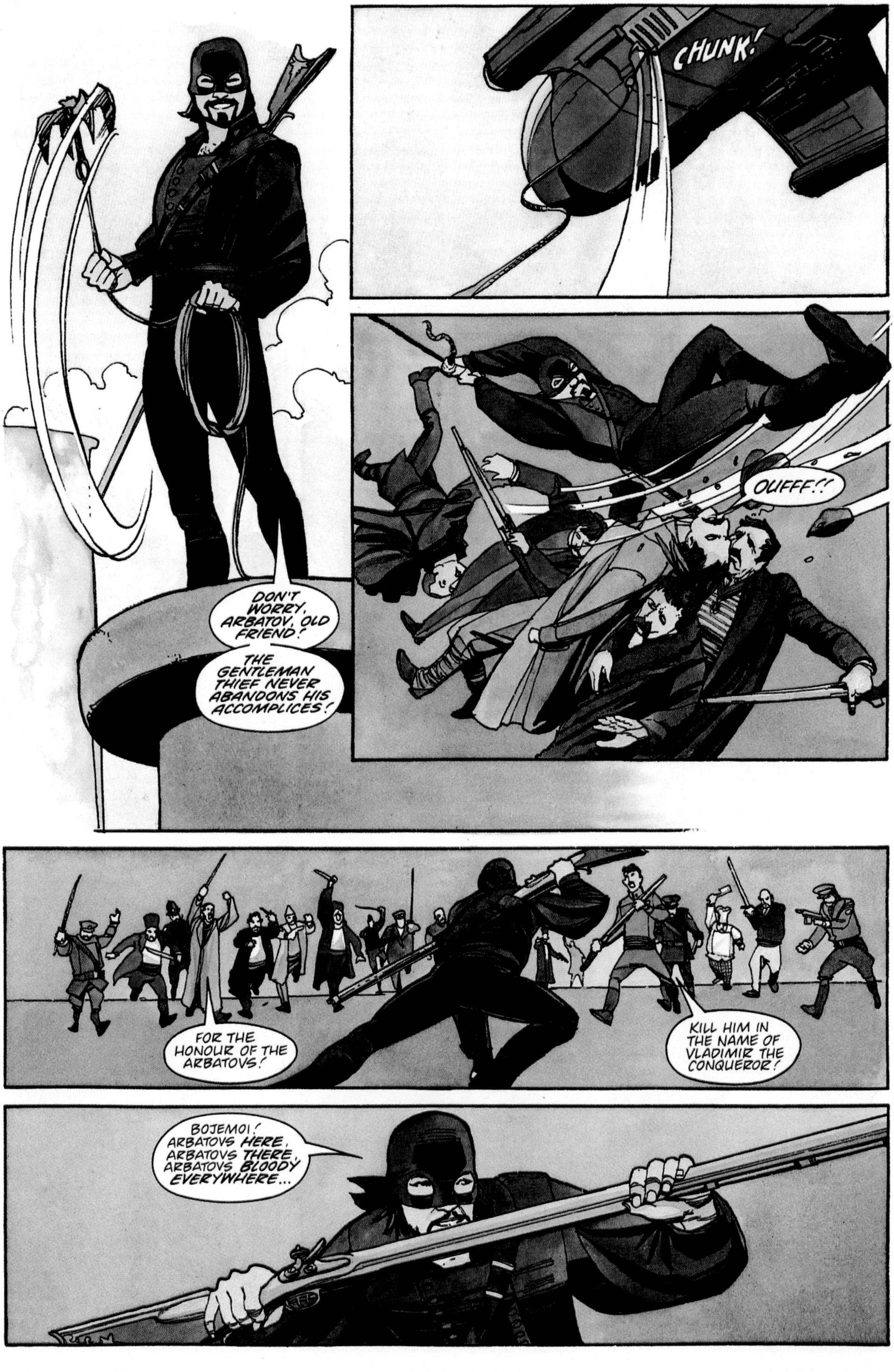
CHUNK!
DON'T WORRY, ARBATOV, OLD FRIEND!
THE GENTLEMAN THIEF NEVER ABANDONS HIS ACCOMPLICES!
OUFFF!!
FOR THE HONOUR OF THE ARBATOVS!
KILL HIM IN THE NAME OF VLADIMIR THE CONQUEROR!
BOJEMOI! ARBATOVS HERE, ARBATOVS THERE, ARBATOVS BLOODY EVERYWHERE...

SWACKKK!

SKRACK!!

DROP YOUR WEAPONS!

ONE MOVE FROM ANY OF YOU AND THE *TSARINA* HERE *ISN'T* GOING TO BE INHERITING THE EMPIRE!

NOW START UP A *RAVENWING* AND SIT THE GOOD CAPTAIN ON IT!

YOU'LL NEVER GET AWAY WITH THIS, *THIEF...*

Ohh, YOU'D BE AMAZED AT WHAT *I* CAN GET AWAY WITH.

?

MAYBE EVEN A LITTLE IMPRESSED IF YOU WEREN'T SO *STUCK-UP.*

THE ONLY THING THAT'LL BE STUCK-UP ANYWHERE IS YOUR *HEAD* IF YOU DON'T LET ME GO — ON A *SPIKE* IN THE IMPERIAL PALACE!

I WOULDN'T BE A *GENTLEMAN* IF I DIDN'T BOW TO A LADY'S WISHES...

BUT I WOULDN'T BE A *THIEF* IF I DIDN'T LEAVE WITH SOMETHING A *LITTLE* MORE VALUABLE THAN CAPTAIN ARBATOV.

SURRENDER, THIEF, OR BE BLOWN OUT OF THE SKIES!

That's an Imperial Raven Corps StrikeHawk, designed for decimating small armies, not lone fugitives.

Though I abhorred your use of the Tsarina as a hostage, Dante, it may have been prudent to hold her captive a little longer...

LET'S HOPE ALL THAT WASN'T JUST *PILLOW TALK.*

KHARA SAID THE HUNTSMAN'S SHELLS INSTANTANEOUSLY ADAPT THEMSELVES INTO THE MOST EFFECTIVE MEANS OF TERMINATING THE ENEMY.

KA-BOOOMM!

DIAVOLO! IT DOES A MAN GOOD TO MEET A WOMAN OF HER WORD.

TSYGANOV BLACK MARKET, ST. PETERSBURG.

OKAY, CAPTAIN, I ADMIT I BANKRUPTED YOUR REGIMENT THROUGH FORGERY *JUST* TO PAY MY HOTEL BILL, BUT I NEVER WANTED YOU TO GET *KILLED* OVER IT.

BUT YOU'RE SAFE NOW. A *FREE MAN.* THE THIEVES' WORLD IS YOUR OYSTER.

NO MORE MILITARY DISCIPLINE, NO MORE *SUCKING UP* TO THE TSAR...

DAMN YOU, DANTE! DAMN YOU TO HELL!

WHOA, I WAS ONLY TRYING TO *HELP!*

HELP!?

YOU'VE *TARNISHED* THE NOBLE REPUTATION OF MY FAMILY! *DESTROYED* MY CAREER, MY *LIFE!* TURNED ME INTO A *COMMON CRIMINAL!*

THE ONLY THING THAT CAN *POSSIBLY* HELP ME--

HEY!

--IS YOUR *DEATH!*

I'D BE CAREFUL WITH THAT...

THE HUNTSMAN 5000 IS CODED *SPECIFICALLY* TO MY GENEPRINT.

IF ANYONE *ELSE* TRIES TO FIRE IT...

THE BULLET AUTOMATICALLY REVERSES TRAJECTORY AND USES THEM FOR TARGET PRACTICE.

DAMN YOU, NIKOLAI DANTE!

SPLUTCH!

Y'KNOW, CREST...

SOME PEOPLE JUST DON'T KNOW WHEN YOU'RE TRYING TO DO THEM A FAVOUR.

THE END

CRUEL BRITANNIA

Script: Robbie Morrison
Art: Simon Fraser
Colours: Alison Kirkpatrick
Letters: Annie Parkhouse

Originally published in *2000 AD* Prog 1084

'In The Year of The Tsar 2667, Britannia — stripped of its arrogant adjective by Imperial decree — is a nation divided, trapped in a mire of political manoeuvring, scandal, sleaze and corruption.

'Nowhere is this more apparent than in the Palace of London itself, which effectively separates the ruling Upperclass from the Underclass.

'King Henry Windsor McKray, the present monarch, while officially answerable to the Tsar, is openly sympathetic to the Romanov Dynasty. He presides over a hostile Parliament manipulated by the Masons, the military, the corporate sector and the Intelligence Services.

'King Henry is the latest descendant of the centuries-old marital union between London's most infamous crime family and an equally infamous royal family.

'Rumours abound that he is also heir to an ailment that frequently assaults both royalty and the criminal fraternity...'

CRUEL BRITANNIA

SCRIPT
ROBBIE MORRISON

ART
SIMON FRASER

COLOURS
ALISON KIRKPATRICK

LETTERS
ANNIE PARKHOUSE

MILORDS, LADIES AND GENTLEMEN, PREPARE TO PAY HOMAGE TO THE KING.

STEP FORWARD AND KISS THE ROYAL RING.

'...madness.' — THE IMPERIAL TIMES.

CHOP TO IT! HOP! HOP!

PUCKER YOUR SUCKERS AND *SNOG, SNOG, SNOG* AWAY!

HOLDING COURT IN THE *NUDE!* IS NOTHING SACRED? OUR NOBLE NATION WILL BE THE LAUGHING STOCK OF THE EMPIRE.

I AGREE. ECCENTRICITY IS TRADITIONAL FOR OUR MONARCHS, BUT *THIS* IS OUTRIGHT *INSANITY.*

LONG LIVE THE KING! HE'S AN *INSPIRATION* TO US ALL!

WHAT?

ARE YOU AS *MAD* AS HE IS, SIR?

MAD? KING HENRY'S A GENIUS OF THE HIGHEST ORDER.

HIS APPEARANCE TODAY STRIKES A BLOW AGAINST HYPOCRISY, AGAINST THE CLASS SYSTEM THAT DIVIDES THIS COUNTRY.

UNITED WE STAND, DIVIDED WE FALL! WITH ONE BRAVE GESTURE, THE KING HAS PROVED THAT WHEN IT COMES RIGHT DOWN TO IT, WE'RE *ALL* THE SAME — KINGS OR COMMONERS.

BRITANNIA MUST UNDERSTAND THAT IF IT IS TO UNITE AND BECOME GREAT AGAIN.

IN FACT, I THINK IT'S ONLY RIGHT AND PROPER THAT WE *ALL* STRIP TO SHOW OUR SUPPORT OF THE KING'S CRUSADE!

EXCELLENT IDEA, *NICOLA!*

EVERYBODY, GET YOUR KEGS OFF!

Perhaps you should participate more actively in politics, Dante. It pains me to pay you a compliment, but you certainly have a way with words.

JUST CALL ME *DR. SPIN,* CREST, JUST CALL ME DR. SPIN...

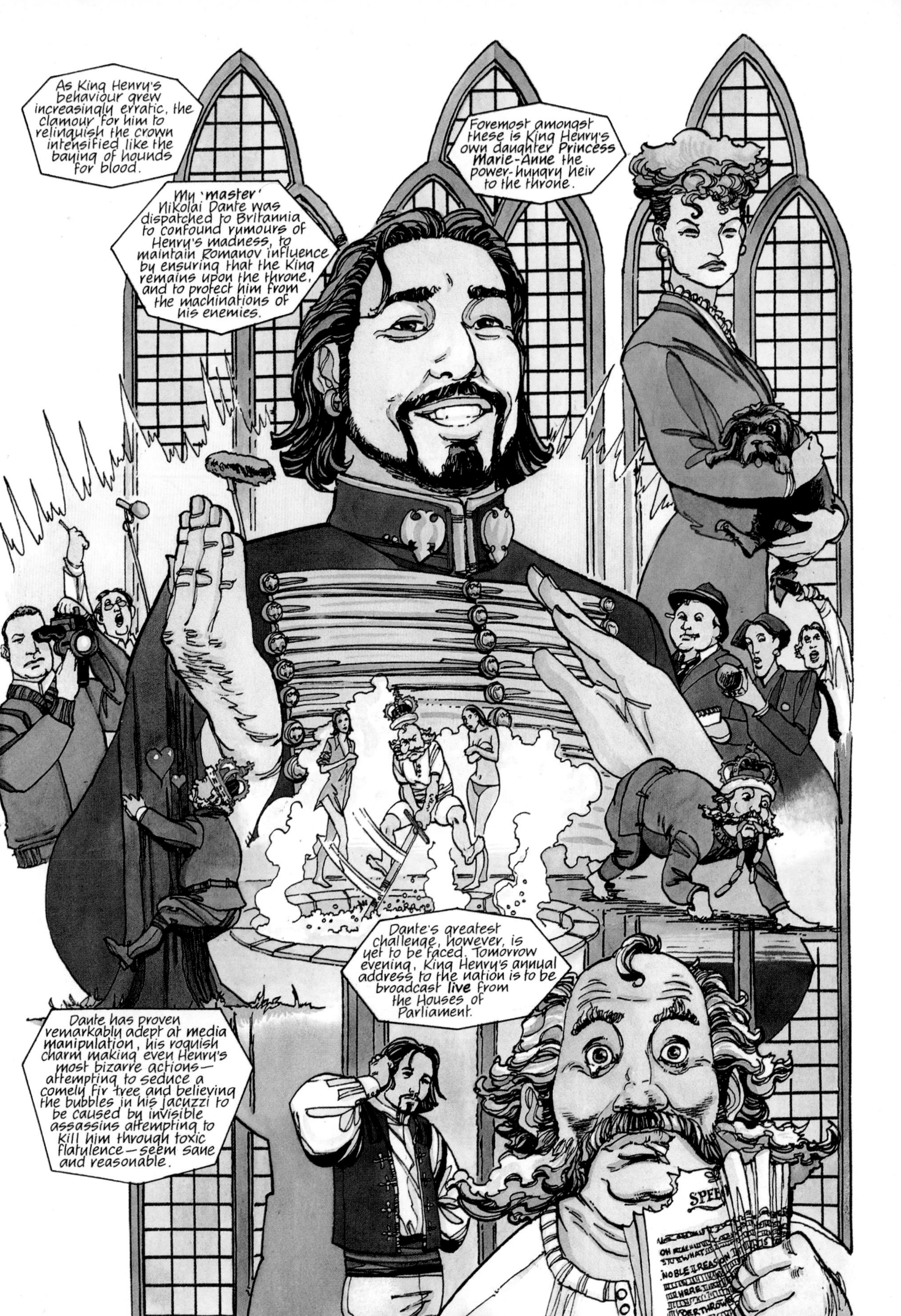
As King Henry's behaviour grew increasingly erratic, the clamour for him to relinquish the crown intensified like the baying of hounds for blood.
My 'master' Nikolai Dante was dispatched to Britannia to confound rumours of Henry's madness, to maintain Romanov influence by ensuring that the King remains upon the throne, and to protect him from the machinations of his enemies.
Foremost amongst these is King Henry's own daughter Princess Marie-Anne the power-hungry heir to the throne.
Dante has proven remarkably adept at media manipulation, his roguish charm making even Henry's most bizarre actions— attempting to seduce a comely fir tree and believing the bubbles in his jacuzzi to be caused by invisible assassins attempting to kill him through toxic flatulence—seem sane and reasonable.
Dante's greatest challenge, however, is yet to be faced. Tomorrow evening, King Henry's annual address to the nation is to be broadcast live from the Houses of Parliament.

PRINCESS MARIE-ANNE, WHAT A *FETCHING* OUTFIT. VERY, UH, *REGAL.*

HOW LONG DO YOU THINK YOU CAN KEEP THIS *FARCE* UP, DANTE?

I *NEVER* HAVE ANY TROUBLE KEEPING MY END UP, MILADY.

WE ARE *NOT* AMUSED.

NO WONDER THE *TABLOIDS* ADORE YOU—YOU WERE OBVIOUSLY RAISED IN THE SAME *GUTTER* AS THEY WERE.

SIR, YOU HAVE THE HONOUR OF BEING *ALLOWED* TO DINE WITH ME THIS EVENING AT MY PALACE.

WHO KNOWS, YOU MAY EVEN BE OF SERVICE TO ME...

TO *SERVE* THE KING AND *SERVICE* THE PRINCESS, EH...

SHOULD I DRESS FOR DINNER OR AM I *APPETISING* ENOUGH AS I AM?

NIKOLA. NIKOLA.

NIKOL*AI*, SIRE...

PERHAPS YOU SHOULD CONSIDER SOME *COMESTIC SURGERY* TO BOOST YOUR ATTRACTIVENESS TO THE OPPOSITE SEX...

I DON'T MEAN TO BE FORWARD, *MADAM*, BUT HOW DO YOU EXPECT TO ATTRACT A HUSBAND WITH A CHEST AS *FLAT* AS A PANCAKE.

NOT TO MENTION ALL THAT *HAIR*...

Too much hair around as it is. Damned country's being *overgrown* by hair. It's a conspiracy!

BOJEMOI...

HOW MUCH *CRAZINESS* CAN YOU TAKE BEFORE YOU *LOSE* IT YOURSELF?

CRIPPEN HOUSE, OVERLOOKING THE RIVER THAMES, HOME TO THE PRINCESS ROYAL.

YOUR FAME PRECEDES YOU, DANTE. MY COOKS HAVE TAKEN YOUR REPUTATION INTO ACCOUNT—THEY'VE PREPARED A *PEASANT'S* FEAST FOR YOU.

TRIPE, HAGGIS, TONGUE, PIGEON, PIGS' TROTTERS, ROAST SWAN, JELLIED EELS...

BRITISH CUISINE, EH, THE *BEST* IN THE WORLD.

MY TASTE BUDS ARE *TINGLING*, MILADY, BUT WHY DON'T WE SKIP THE MAIN COURSE AND GET STRAIGHT DOWN TO *DESSERT*?

YOU REALLY ARE THE MOST *ARROGANT* FOOL.

I DIDN'T BRING YOU HERE TO *SEDUCE* YOU. THE ONLY SERVICE YOU CAN PERFORM FOR ME IS TO *DIE HORRIBLY*.

MANY POWERFUL, *PATRIOTIC* BRITONS WISH TO SEE MY FATHER OVERTHROWN. IT'S REMARKABLE WHAT YOU CAN ACHIEVE IF YOU WORK TOGETHER.

UNITED WE STAND, DIVIDED WE FALL, ISN'T THAT WHAT *YOU* SAID?

MY ALLIES AND I CONSPIRED TO BRING THE KING'S SPEECH FORWARD WITHOUT YOUR KNOWLEDGE. IT BEGINS IN *20 MINUTES*.

WITHOUT YOU TO PROTECT HIM, MY FATHER WILL BE *CONDEMNED* BY HIS OWN MADNESS. *LIVE* ON DIGITAL-VISION.

I WOULD INVITE YOU TO MY *CORONATION*, DANTE, BUT WHEN *THE RIPPERS* HAVE FINISHED WITH YOU, THE ONLY WAY YOU'LL BE ABLE TO ATTEND IS IN *PIECES*.

TOODLE-PIP!

'With interest in the King's mental stability riding at fever pitch, the Bolshoi Channel reported that an astounding 97% of the viewing public tuned into Henry's broadcast...'

PARLIAMENT TODAY. *WITH* ZACHARIA DIMBLEBY III

PARLIAMENT TODAY *WITH* ZACHARIA DIMBLEBY III

'Over ten times the number who usually follow political programming.' — *THE IMPERIAL TIMES.*

PRINCESS MARIE-ANNE, YOU'RE JUST IN TIME. THE KING IS ABOUT TO BEGIN HIS ADDRESS.

HOW THRILLING, GUARDSMAN.

WHAT WORDS OF WISDOM WILL MY FATHER ENLIGHTEN US WITH TODAY, I WONDER?

FRIENDS! BRITONS! COUNTRYMEN! HENRY LOVES YOU, HENRY LOVES YOU ALL!

BUT I'M NOT HERE JUST TO WHISPER SWEET NOTHINGS INTO YOUR EARS, I HAVE MOMENTOUS CHANGES TO MAKE TO OUR CONSTITUTION.

HENCEFORTH, ANYONE EXPRESSING A DESIRE TO ENTER POLITICS WILL AUTOMATICALLY BE BANNED FROM DOING SO!

BALDNESS WILL BE OUTLAWED — IF YOU'RE NOT HAIRY, YOU BETTER BE WARY!

A NEW WELFARE STATE WILL BE CREATED TO CARE FOR THE UNDERCLASS!

THE NATIONAL ANTHEM WILL BE REPLACED BY THAT GOOD-TIME CLASSIC 'THE KING OF THE SWINGERS'!

DISCRIMINATION!

I THINK MY FATHER'S DUG HIMSELF A DEEP ENOUGH GRAVE, GENTLEMEN. IT ONLY REMAINS FOR US TO FILL IT IN.

MADNESS! HE'LL RUIN THE LAND!

MEANWHILE, AT CRIPPEN HOUSE...

SURGERY'S UP, BOYS! I'LL 'AVE 'IS 'EART!

BAGS 'IS KIDNEYS!

WHO ARE THESE FREAKS, CREST? THE UNDERTAKERS FROM HELL?

I'M TEMPTED TO CARRY ME OUT A LITTLE VASECTOMY!

The Rippers. Covert assassins attached to Britannia's Secret Service, often used in a death squad capacity.

They're genetically engineered for stealth and sadism.

Their appearance is carefully designed to strike fear into the Underclass by tapping into hereditary memories of the original Ripper murders.

Dante, sometimes discretion is the better part of valour.

MEANING THAT, SINCE I'M NEITHER DISCREET OR VALIANT, I SHOULD GET THE HELL OUT OF THE DUELLING BUSINESS AND RUN FOR PARLIAMENT.

Something like that.

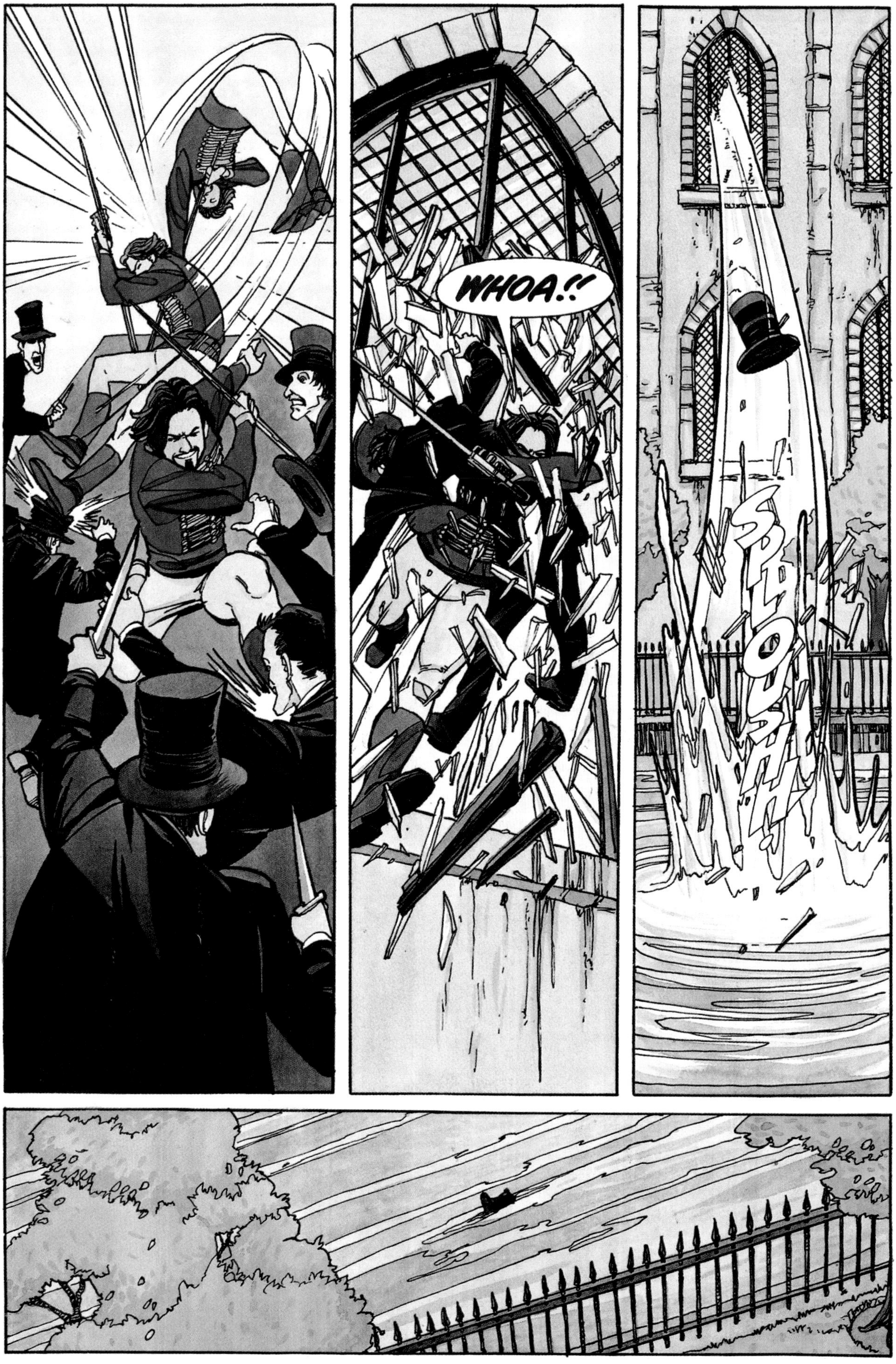
WHOA.!!
SPLOOSH!

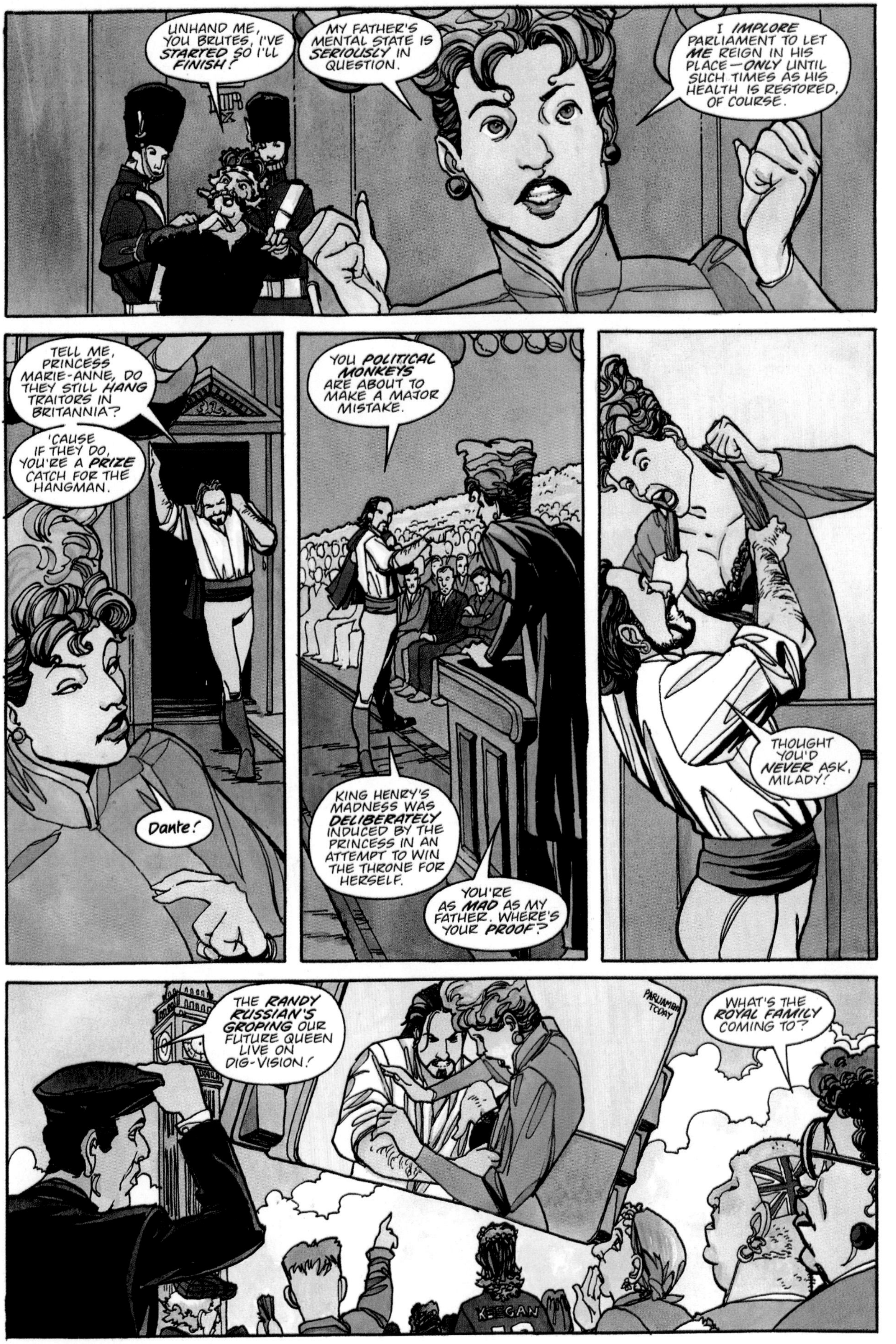
UNHAND ME, YOU BRUTES, I'VE STARTED SO I'LL FINISH!
MY FATHER'S MENTAL STATE IS SERIOUSLY IN QUESTION.
I IMPLORE PARLIAMENT TO LET ME REIGN IN HIS PLACE—ONLY UNTIL SUCH TIMES AS HIS HEALTH IS RESTORED, OF COURSE.
TELL ME, PRINCESS MARIE-ANNE, DO THEY STILL HANG TRAITORS IN BRITANNIA?
'CAUSE IF THEY DO, YOU'RE A PRIZE CATCH FOR THE HANGMAN.
Dante!
YOU POLITICAL MONKEYS ARE ABOUT TO MAKE A MAJOR MISTAKE.
KING HENRY'S MADNESS WAS DELIBERATELY INDUCED BY THE PRINCESS IN AN ATTEMPT TO WIN THE THRONE FOR HERSELF.
YOU'RE AS MAD AS MY FATHER. WHERE'S YOUR PROOF?
THOUGHT YOU'D NEVER ASK, MILADY!
THE RANDY RUSSIAN'S GROPING OUR FUTURE QUEEN LIVE ON DIG-VISION!
WHAT'S THE ROYAL FAMILY COMING TO?
KEEGAN

THE DRUG *PSYKO : RANGE 27.* YOUR OWN SECRET SERVICE USES IT FOR PRISONER INTERROGATIONS.

A CONTINUAL DOSAGE EVENTUALLY DRIVES THE PATIENT INSANE AND LEAVES LITTLE TRACE OF HAVING BEEN ADMINISTERED.

?

AND *WHO BETTER* TO POISON A KING THAN A *PRINCESS?*

IF YOU DON'T BELIEVE THE PROOF OF HER OWN *BOSOM,* SEARCH HER MANSION — YOU'LL FIND *PLENTY* OF *EVIDENCE* THERE.

'The tensest moments in Britannia's history unfolded to King Henry's rendition of the new national anthem, as Guardsmen were sent to Crippen House!'

♪ I'M THE KING OF THE SWINGERS, YEAH! BRITANNIA'S V.I.P.! ♪

YOU SHOULD BE CAREFUL *WHO* YOU HONOUR WITH DINNER INVITATIONS, MILADY, THERE'S A LOT OF *DISREPUTABLE* PEOPLE AROUND.

LONG LIVE THE KING!

'Parliament declared its loyalty with loud insincerity as the Guardsmen returned with evidence to substantiate Dante's claims.'

AND A *NICKETY-KNACKETY-NOO* TO YOU, TOO...

'The disgraced Princess Marie-Anne was sentenced to the Tower of London' — *THE IMPERIAL TIMES.*

YOU HAVE NO *HONOUR,* SIR.

NEITHER HAS THE REST OF THIS COUNTRY. WHY SHOULD I BREAK THE MOULD?

However did you deduce such an *insidious* plot, Dante?

WHERE'S MY *SCRIBE?* I WISH TO CREATE A NEW POSITION ON MY STAFF—THE *ROYAL BACK-SHAVER!*

ELEMENTARY, MY DEAR CREST, AS YOU WELL KNOW.

I MADE IT ALL UP AND PLANTED THE EVIDENCE MYSELF.

THE KING REALLY IS *PANTS-ON-HIS-HEAD-MAD.* EVER MET ANYONE IN POWER WHO *WASN'T?*

THE GREAT GAME

Script: Robbie Morrison
Art: Simon Fraser
Colours: Alison Kirkpatrick
Letters: Annie Parkhouse

Originally published in *2000 AD* Progs 1101-1110

THE YEAR OF THE TSAR 2660. THE HOTEL APARTMENTS OF THE CASINO ROYALE. MONACO.

THE GREAT GAME PART 1

'Even without the influence of the Romanov Dynasty, Nikolai Dante's place in Imperial history would have been assured, for his reputation as a thief and an adventurer was second to none.'

'From the age of twelve, Dante survived alone in the Thieves' World, learning the criminal arts from a number of infamous outlaws who helped turn him into the living embodiment of that ancient adage...

'"Never trust a thief."' — FROM 'NIKOLAI DANTE: A CHARACTER ASSASSINATION' — BY VARIOUS CONTRIBUTORS.

AOWW!

YOU SAID YOU'D BE GENTLE...

STOP BUCKING AROUND UNDER ME, KOLYA. NO MATTER HOW MUCH YOU BOAST ABOUT IT, YOU'RE NOT A STALLION.

WHAT DO I WANT AN EARRING FOR, ANYWAY?

IT'LL JUST BE ANOTHER DISTINGUISHING MARK FOR THE LAW TO IDENTIFY ME WITH.

IT LOOKS GOOD. KIND OF ROGUISH.

IF YOU WANT TO BE TOO COOL TO KILL, YOU BETTER START LOOKING THE PART.

I WISH WE COULD STAY HERE. THESE LAST FEW WEEKS HAVE BEEN, WELL, Y'KNOW...

KEEP ON MOVING, ELLIE, IT'S THE FIRST RULE OF THIEVERY. WELL, APART FROM NOT GETTING CAUGHT.

SCRIPT ROBBIE MORRISON
ART SIMON FRASER
COLOURS ALISON KIRKPATRICK
LETTERS ANNIE PARKHOUSE

THERE'S A BIG, WIDE WORLD OUT THERE—WE'LL GO SEE IT *TOGETHER*. WE'LL SKIP OUT OF THE CASINO ROYALE—

WITHOUT PAYING OUR BILL, I HOPE...

NATURALLY. WE'LL BUY A YACHT WITH THE MONEY WE'VE STOLEN AND SAIL OFF INTO THE SUNSET.

YOU CAN SAIL?

I'M THE *SON* OF A *PIRATE-QUEEN!*

I CAN SAIL THE PANTS OFF *CORTO MALTESE* AND OUT-SWIM A *SHARK!*

YEAH, AND SOMETIMES YOU *SMILE* LIKE ONE AS WELL.

I CAN *NEVER* TELL WHEN YOU'RE LYING, YOU KNOW THAT?

I'VE *NEVER* LIED TO YOU. I'VE BEEN *TRYING*, JUST DOESN'T WORK. *CAN'T* DO IT.

IF WE'D MET A YEAR AGO, YOU'D'VE PROBABLY *HATED* ME. I DIDN'T ALWAYS LIVE LIKE THIS.

NOBODY CAN ACCUSE *ME* OF BEING A SAINT EITHER.

WE'RE TOO YOUNG TO WORRY ABOUT THE PAST, ELLIE, *OR* THE FUTURE.

YOU ONLY LIVE *ONCE*, SO LIVE *DANGEROUSLY*...

SKASHH

YOU COVER YOUR TRACKS WELL. ANYONE WOULD HAVE THOUGHT WE WERE TRAILING *PROFESSIONAL CRIMINALS.*

WE ARE *THE WARLORDS,* BOY.

YEAH, YEAH, YEAH. *IMPERIAL MERCENARIES.*

WHO HIRED YOU?

THE *CASINO* 'CAUSE WE BROKE THE BANK TWICE, THE *CABINET NOIRE* 'CAUSE I SOLD THE *EIFFEL TOWER* OUT FROM UNDER THEM, OR *BARONESS LUFTHANZA* 'CAUSE I STOLE THE SAPPHIRE SHE USED AS A *GLASS EYE?*

THIS ISN'T BUSINESS, THIEF, THIS IS *PERSONAL.* I AM *ELENA DI JANISSAIRE,* COMMANDER-IN-CHIEF OF THE WARLORDS.

GET YOUR *FILTHY* HANDS OFF MY *DAUGHTER.* NOW!

daughter?

THERE'S A *FEW* THINGS I'VE BEEN MEANING TO TELL YOU, NIKOLAI...

BRING ELOISE TO ME, GENERAL KVASS.

AND *DANTE?*

I'M STILL TRYING TO DECIDE WHETHER TO *KILL* HIM OR MERELY *CUT OFF* ALL THE PARTS OF HIS BODY WHICH CAME IN CONTACT WITH HER.

IF *YOU* GROW UP TO BE LIKE YOUR MOTHER, YOU'RE *DUMPED.*

WHY DO YOU THINK I *RAN AWAY* IN THE FIRST PLACE?

RESCUE ME, KOLYA?

SURE.

NO PROBLEM.

ARGHH!

SMACK!

I'VE GOT YOU, AND *WE'VE* GOT THE MONEY. NOW GIVE ME A *KISS.*

FOR *LUCK*?

Nah, JUST FOR THE *SHEER HELL* OF IT...

KRAKK

HELL'S WHERE YOU'RE GOING, BOY— IF YOU'RE FOOLISH ENOUGH TO BELIEVE IN SUCH THINGS.

AND *YOU,* *LITTLE* *ELOISE...*

IF YOU HUMILIATE THE WARLORDS AGAIN, I WILL *PERSONALLY* EXECUTE YOU, *REGARDLESS* OF YOUR MOTHER'S COMMANDS.

N-*Nikolai...* Help me...

OUR *MONEY...*

FORGET THE MONEY, KOLYA! *HELP ME—* BEFORE IT'S *TOO LATE!*

Ellie...

WITHDRAW THE MEN, KVASS.

AND PLEASE *COMPOSE* YOURSELF, ELOISE, YOU'RE THE FUTURE COMMANDER OF THE WARLORDS. YOU *CAN'T* ESCAPE *THAT.*

Damn you, Kolya, damn you to Hell.

I'LL *COME* FOR YOU, ELLIE, I'LL *RESCUE* YOU.

I - I promise...

DON'T RIDDLE YOURSELF WITH *HATRED*, ELOISE, YOU SHOULD BE *GRATEFUL* FOR WHAT THE BOY'S DONE.

HE TAUGHT YOU A *LESSON...*

'NEVER TRUST A THIEF.'

Seven years later... Imperial Russia exists in a climate of fear.

Open hostilities between Tsar Vladimir The Conqueror and the House of Romanov have withdrawn once more into the Machiavellian intrigue of politics and espionage.

The transactions of the Thieves' World continue under a veil of suspicion, for spies are rumoured to be everywhere...

Where there are spies, assassins are never far behind.

OVER THE YEARS, THE MAKAROV DYNASTY HAS *EXCELLED* IN MAKING ME FEEL UNAPPRECIATED. FOR THE *EARTHSHATTERING* INFORMATION I NOW POSSESS, I EXPECT TO BE *HANDSOMELY* REWARDED.

A CITY STATE TO RULE. A REGIMENT OF THE RAVEN CORPS FOR MY PROTECTION. IMPERIAL SEDUCTRESSES FOR MY PLEASURE.

INDEED, I WOULDN'T BE SURPRISED IF THE TSAR'S GRATITUDE DIDN'T EXTEND TO OFFERING ME ONE OF HIS DAUGHTERS' HANDS IN *MARRIAGE*

ONE OF YOUR *SISTERS*, PERHAPS. OR—IF I MAY BE SO BOLD, *LADY JENA*—YOURS.

NEW MOSCOW. THE FACE OF THE EMPIRE. THE *VISAGE OF POWER*.

GNNHH!

LET ME *CLARIFY* YOUR POSITION, *AGENT KAINE!*

YOU'RE A SPY. I *ABHOR* SPIES.

SAD, PATHETIC, NONDESCRIPT LITTLE PEOPLE, WILLING TO BETRAY IDEALS GREATER THAN THEMSELVES FOR THE *PETTIEST* OF MOTIVATIONS —GREED, JEALOUSY, SEXUAL GRATIFICATION...

THEY ARE, HOWEVER, A *NECESSARY* EVIL, ONE NO *DYNASTY* CAN DO WITHOUT.

YOUR *EXALTED* POSITION IN OUR SPY NETWORK IS SUCH THAT I WOULDN'T *SPIT* IN YOUR MOUTH IF YOU WERE DYING OF *THIRST* IN A DESERT.

WE PLANTED YOU AMONGST *THE DRAGUTIN*, THE EMPIRE'S GREATEST ARMS DEVELOPERS, AS A MATTER OF COURSE.

THE DRAGUTIN OFFER MY FATHER AN EXCLUSIVE CLAIM TO *ALL* NEW WEAPONS BEFORE PUTTING THEM ONTO THE OPEN MARKET.

YOU TELL US *NOTHING* THAT THE DRAGUTIN HAVEN'T ALREADY TOLD US *FIRST*. THEY'RE THE *MOST LOYAL* DYNASTY IN THE EMPIRE.

ISN'T THAT THE MOST *SUCCESSFUL* FORM OF SUBTERFUGE, MILADY?

TO MAKE YOUR MASTERS THINK ONE THING, WHEN IN FACT *THE OPPOSITE* IS TRUE?

WHAT IF I TOLD YOU THE DRAGUTIN HAD CREATED A WEAPON THAT COULD *TEAR* THIS WORLD APART, THAT COULD *CONQUER* THE EMPIRE OF *VLADIMIR THE CONQUEROR*?

I THOUGHT THREATENING YOUR INHERITANCE MIGHT GRAB YOUR ATTENTION.

DOES THIS *RAISE* MY BARGAINING POWER?

OH, IT MOST *CERTAINLY* DOES.

HHANK

GLANCE OVER YOUR SHOULDER, AND YOU'LL SEE *HOW HIGH*.

NOW, TELL ME ABOUT THE DRAGUTIN WEAPON, AND I'LL TELL YOU WHETHER YOU *LIVE* OR *DIE*.

THE DARKSTAR!

THEY CALL IT THE--

PLEASE ACCEPT OUR **APOLOGIES**. IF WE HAD ARRIVED BEFORE THE TRAITOR KAINE BEGAN HIS CONFESSION, **HIS** DEATH ALONE WOULD HAVE BEEN ENOUGH.

NOW, WE MUST CLAIM **ALL** YOUR LIVES.

I WISH YOU **LUCK!**

RAVENS!

THROW THEIR CORPSES FROM THE ROOF! THEY'RE ASSASSINATION DROIDS! THEY COULD BE PRIMED TO--

...self-destruct!

SKY-BOOM!

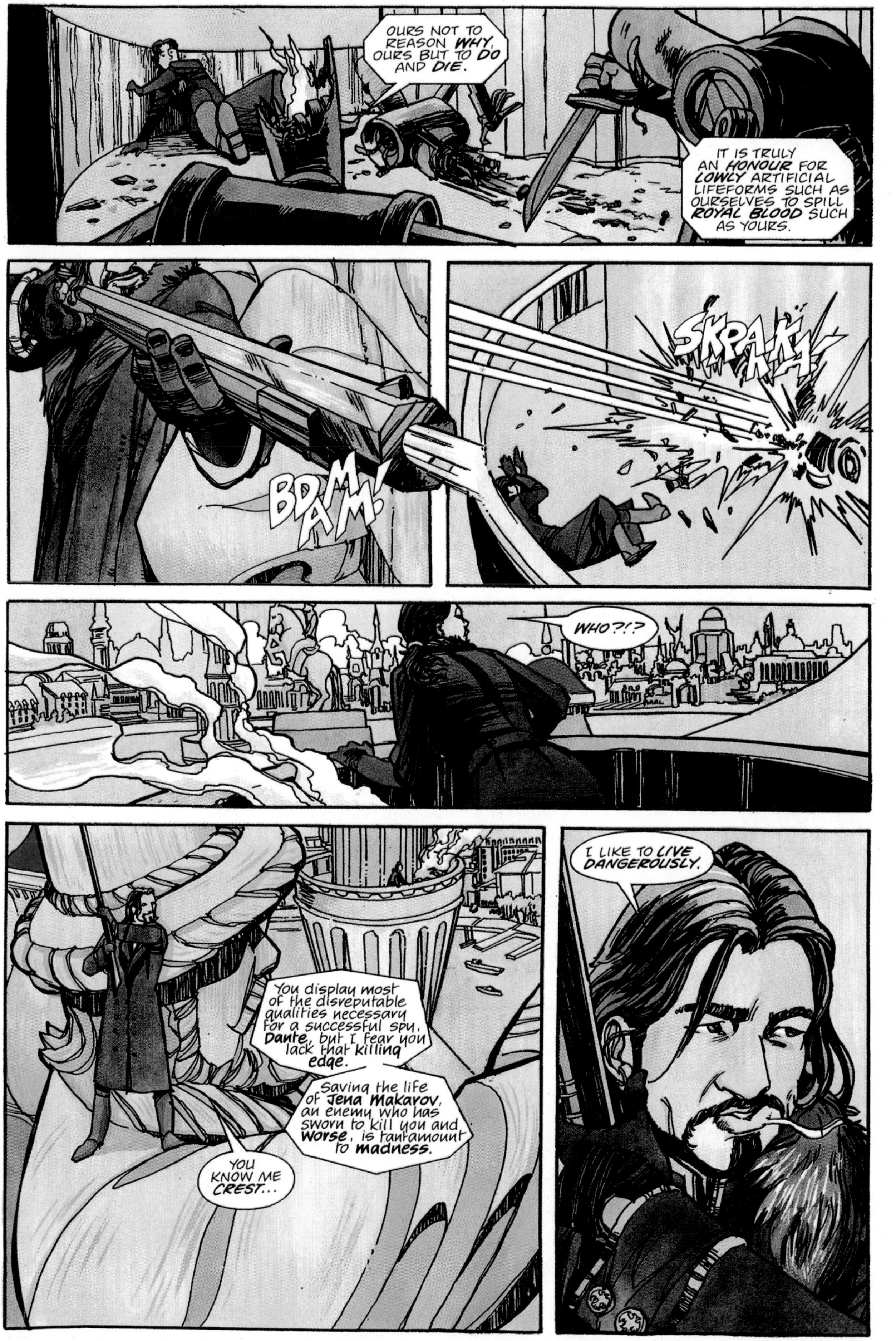

OURS NOT TO REASON WHY, OURS BUT TO DO AND DIE.
IT IS TRULY AN HONOUR FOR LOWLY ARTIFICIAL LIFEFORMS SUCH AS OURSELVES TO SPILL ROYAL BLOOD SUCH AS YOURS.
BDAM AM!
SKRAKAM!
WHO?!?
You display most of the disreputable qualities necessary for a successful spy, Dante, but I fear you lack that killing edge.
Saving the life of Jena Makarov, an enemy who has sworn to kill you and worse, is tantamount to madness.
YOU KNOW ME CREST...
I LIKE TO LIVE DANGEROUSLY.

NIKOLAI DANTE

Perhaps a re-appraisal of your character is in order, Dante. You've certainly displaying hidden depths today...

Indeed, I doubt any other man in the Empire could sink so low.

This orgy is dirty, degrading and decadent.

Exactly, Crest...

That's why it's so much fun!

THE GREAT GAME PART 2

BY ANASTASIA'S BONES!

YOU'VE GONE TOO FAR THIS TIME, BOY!

Ahh, Fuoco...

UH, LORD DMITRI, I CAN EXPLAIN.

YOU WEREN'T HERE WHEN I ARRIVED, SO I USED MY WEAPONS CREST JUST TO, Y'KNOW, CHECK OUT HOW LIFELIKE THE HOLOGRAPHIC FACILITIES WERE...

WAR ROOM. DESTROY DANTE'S PROGRAMME. NOW.

THIS IS THE MILITARY MIND OF THE ROMANOV DYNASTY, NOT A PLAYGROUND FOR YOUR CRUDE FANTASIES.

AND A WEAPONS CREST IS A HIGHLY SOPHISTICATED BIO-WEAPON, NOT A VIRTUAL PIMP.

TREAT THEM BOTH WITH THE RESPECT THEY DESERVE.

WAR ROOM: GIVE ME A UNIVERSAL SCHEMATIC OF THE EMPIRE.

SCRIPT
ROBBIE MORRISON

ART
SIMON FRASER

COLOURS
ALISON KIRKPATRICK

LETTERS
ANNIE PARKHOUSE

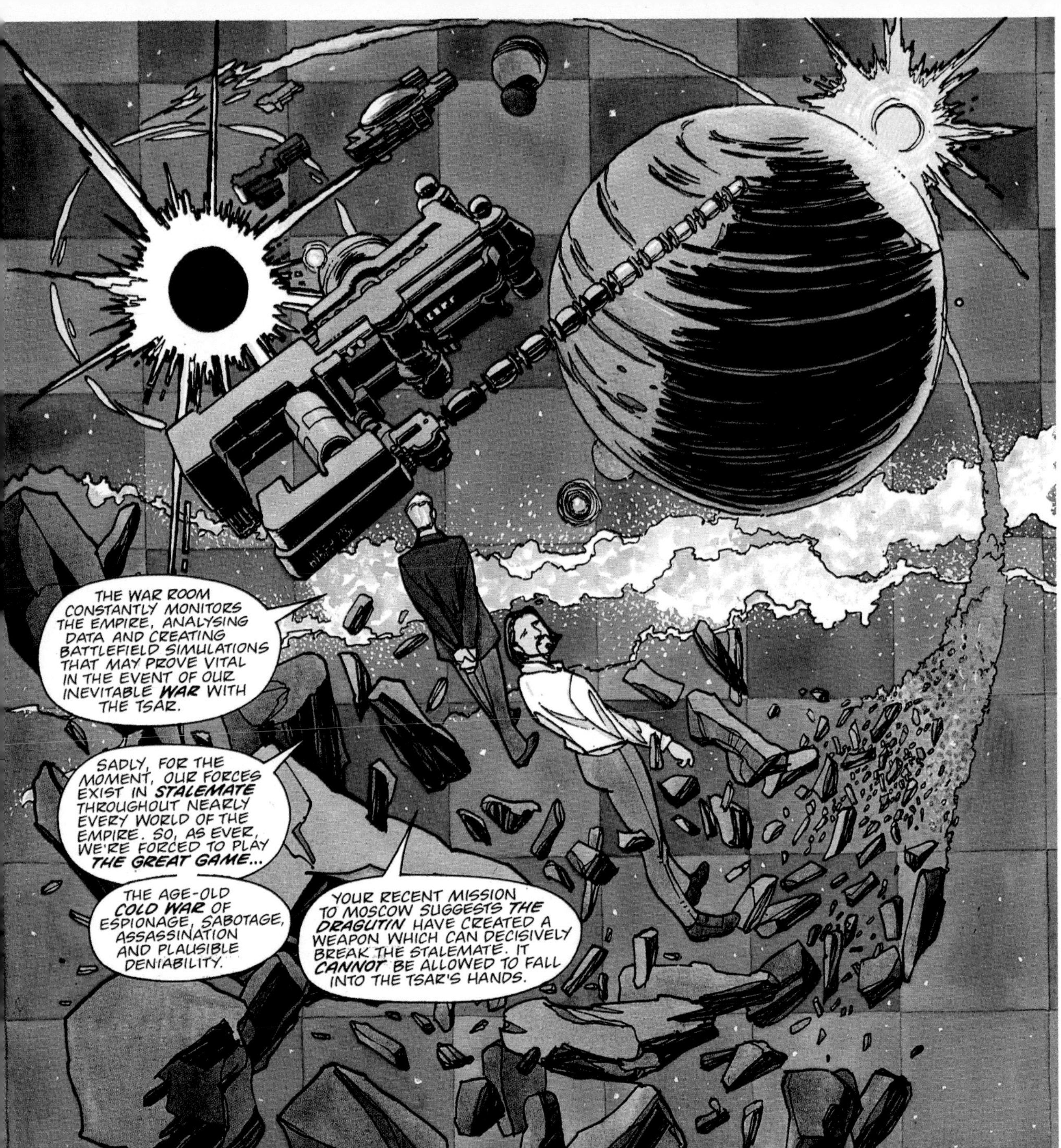
THE WAR ROOM CONSTANTLY MONITORS THE EMPIRE, ANALYSING DATA AND CREATING BATTLEFIELD SIMULATIONS THAT MAY PROVE VITAL IN THE EVENT OF OUR INEVITABLE WAR WITH THE TSAR.
SADLY, FOR THE MOMENT, OUR FORCES EXIST IN STALEMATE THROUGHOUT NEARLY EVERY WORLD OF THE EMPIRE. SO, AS EVER, WE'RE FORCED TO PLAY THE GREAT GAME...
THE AGE-OLD COLD WAR OF ESPIONAGE, SABOTAGE, ASSASSINATION AND PLAUSIBLE DENIABILITY.
YOUR RECENT MISSION TO MOSCOW SUGGESTS THE DRAGUTIN HAVE CREATED A WEAPON WHICH CAN DECISIVELY BREAK THE STALEMATE. IT CANNOT BE ALLOWED TO FALL INTO THE TSAR'S HANDS.

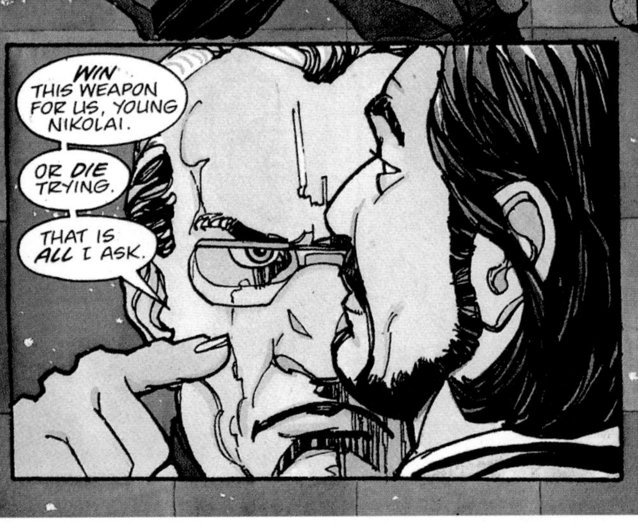
WIN THIS WEAPON FOR US, YOUNG NIKOLAI.
OR DIE TRYING.
THAT IS ALL I ASK.

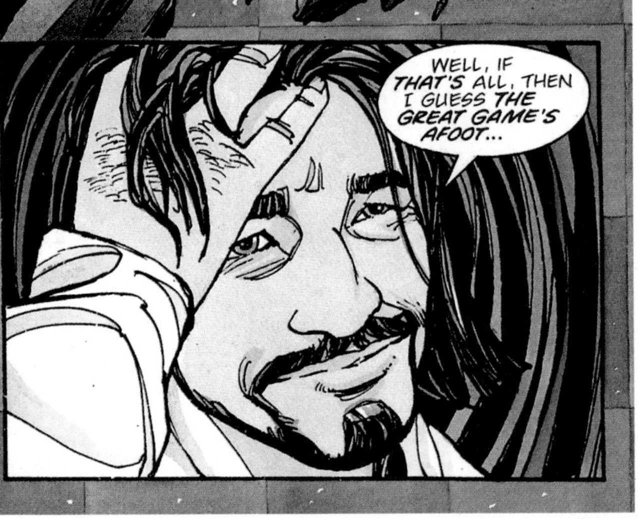
WELL, IF THAT'S ALL, THEN I GUESS THE GREAT GAME'S AFOOT...

'The Colony World of Draguta regularly plays host to highly lucrative arms bazaars which cater shamelessly for the favourite pastimes of sentient beings throughout the Empire...

...sex and violence'—
IMPERIAL TIMES TRAVELOGUE, 2667.

NOW, A FEW MORE WEAPONS WITHOUT WHICH NO ARSENAL WOULD BE COMPLETE:

THE *BRAINBYTER™ AXE*, LATEST INCARNATION OF A SAVAGE OLD FAVOURITE.

THE MARK VI *FIRESTORM™ BLASTER*— PLACE YOUR ORDERS 'CAUSE IT'S *HOT, HOT, HOT!*

AND LAST, BUT CERTAINLY NOT LEAST, THE *THUNDERTHIGHS™ EXO-SKELETON*— CRUSH A FEW SKULLS, WHY DON'T YOU?

TSARINA JENA, YOU SHOULD HAVE INFORMED US OF YOUR VISIT— THIS BAZAAR IS AIMED AT THE *LOWER* END OF THE MARKET, NOT AT CUSTOMERS OF YOUR *DISTINCTION.*

SURPRISE VISITS PROVIDE THE NOBLE HOUSES WITH IMPROMTU 'OPPORTUNITIES TO EXPRESS THEIR *LOYALTY...*

TO PROVE THAT THEY ARE STILL *WORTHY* OF THE TSAR'S BENEVOLENCE.

IS DRAGUTIN LOYALTY *BEYOND* QUESTION?

IT MOST ASSUREDLY *IS,* MILADY!

PLEASE DON'T GET UP, *PRESIDENT ADJANI,* YOU'RE ALREADY IN THE *PERFECT* POSITION FOR A MAN FACING *EXECUTION.*

NLP!

ONE WORD. DARKSTAR.

WHAT IS IT, AND WHY ARE YOU HIDING IT FROM US?

D-DARKSTAR?

I-I DON'T KNOW WHAT YOU'RE TALKING ABOUT, MILADY, I-I SWEAR.

DO YOU RECOGNISE THE PISTOL? A FINE WEAPON, ALMOST ARTISTIC.

IT WAS A GIFT FROM YOUR PREDECESSOR, AND WE ALL KNOW WHAT HAPPENED TO HER.

LAST CHANCE. WHERE IS THE --

SKRASH!

WE'RE UNDER ATTACK! THIS IS UNSPEAKABLE!

THE DRAGUTIN ARE NEUTRAL—OUR WHOLE PHILOSOPHY IS BASED UPON NON-PARTICIPATION IN CONFLICT!

DARK LEADER TO ASSAULT SQUAD!

INDISCRIMINATE STRAFING! KILL THEM ALL—WE'RE ON A TIGHT SCHEDULE.

BLAMM!

BDAM

SPAFFE

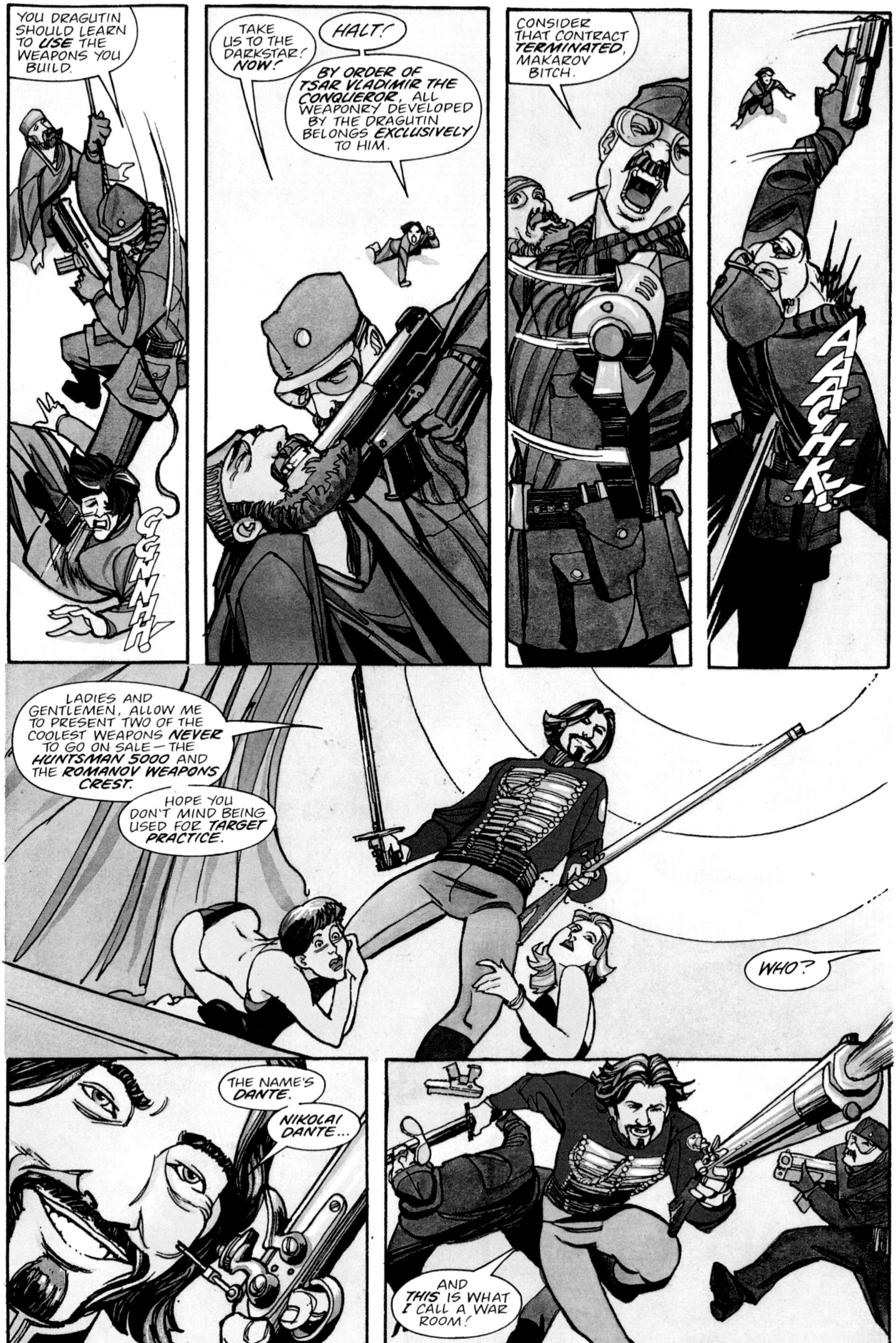

YOU DRAGUTIN SHOULD LEARN TO USE THE WEAPONS YOU BUILD.
GGHNNH!
TAKE US TO THE DARKSTAR! NOW!
HALT!
BY ORDER OF TSAR VLADIMIR THE CONQUEROR, ALL WEAPONRY DEVELOPED BY THE DRAGUTIN BELONGS EXCLUSIVELY TO HIM.
CONSIDER THAT CONTRACT TERMINATED, MAKAROV BITCH.
AAAGHK!
LADIES AND GENTLEMEN, ALLOW ME TO PRESENT TWO OF THE COOLEST WEAPONS NEVER TO GO ON SALE — THE HUNTSMAN 5000 AND THE ROMANOV WEAPONS CREST.
HOPE YOU DON'T MIND BEING USED FOR TARGET PRACTICE.
WHO?
THE NAME'S DANTE.
NIKOLAI DANTE...
AND THIS IS WHAT I CALL A WAR ROOM!

'My investigation on Draguta was interrupted by a full-scale military assault from forces unknown which ruthlessly devastated the city.'

'I might have been impressed if I wasn't one of the targets.' — LADY JENA MAKAROV, THE DARKSTAR JOURNALS.

ADMIT IT, JENA, THINGS WERE LOOKING PRETTY BAD FOR YOU BEFORE I TURNED UP.

THINGS'RE NEVER SO BAD THAT THEY CAN'T GET WORSE—NOT WHERE YOU'RE CONCERNED, DANTE!

IS THAT ALL THE THANKS I GET FOR SAVING YOUR ASS?

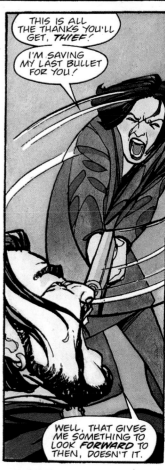

THIS IS ALL THE THANKS YOU'LL GET, THIEF!

I'M SAVING MY LAST BULLET FOR YOU!

WELL, THAT GIVES ME SOMETHING TO LOOK FORWARD TO THEN, DOESN'T IT.

KISSING A BULLET'S MORE FUN THAN KISSING YOU!

NOT HALF AS MUCH FUN AS PULLING THE TRIGGER!

THIS WAY! THE SECURITY DOORS WILL HOLD THEM!

SCRIPT
ROBBIE MORRISON
ART
SIMON FRASER
COLOURS
ALISON KIRKPATRICK
LETTERS
ANNIE PARKHOUSE

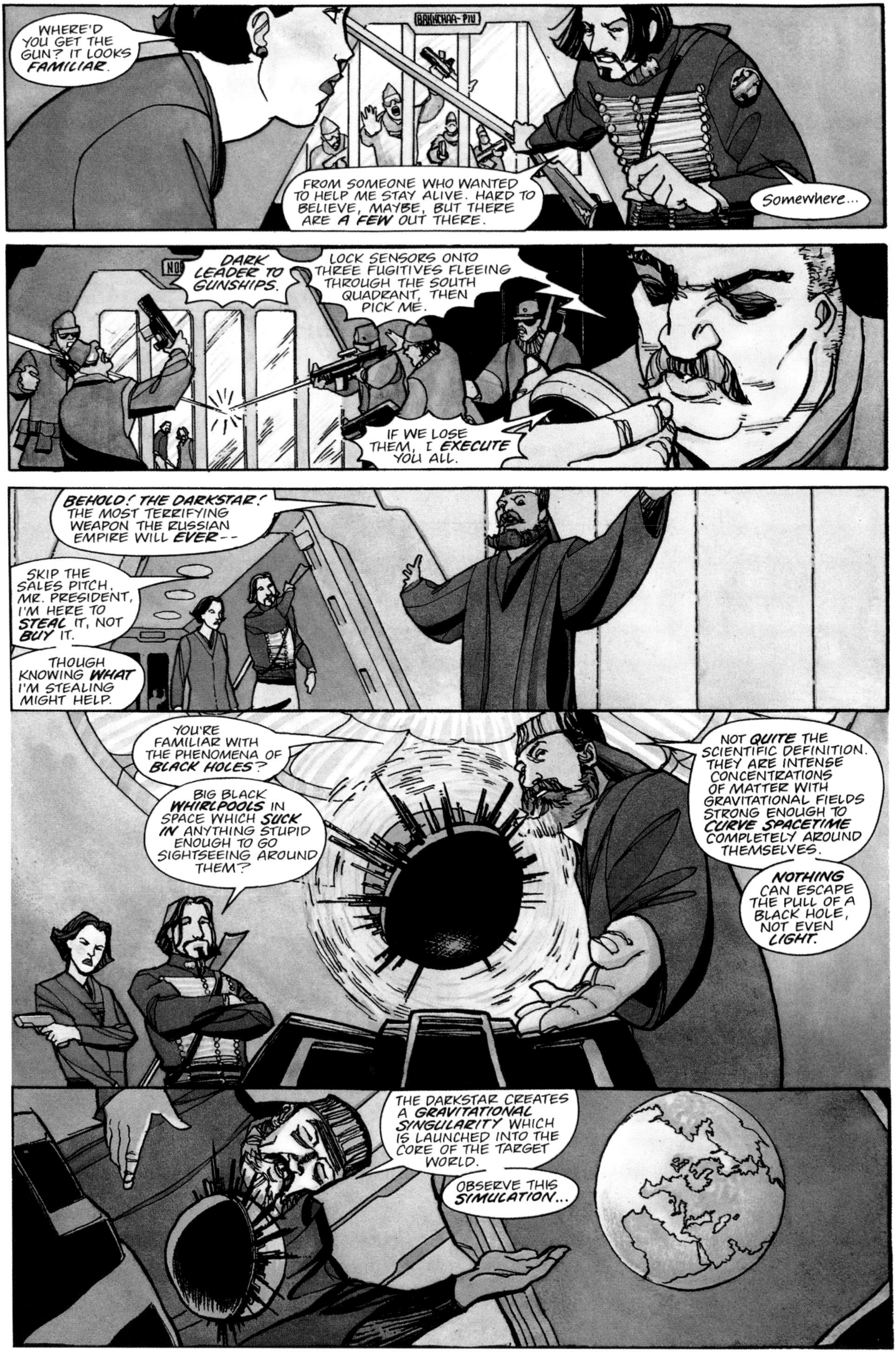
BAKHCHAA-PIU
WHERE'D YOU GET THE GUN? IT LOOKS FAMILIAR.
FROM SOMEONE WHO WANTED TO HELP ME STAY ALIVE. HARD TO BELIEVE, MAYBE, BUT THERE ARE A FEW OUT THERE.
Somewhere...
DARK LEADER TO GUNSHIPS.
LOCK SENSORS ONTO THREE FUGITIVES FLEEING THROUGH THE SOUTH QUADRANT, THEN PICK ME.
IF WE LOSE THEM, I EXECUTE YOU ALL.
BEHOLD! THE DARKSTAR! THE MOST TERRIFYING WEAPON THE RUSSIAN EMPIRE WILL EVER--
SKIP THE SALES PITCH, MR. PRESIDENT, I'M HERE TO STEAL IT, NOT BUY IT.
THOUGH KNOWING WHAT I'M STEALING MIGHT HELP.
YOU'RE FAMILIAR WITH THE PHENOMENA OF BLACK HOLES?
BIG BLACK WHIRLPOOLS IN SPACE WHICH SUCK IN ANYTHING STUPID ENOUGH TO GO SIGHTSEEING AROUND THEM?
NOT QUITE THE SCIENTIFIC DEFINITION. THEY ARE INTENSE CONCENTRATIONS OF MATTER WITH GRAVITATIONAL FIELDS STRONG ENOUGH TO CURVE SPACETIME COMPLETELY AROUND THEMSELVES.
NOTHING CAN ESCAPE THE PULL OF A BLACK HOLE, NOT EVEN LIGHT.
THE DARKSTAR CREATES A GRAVITATIONAL SINGULARITY WHICH IS LAUNCHED INTO THE CORE OF THE TARGET WORLD.
OBSERVE THIS SIMULATION...

"THE PLANET *IMPLODES* AROUND THE SINGULARITY, ITS *ENTIRE* MASS AND ENERGY COMPACTING INTO AN ALMOST INFINITESIMAL POINT, CREATING A BLACK HOLE...

"AND *OBLITERATING EVERY* LIVING THING ON THAT WORLD, PERHAPS EVEN THE *STAR SYSTEM* AROUND IT."

NOW DO YOU UNDERSTAND WHY WE CONCEALED ITS EXISTENCE? NO DYNASTY, *NO* WORLD, *NO* EMPIRE COULD BE TRUSTED WITH SUCH A WEAPON.

WHOEVER *HOLDS* THE DARKSTAR HOLDS THE *UNIVERSE*.

STRAFING FIRE. SHORT BURSTS.

DRIVE THEM AWAY FROM MISSION OBJECTIVE, THEN PICK THEM OFF AT LEISURE.

THOSE SHIPS...

I *KNOW* THOSE SHIPS.

HAAGHKK!

SPRAKK!

SPRAKK!

SPRAKK!

SPRAKK!

GUESS THE *STAKES* IN THE *GREAT GAME* JUST GOT A LITTLE *HIGHER*.

MAYBE WE SHOULD THINK ABOUT WORKING TOGETHER FOR A CHANGE...

BETTER THE DEVIL YOU KNOW, YOU MEAN?

SOMETHING LIKE THAT.

ONLY UNTIL OUR PRESENT SITUATION IS SATISFACTORILY RESOLVED?

OF COURSE. I'M NOT INTO *HEAVY*, *LONG-TERM* RELATIONSHIPS.

CHOOM! CHOOM! CHOOM!

RUN!!

SKRASHH!

SQUAD, TRANSPORT THE DARKSTAR TO THE CRUISER AND PROCEED TO THE RENDEZVOUS WORLD.

I'LL INFORM OUR NOBLE CLIENT THAT THE OPERATION WAS A SUCCESS.

THANK HIM FOR GIVING ME THE OPPORTUNITY TO REACQUAINT MYSELF WITH AN OLD FRIEND.

MUCH AS I'M ENJOYING THE *VIEW*, JENA, THINK YOU COULD HURRY IT UP A BIT?

SHUT UP. WE DIDN'T ALL SPEND OUR TEENAGE YEARS CLIMBING OUT OF LONELY OLD WIDOWS' BEDCHAMBERS AFTER *STEALING* THEIR *JEWELLRY.*

OLD *WIDOWS*?

I HAD MORE SELF-RESPECT THAN THAT—*YOUNG HEIRESSES* WERE MY SPECIALITY.

THE WHOLE EMPIRE'S IN DANGER BECAUSE I *FAILED* HERE TODAY...

RELAX, MILADY, *I'M* ON THE CASE.

WE'LL INFORM OUR HOUSES OF THE THREAT, THEN USE MY WEAPONS CREST TO ANALYSE --

WE?

UH, YEAH. WORKING *TOGETHER*? BETTER THE DEVIL YOU KNOW?

JENA, I, UH, DON'T LIKE THE *LOOK* ON YOUR FACE...

NO? I *LOVE* THE ONE ON YOURS.

I HAVE ALLIED MYSELF WITH *UNSAVOURY* CHARACTERS IN THE PAST, THAT'S *POLITICS*.

BUT YOU'RE THE *LAST* DEVIL I'D EVER MAKE A DEAL WITH!

WHOA!!

Y'KNOW, *CREST*, I'M BEGINNING TO THINK I'VE GOT A PROBLEM WITH WOMEN.

THE MORE THEY *DUMP* ON ME, THE MORE I *FANCY* THEM!

'The theft of the Darkstar weapon put the entire Empire in jeopardy.'

'The full military might of both the Tsar and the House of Romanov came into play as the stakes in the Great Game were raised to a terrifying level.'
— PRINCESS JENA MAKAROV, THE DARKSTAR JOURNALS.

BATTLESHIP POTEMKIN TO SHUTTLECRAFT DRAGO, YOU ARE CLEARED FOR DOCKING.

INFORM LORD DANTE THAT HE WILL BE MET UPON DISEMBARKATION.

ПОТЕМКИН

SCRIPT
ROBBIE MORRISON
ART
SIMON FRASER
COLOURS
ALISON KIRKPATRICK
LETTERS
ANNIE PARKHOUSE

LORD NIKOLAI, I AM THE DIRECTOR-GENERAL OF ROMANOV OFFWORLD INTELLIGENCE.

YOU MAY ADDRESS ME AS MADAM, DIRECTOR, OR MADAM-DIRECTOR. MY NAME ISN'T IMPORTANT.

WHAT I DON'T KNOW CAN'T HURT ME, HUH?

THE DYNASTY TRUSTS NO ONE, NIKOLAI, THAT'S HOW WE MAINTAIN POWER.

IT'S BEST THAT WE REMAIN A FACELESS ORGANISATION.

EMOTIONAL INVOLVEMENT AND PERSONAL ATTACHMENTS ARE A LIABILITY IN THE GAME.

NICE PLACE!

IT SUITS OUR PURPOSES.

THE POTEMKIN IS THE OPERATIONAL COMMAND OF THE ROMANOV OFFWORLD INTELLIGENCE NETWORK AND POSSESSES THE FIREPOWER OF A SMALL DYNASTY.

IT SERVES AS A CENTRALISED BASE FOR TRAINING OPERATIVES IN THE SKILLS NEEDED TO SURVIVE AND SUCCEED IN THE GAME...

BLACKMAIL, DECEPTION, CUNNING, THEFT, SABOTAGE, SKILL-AT-ARMS, SEDUCTION, ASSASSINATION.

GUESS SOME PEOPLE HAVE TO WORK *HARD* AT THAT SORT OF STUFF, AND SOME OF US IT JUST COMES *NATURALLY* TO.

CHILO, IF YOUR FLIPPANCY MASKS NERVOUSNESS, THEN PLEASE RELAX, I AM NOT YOUR ENEMY.

BEG YOUR PARDON, *MA'AM*. I'LL ENSURE THAT MY MANNERS ARE DECOROUS AND PRAISEWORTHY FROM––

WHOA!

I WANT ONE OF *THEM* WHEN I GROW UP.

THE *ROMANOVA STRIKEHAWK*, PERSONAL SPACECRAFT OF THE ROMANOV ELITE, OPERATED VIA THE PILOT'S WEAPONS CREST.

STATE-OF-THE-ART WEAPONRY, FASTER THAN A SOLAR YACHT AND MORE *MANOEUVRABLE* THAN A *RAVENWING*.

WHERE'S *MINE*? I'M THE *HERO* OF *RUDINSHTEIN*, DON'T *I* GET ONE?

CHILD, TO GAIN YOURSELF A HAWK YOU'D HAVE TO SELL THE CITY OF RUDINSHTEIN *TEN TIMES OVER*—NOT THAT *ANYONE* WOULD BUY IT.

EXCLUSIVE TO THE *BOLSHOI UNI-NEWS CHANNEL*—THE FIRST FOOTAGE OF THE *DRAGUTIN DISASTER*.

IMPERIAL SOURCES HAVE BLAMED A WEAPONS TESTING PROCEDURE WHICH MALFUNCTIONED FOR THE EXPLOSIONS WHICH LAID WASTE TO THE CITY.

Hmph.

THE TSAR'S *SPIN DOCTORS* ARE ALREADY WORKING OVERTIME, MADAM-DIRECTOR.

IN OTHER NEWS, THE RECENTLY DISCOVERED *VOIGHT-KAMPF COMET* PASSED THROUGH THE ANDROMEDA SYSTEM WITHOUT INCIDENT.

COSMOLOGISTS PREDICT THAT ALTHOUGH IT WILL PASS CLOSE ENOUGH TO IMPERIAL EARTH TO BE SEEN WITH THE NAKED EYE, THERE IS *NO* CHANCE OF COLLISION.

IN *ANCIENT* TIMES, THE APPEARANCE OF A COMET WAS REGARDED AS AN OMEN OF *DOOM*.

I HOPE THAT ISN'T PROVED TRUE IN LIGHT OF YOUR FAILURE TO SECURE THE DARKSTAR FOR US.

ROMANOV. VALENTINE ROMANOV.

I WISH I COULD SAY IT WAS A PLEASURE TO FINALLY MAKE YOUR ACQUAINTANCE, BUT I HAVE *FEW* PLEASURES LEFT, AND MEETING MY FATHER'S *BASTARD* ISN'T ONE OF THEM.

I, UH, THOUGHT I KNEW ALL THE FAMILY.

THERE'S A GREAT DEAL YOU DON'T KNOW.

I'M WHAT YOU MIGHT CALL THE *BLUNT INSTRUMENT* OF THE ROMANOV DYNASTY.

VALENTINE IS OUR PRIME *EXECUTIVE ACTION* AGENT, AS DEDICATED TO THE DYNASTY AS HIS FATHER *DMITRI*.

WHAT'S WITH THE *HOLO-IMPLANT*?

COSMETIC REASONS.

THE GAME LEAVES ITS MARK ON A MAN, AND NO MAN HAS *BLED MORE* IN THE NAME OF ROMANOV THAN VALENTINE.

MY *ONE* CONCESSION IN LIFE. I WEAR MY SCARS WITH *PRIDE*, IT'S THE REST OF THE EMPIRE THAT CAN'T *STOMACH* THEM.

YEAH? I JUST FIGURED YOU WERE AN *UGLY* BASTARD...

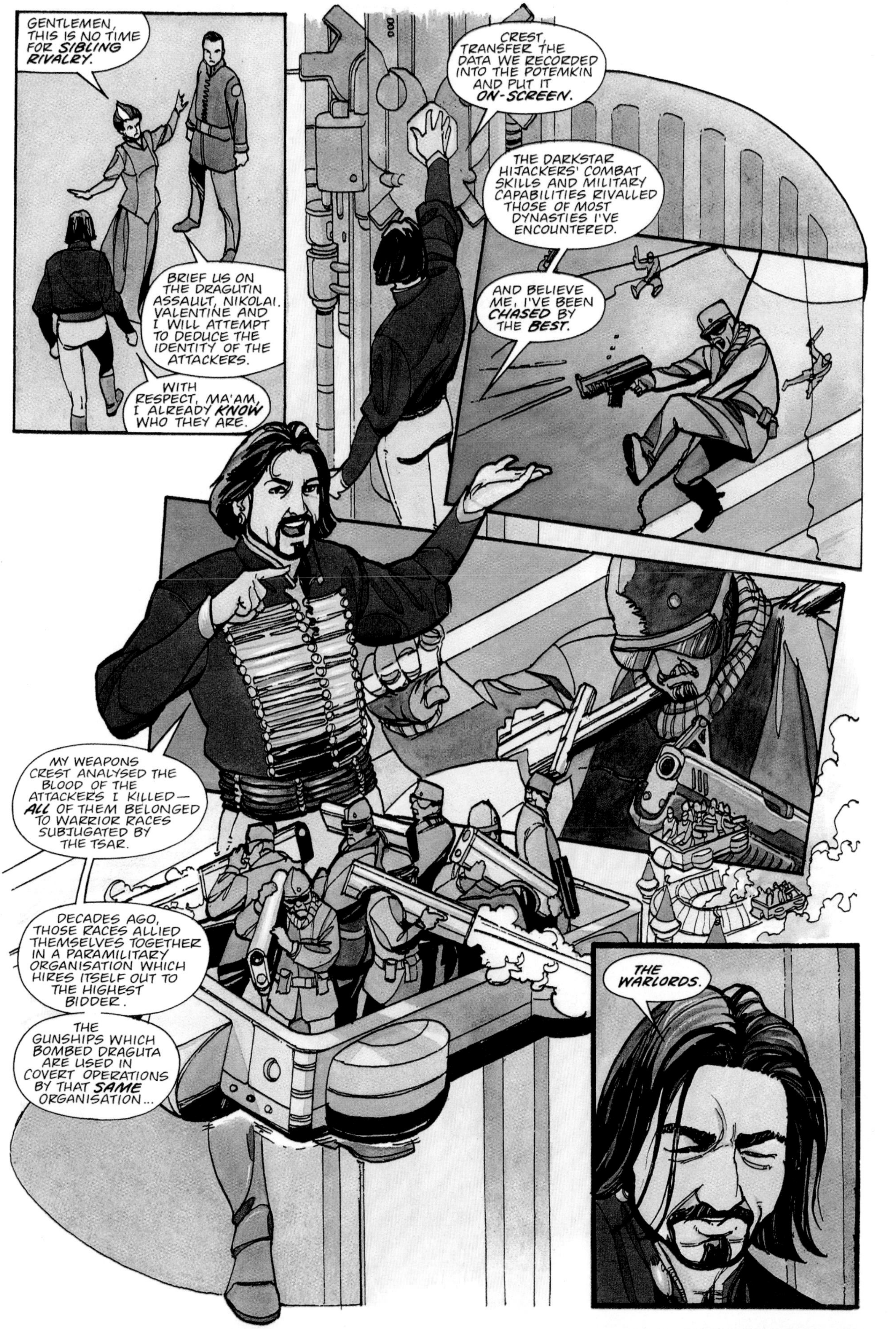
GENTLEMEN, THIS IS NO TIME FOR SIBLING RIVALRY.
BRIEF US ON THE DRAGUTIN ASSAULT, NIKOLAI. VALENTINE AND I WILL ATTEMPT TO DEDUCE THE IDENTITY OF THE ATTACKERS.
WITH RESPECT, MA'AM, I ALREADY KNOW WHO THEY ARE.
CREST, TRANSFER THE DATA WE RECORDED INTO THE POTEMKIN AND PUT IT ON-SCREEN.
THE DARKSTAR HIJACKERS' COMBAT SKILLS AND MILITARY CAPABILITIES RIVALLED THOSE OF MOST DYNASTIES I'VE ENCOUNTERED.
AND BELIEVE ME, I'VE BEEN CHASED BY THE BEST.
MY WEAPONS CREST ANALYSED THE BLOOD OF THE ATTACKERS I KILLED— ALL OF THEM BELONGED TO WARRIOR RACES SUBJUGATED BY THE TSAR.
DECADES AGO, THOSE RACES ALLIED THEMSELVES TOGETHER IN A PARAMILITARY ORGANISATION WHICH HIRES ITSELF OUT TO THE HIGHEST BIDDER.
THE GUNSHIPS WHICH BOMBED DRAGUTA ARE USED IN COVERT OPERATIONS BY THAT SAME ORGANISATION...
THE WARLORDS.

PERHAPS THE WARLORDS HAVE RELINQUISHED THE SAFETY OF COMMERCIAL PURSUITS AND MERCENARY IDEALS FOR A POLICY OF AGGRESSION.

SURPRISED IT DIDN'T HAPPEN *YEARS* AGO—FROM WHAT I HEAR, *ELENA DI JANISSAIRE'S* ONE HARD BITCH.

ELENA DI JANISSAIRE IS NO LONGER THEIR COMMANDER-IN-CHIEF. SHE... *COMMITTED SUICIDE* TWO YEARS AGO. HER *DAUGHTER'S* BEEN IN CHARGE SINCE THEN.

DIAVOLO...

SHE NEVER STRUCK ME AS THE *SUICIDAL* TYPE.

ANY *FOOL* CAN COMMIT A *MURDER*, DANTE, BUT IT TAKES A TRUE *ARTIST* TO COMMIT A *SUICIDE*.

I'M SURE HER DAUGHTER—THE LOVELY *ELOISE*—WILL PROVE *MOST* COOPERATIVE WHEN I CONVINCE HER HOW EASILY A PERSON CAN BE MADE TO TAKE THEIR OWN LIFE.

WHOA. NO WAY.

SEND ME IN INSTEAD OF *MR. LICENSED-TO-KILL*, MA'AM.

I'LL CHARM THE PANTS OFF HER TO FIND OUT WHATEVER WE NEED TO KNOW. NO ONE HAS TO DIE.

I HOPE YOU'RE NOT HIDING SOMETHING FROM ME, DANTE. AFTER ALL, WE ARE *FAMILY*.

YOU DO SEEM REMARKABLY *COCKSURE*, CHILD. DO YOU AND ELOISE DI JANISSAIRE *KNOW* EACH OTHER?

YOU, UH, COULD SAY THAT...

WE'RE MARRIED.

NIKOLAI DANTE

THE GREAT GAME — PART 5

SCRIPT
ROBBIE MORRISON
ART
SIMON FRASER
COLOURS
ALISON KIRKPATRICK
LETTERS
ANNIE PARKHOUSE

FORTRESS ARES, OPERATIONAL COMMAND OF THE WARLORD MERCENARIES, STOLIETOV'S WORLD.

'Over the last century, thousands of worlds have fallen to the forces of Tsar Vladimir The Conqueror.'

'Defeated military personnel from many of these societies formed the Warlords, the mercenary organisation which grew notorious under the late Elena Di Janissaive.'

'Entry to the Warlords can only be gained through fierce gladiatorial trials which celebrate the disciplines of warfare.' — 'FOR LOVE AND MONEY: A HISTORY OF MERCENARY WARFARE,' BY LORD PETER FLINT.

I WON! I'M A WAR-WARLORD!

ORDER A REVIEW OF OUR RECRUITMENT PROCEDURES.

WE SPEND MORE ON MEDICAL TREATMENT FOR OUR NEW WARRIORS THAN WE WOULD TRAINING THEM FROM SCRATCH.

COMMANDER DI JANISSAIRE, THERE'S A CANDIDATE IN THE SHOOTIST TRIALS YOU MIGHT WANT TO SEE — HE'S ABOUT TO FACE THREE SNIPER DRONES IN A SHOWDOWN SCENARIO.

THREE?

BRUTUS, BOTH GENERAL KVASS AND I HAVE TAKEN DOWN FIVE.

BLINDFOLDED?

I HOPE YOU DON'T THINK THIS AFFECTS THE *IMPARTIALITY* OF MY JUDGEMENT, SIR, BUT THAT'S A *FINE* OUTFIT YOU'RE WEARING. MAY I *APPROPRIATE* IT IN THE EVENT OF YOUR DEATH?

SURE, *FIRE AWAY.* I'LL TRY NOT TO GET *TOO* MANY BULLETHOLES IN IT.

FINE FELLOW! I'LL COUNT TO THREE, THEN GIVE THE ORDER...

ONE... TWO... THREE...

FIRE!

TESTING YOUR MARKSMANSHIP LIKE THAT'S A GOOD WAY TO GET YOURSELF *KILLED*, STRANGER...

I'M *TOO COOL* TO KILL.

SOMEONE TOLD ME THAT A FEW YEARS BACK. THINK SHE *STILL* FEELS THE SAME WAY?

Nikolai Dante...

THE PENTHOUSE APARTMENTS OF COMMANDER ELOISE DI JANISSAIRE.

NIKOLAI DANTE...

OF ALL THE CITIES IN ALL THE WORLDS OF THE EMPIRE, I JUST *KNEW* YOU'D COME CRAWLING INTO MINE ONE DAY...

GIVE ME ONE REASON WHY I SHOULDN'T DRAG YOU BEFORE A *FIRING SQUAD* — OTHER THAN IT WOULD BE TOO *QUICK* AND *EASY* A DEATH.

BECAUSE IF YOU DID THAT, YOU REALLY WOULD HAVE GROWN UP TO BE LIKE YOUR *MOTHER*, AND I'D HAVE TO *DUMP* YOU.

DUMP ME? YOU'RE LUCKY I DIDN'T DUMP *YOU* INTO A GRAVE BACK AT THE ARENA.

SENT A LOT OF MEN TO THEIR GRAVES SINCE *MONACO*?

NOT *PERSONALLY.* YOU MIGHT BE THE EXCEPTION...

WHY ARE YOU HERE, NIKOLAI?

WE'RE *MARRIED*, ELLIE. WE CAN'T *HIDE* FROM THAT FOREVER.

NO! JUST FOR *SEVEN YEARS!*

AND WAKING UP WITH A *KILLER HANGOVER* AND NO MEMORY OF THE EVENT OTHER THAN A *SCRAWLED* LICENCE AND A HOLO-IMAGE OF IT DOESN'T CONSTITUTE A *MARRIAGE* IN MY BOOK.

IF YOU CAN'T FORGIVE ME, THEN YOU MIGHT AS WELL *KILL* ME, 'CAUSE I'M DEAD WITHOUT YOU.

YOU'RE MY *WIFE*, ELOISE DI JANISSAIRE. I WANT US TO BE *TOGETHER*. FOREVER.

GGNNURGH RGH!

NICE *TRY*, NIKOLAI, BUT I'M NOT A *LITTLE GIRL* ANYMORE.

SO, WHAT'S THE GAME?

NOW THAT I'M A WOMAN OF *SUBSTANCE*, YOU'LL OOZE BACK IN THERE LIKE A *SLUG*, THEN *DIVORCE* ME AND TAKE *HALF* OF EVERYTHING I OWN?

I GUESS I *DESERVED* THAT.

I NEVER COULD *LIE* TO YOU...

NO?

YOU SAID YOU'D COME *BACK* FOR ME, AND YOU *NEVER* DID. YOU SAID YOU'D *RESCUE* ME, AND YOU *RAN*.

HMPHH!

I AM *BACK!*

NOW SHUT UP AND LET ME RESCUE YOU!

THE ROMANOV DYNASTY IS ON THE VERGE OF DECLARING **WAR** ON YOU, EXCEPT IT WON'T BE A WAR, IT'LL BE A **MASSACRE**.

I'VE NO QUARREL WITH THE ROMANOVS, WITH **ANY** NOBLE HOUSE.

THE **DARKSTAR**, ELOISE, THE MOST POWERFUL WEAPON IN THE EMPIRE. YOU STOLE IT FROM THE DRAGLITIN—IT'S **ONBOARD** ONE OF YOUR CRUISERS RIGHT NOW.

I'VE NEVER HEARD OF ANY DARKSTAR, NIKOLAI, AND I SANCTIONED NO MISSIONS TO DRAGUTA.

TRUST ME, I WAS **THERE**.

Never trust a thief...

COMPUTER. PINPOINT EVERY SHIP CURRENTLY ON ASSIGNMENT.

THE CRUISER **ERICH VON STALHEIN'S** SUPPOSED TO BE IN DRY-DOCK.

WHERE'S IT GOING? AND ON WHOSE ORDERS?

DESTINATION: SHAKAN T. AUTHORISATION: GENERAL KVASS.

I FORGOT, YOU'RE NOT A THIEF ANYMORE, YOU'RE AN ARISTOCRAT OF THE ROMANOV DYNASTY, AND I'M THE LEADER OF AN ORGANISATION WHICH RAPES AND MURDERS FOR MONEY.

We both **became** what we **always** hated, Kolya...

HOW **TOUCHING**...

THE YOUNG **LOVERS**, KISSING AND MAKING UP.

WHAT'S GOING ON, **KVASS**?

IT'S CALLED A **COUP**, ELOISE.

AND DON'T THINK IT'S GOING TO BE **BLOODLESS**.

"While I pursued the hijackers of the Darkstar weapon through more surreptitious channels, Nikolai Dante stepped straight into the line of fire.

'Some people never learn' — PRINCESS JENA MAKAROV, THE DARKSTAR JOURNALS.

NIKOLAI DANTE

THE GREAT GAME PART 6

WHY?

BECAUSE OF YOUR WEAKNESS, ELOISE! BECAUSE WE ARE THE WARLORDS!

WE ARE THE MASTERS OF CONFLICT. THE MASTERS! WE SHOULDN'T PROSTITUTE OUR SKILLS TO SCUM WHO AREN'T WORTHY OF THEM.

POSSESSION OF THE DARKSTAR WILL ALLOW US TO CONTROL OUR OWN DESTINY, TO BECOME A MILITARY POWER STRONG ENOUGH TO OVERTHROW ANYONE.

STARTING WITH ME?

I WOULD'VE FOLLOWED YOUR MOTHER TO HELL AND BACK, ELOISE.

BUT YOU TRIED TO FORMULATE AN 'ETHICAL APPROACH' TO OUR BUSINESS, AND ETHICS HAVE NO PLACE IN WARFARE.

IT'LL BE SUCH A TRAGEDY WHEN THEY FIND YOUR CORPSES—TWO YOUNG LOVERS WHO KILLED EACH OTHER IN A FIT OF PASSION.

AT LEAST, THAT'S HOW WE'LL MAKE IT LOOK.

HELL, KVASS, IF YOU'D WAITED A LITTLE LONGER WE PROBABLY WOULD HAVE...

STAY WHERE YOU ARE, THIEF.

DON'T EVEN THINK OF GOING FOR THAT RIFLE.

HEY, WHO NEEDS THE HUNTSMAN?

THESE HANDS ARE DEADLY WEAPONS...

SCRIPT
ROBBIE MORRISON

ART
SIMON FRASER

COLOURS
ALISON KIRKPATRICK

LETTERS
ANNIE PARKHOUSE

YOU TOO, BRUTUS?

BEFORE HE DIED, MY FATHER TAUGHT ME THAT—NO MATTER *WHAT* THE SPECIES—THE FEMALE IS *ALWAYS* WEAKER THAN THE MALE.

YOU'VE DONE *NOTHING* TO DISPROVE THE THEORY.

NO? GIVE HIM MY *REGARDS!*

HACK!

SEE? WHAT DID I TELL YOU?

SHIK!

NIKOLAI! DOWN!

KRAKK!

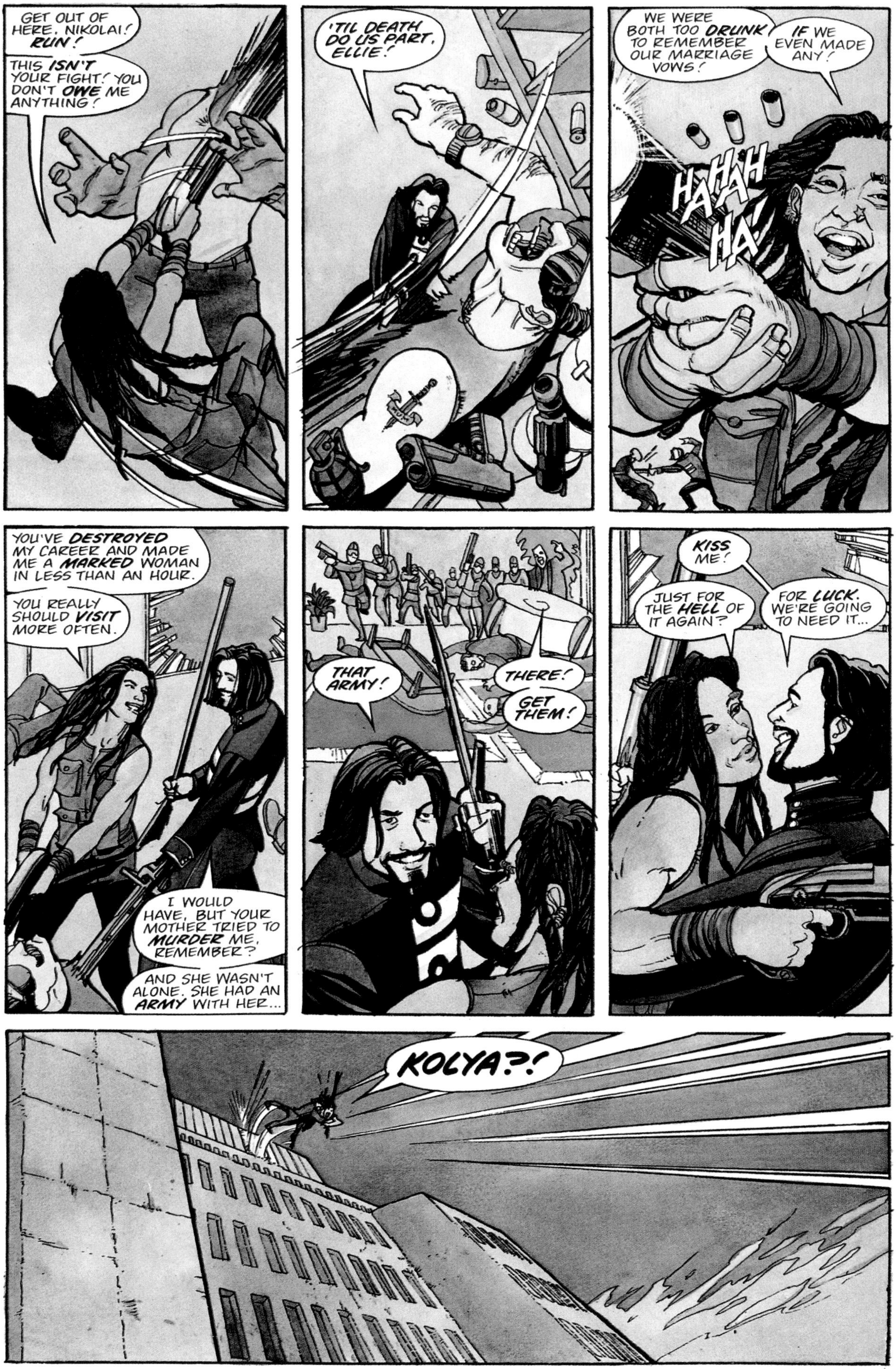
GET OUT OF HERE, NIKOLAI! RUN!
THIS ISN'T YOUR FIGHT! YOU DON'T OWE ME ANYTHING!
'TIL DEATH DO US PART, ELLIE!
WE WERE BOTH TOO DRUNK TO REMEMBER OUR MARRIAGE VOWS!
IF WE EVEN MADE ANY!
HAHAHAHA!
YOU'VE DESTROYED MY CAREER AND MADE ME A MARKED WOMAN IN LESS THAN AN HOUR.
YOU REALLY SHOULD VISIT MORE OFTEN.
I WOULD HAVE, BUT YOUR MOTHER TRIED TO MURDER ME, REMEMBER?
AND SHE WASN'T ALONE. SHE HAD AN ARMY WITH HER...
THAT ARMY!
THERE!
GET THEM!
KISS ME!
JUST FOR THE HELL OF IT AGAIN?
FOR LUCK. WE'RE GOING TO NEED IT...
KOLYA?!

CREST!

Oh! You've finally remembered I exist...

Strange how you **ignore** me when you're in the company of women, but feel the urge to communicate whenever your **life** is in danger.

THIS IS NO TIME TO BE GETTING **JEALOUS** ON ME, CREST!

CALL IN THE **STRIKEHAWK!** NOW!

As **ever**, Dante, I'm one step ahead of you...

Jealous, indeed!

DANTE TO BATTLESHIP POTEMKIN! THE WARLORDS DID HIJACK THE **DARKSTAR**—IT'S EN ROUTE TO **SHAKAN 7** ABOARD THE CRUISER **ERICH VON STALHEIN.**

I'M GOING TO TRY AND INTERCEPT THEM...

WILL WONDERS NEVER CEASE? THE **HERO OF RUDINSHTEIN** TURNS OUT TO BE THE **GENUINE** ARTICLE AFTER ALL...

GOOD WORK, LITTLE BROTHER. I'LL SEE YOU ON **SHAKAN 7.**

THAT WAS, UH, QUITE A **RIDE.**

YOU KNOW ME.

KISS KISS, BANG BANG.

IN THE NAME OF TSAR VLADIMIR THE CONQUEROR! DEATH TO THE WARLORDS!

RAVEN CORPS! ATTACK!

JENA MAKAROV!?

WARLORDS! DEFEND THE DARKSTAR WITH YOUR LIVES!

IF THIS IS *YOUR* DOING, DANTE...

AAAAGHKK!

THE *TRUTH'S* OUT NOW, eh?

Bojemoi...

LOOK WHAT THEY'VE *DONE* TO ME, OUR PRECIOUS FAMILY...

I WAS THE *FIRST* TO BEAR THE CREST, BUT THE BIOTECHNOLOGY WASN'T PERFECTED. THE HEALING FACTOR DIDN'T *QUITE* WORK.

EVERY TIME I USE MY CREST, IT *TEARS* ME APART. EVERY TIME *I* KILL, IT KILLS *ANOTHER* PART OF ME.

NO ONE HAS *BLED MORE* FOR THE ROMANOV DYNASTY THAN I...

IT'S TIME THEY BLED FOR ME!

OOF!

HOW SHOULD WE *THANK* DANTE FOR LEADING US TO THE DARKSTAR, LADY JENA?

A BULLET IN THE *BRAIN*, OR ONE *STRAIGHT* BETWEEN THE LEGS?

THAT *IS* WHERE HIS BRAINS ARE, LIEUTENANT!

GIVE IT UP, VALENTINE! *LET HER GO!*

YOU KNOW THE *HUNTSMAN'S* CAPABILITIES! IT'LL *DESTROY* THE DARKSTAR!

NO, BOY. *YOU* GIVE UP. DROP THE RIFLE...

OR I'LL *SLIT* HER THROAT AND *SHOWER* YOU WITH *BLOOD*.

DON'T LISTEN TO HIM, *KOLYA!* DO IT! SHOOT IT AND GET AWAY, GET OUT OF HERE!

ELLIE...

LEAVE ME...

BLOW IT AWAY TO HELL AND *RUN*...

Please...

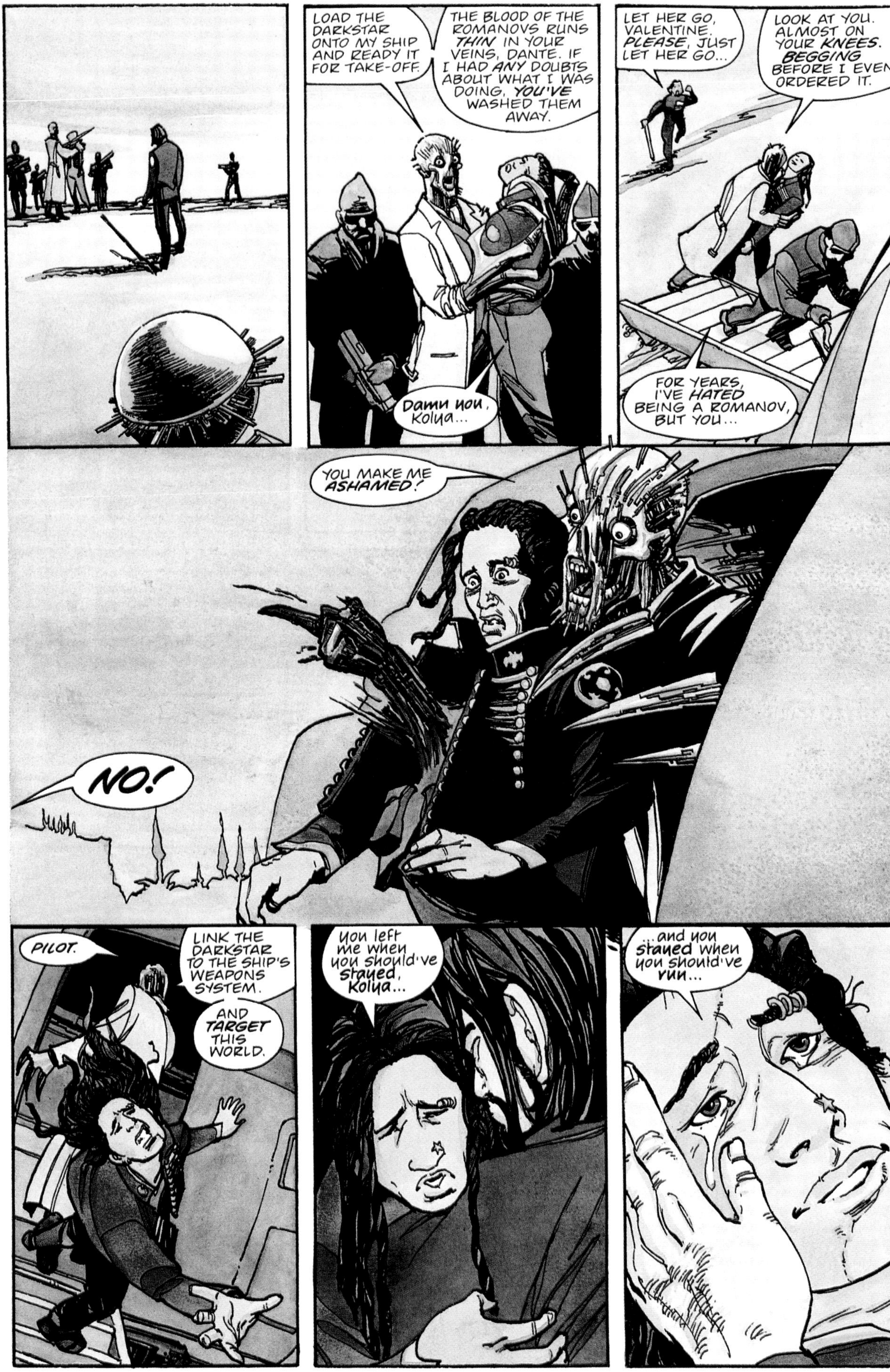
LOAD THE DARKSTAR ONTO MY SHIP AND READY IT FOR TAKE-OFF.
THE BLOOD OF THE ROMANOVS RUNS THIN IN YOUR VEINS, DANTE. IF I HAD ANY DOUBTS ABOUT WHAT I WAS DOING, YOU'VE WASHED THEM AWAY.
Damn you, Kolya...
LET HER GO, VALENTINE. PLEASE, JUST LET HER GO...
LOOK AT YOU. ALMOST ON YOUR KNEES. BEGGING BEFORE I EVEN ORDERED IT.
FOR YEARS, I'VE HATED BEING A ROMANOV, BUT YOU...
YOU MAKE ME ASHAMED!
NO!
PILOT.
LINK THE DARKSTAR TO THE SHIP'S WEAPONS SYSTEM.
AND TARGET THIS WORLD.
You left me when you should've stayed, Kolya...
...and you stayed when you should've run...

Ellie...

THE DARKSTAR'S ACTIVATED, SIR, BUT WE'VE STILL GOT MEN ON THE GROUND.

THEY'RE *SOLDIERS.* IT'S THEIR *DUTY* TO DIE IF THEY'RE *ORDERED* TO. IF THEY'RE UNHAPPY WITH THAT, THEY DON'T *DESERVE* TO LIVE.

FIRE THE DARKSTAR!

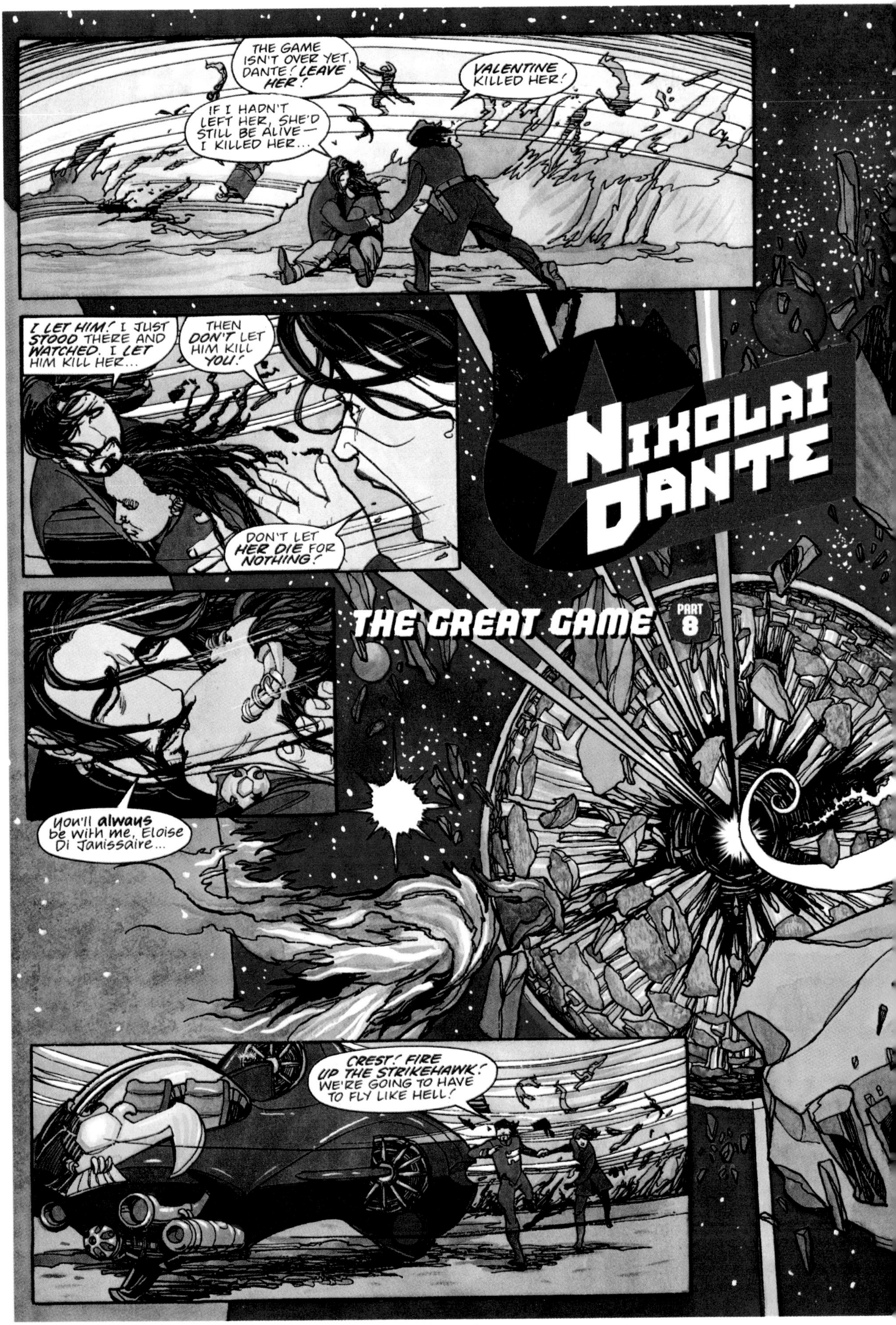

THE GAME ISN'T OVER YET, DANTE! LEAVE HER!
IF I HADN'T LEFT HER, SHE'D STILL BE ALIVE — I KILLED HER...
VALENTINE KILLED HER!
I LET HIM! I JUST STOOD THERE AND WATCHED. I LET HIM KILL HER...
THEN DON'T LET HIM KILL YOU!
DON'T LET HER DIE FOR NOTHING!
NIKOLAI DANTE
THE GREAT GAME PART 8
You'll always be with me, Eloise Di Janissaire...
CREST! FIRE UP THE STRIKEHAWK! WE'RE GOING TO HAVE TO FLY LIKE HELL!

'The Darkstar weapon creates a gravitational singularity which is launched into the core of the target world.'

'The planet implodes around the singularity, its entire mass and energy compacting into an almost infinitesimal point, creating a Black Hole and obliterating every living thing on that planet.'

'Valentine Romanov targeted the Darkstar upon Shakan 7 at 19:47 hours, Imperial time. By 20:10, Shakan 7 ceased to exist as a planetary body.'

'Observing the Darkstar chain-reaction on computer simulation had been impressive enough. Getting caught in the middle of it was an earth-shattering experience.' — *PRINCESS JENA MAKAROV, THE DARKSTAR JOURNALS.*

SCRIPT
ROBBIE MORRISON

ART
SIMON FRASER

COLOURS
ALISON KIRKPATRICK

LETTERS
ANNIE PARKHOUSE

THE BATTLESHIP POTEMKIN, ORBITING THE SHAKAN 7 BLACK HOLE AT A SAFE DISTANCE.

I THOUGHT YOU WERE THE *LOVE-THEM-AND-LEAVE-THEM* TYPE, DANTE, THE KIND THAT DOESN'T RISK HIS LIFE FOR *ANYONE*, LET ALONE A *WOMAN*.

YEAH, WELL, IT'S NOT OFTEN YOU GET A CHANCE TO KISS AND MAKE UP WITH YOUR WIFE AFTER SEVEN YEARS.

YOUR *WIFE*?

ELOISE DI JANISSAIRE WAS YOUR *WIFE*?

YEAH, FOR A *LITTLE* WHILE THERE, SHE *REALLY WAS...*

DID YOU..?

DID YOU *LOVE* HER?

WHAT'S *LOVE*, JENA?? TELL ME WHAT IT IS.

THE ONLY *LOVE* I'VE EVER SEEN IN ANYONE — *YOU*, THE *ROMANOVS*, THE *TSAR* — IS FOR *POWER* AND *WEALTH* AND WHAT THEY LET YOU *DO* TO THE PEOPLE THAT DON'T HAVE THEM.

WHO ARE *YOU* TO JUDGE *ANYONE*, NIKOLAI??

YOU DON'T *KNOW* ME...

NO, I don't know anything...

DANTE. LADY JENA.

THE *HOLO-CONFERENCE* WITH OUR DYNASTIES IS ABOUT TO BEGIN. I'M SURE I DON'T NEED TO STRESS THE *IMPORTANCE* OF ATTENDING.

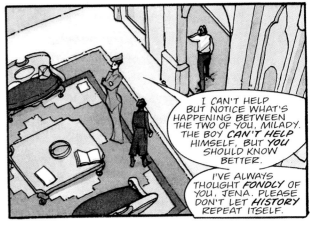

I CAN'T HELP BUT NOTICE WHAT'S HAPPENING BETWEEN THE TWO OF YOU, MILADY. THE BOY *CAN'T HELP* HIMSELF, BUT *YOU* SHOULD KNOW BETTER.

I'VE ALWAYS THOUGHT *FONDLY* OF YOU, JENA. PLEASE DON'T LET *HISTORY* REPEAT ITSELF.

IT'S *ALWAYS* A PLEASURE TO FIND MYSELF IN YOUR COMPANY, MADAME-DIRECTOR.

YOU REMAIN, AS EVER, THE *ONLY* WOMAN IN THE EMPIRE WHOSE HAND I BOW TO KISS.

IF ONLY WE WEREN'T PALE HOLOGRAPHIC SHADOWS OF OUR TRUE SELVES.

AND YOU, *TSAR VLADIMIR*, ARE AS INFURIATING AS YOU EVER WERE. IT'S A SHAME ONLY A *MAJOR CRISIS* CAN MAKE OUR HOUSES WORK TOGETHER.

A SEARCH DRONE LOCATED VALENTINE'S SHIP. SEEMS HE TRIED TO DESTROY IT BY ABANDONING IT IN THE PATH OF THE *VOIGHT-KAMPF COMET*.

WE'RE SENDING A TEAM TO INVESTIGATE, BUT I DOUBT WE'LL FIND ANY CLUES TO HIS LOCATION.

FAMILIES, THEY ALWAYS *HURT* THE ONES THEY *LOVE*.

DANTE, YOU AND THE LADY JENA WILL RETURN TO EARTH WITH THE POTEMKIN. THE TSAR AND I ARE TAKING CHARGE OF THE DARKSTAR AFFAIR.

PERSONALLY.

YOU ARE, AS THEY USED TO SAY IN ANCIENT TIMES, *OFF THE CASE.*

FUOCO!

TRANSMISSION'S OVER.

THAT WAS *SHORT* AND *SWEET.*

NIKOLAI, IF YOU WISH TO PURSUE VALENTINE IN A *RENEGADE* CAPACITY, IN DEFIANCE OF DYNASTIC DECREE, I *WON'T* STOP YOU.

ALL I WANT TO KNOW IS WHAT YOU'LL *DO* IF YOU FIND HIM.

I'LL *KILL* HIM OR HE'LL *KILL* ME.

ISN'T THAT WHAT *EVERYBODY* WANTS?

OF COURSE...

BUT I DOUBT THERE'S MANY *MOTHERS* WHO CAN HAPPILY CONDEMN THEIR SONS TO *DEATH*, NO MATTER *WHAT* THEIR CRIMES.

HUH!?

MY SON. THEY'RE *ALL* MY CHILDREN. *VALENTINE*, *KONSTANTIN*, *LULU*, *ANDREAS*, *VIKTOR*, *NASTASIA*. ALL OF THEM.

DMITRI IS THE *PATRIARCH* OF THE ROMANOV DYNASTY. I AM THE *MATRIARCH*.

Heh, DOES THIS MEAN I HAVE TO START CALLING YOU *MAMA* INSTEAD OF *MA'AM*?

I THINK WE CAN *BOTH* LIVE WITHOUT THAT, CHILD.

GO, BEFORE I CHANGE MY MIND. AND FORGIVE ME IF I *DON'T* WISH YOU LUCK...

YOU *STILL* FOLLOWING ME, JENA?

I- I DON'T KNOW...

I'VE NEVER DISOBEYED AN ORDER FROM MY FATHER BEFORE...

NO?

I'VE *NEVER* OBEYED AN ORDER FROM ANYONE IN MY LIFE!

ANALYSIS, CREST?

This destruction did not result from a collision with the *Voight-Kampf Comet*, Dante.

I'm familiar with the destructive capabilities of all known Imperial weapons. This is the work of a warship-calibre *Plasma Cannon.*

And another thing...

NIKOLAI DANTE

THE GREAT GAME PART 9

I believe the *Voight-Kampf* may hold a great deal *more* than ice and dust.

Its ion tail contains certain trace elements normally only produced by a *starship.*

GUESS THERE'S ONLY ONE THING FOR IT, THEN...

FOLLOW THAT STAR!

DO YOU HAVE ANY IDEA HOW *IRRITATING* IT IS TRYING TO EAVESDROP ON A *ONE*-SIDED CONVERSATION?

DON'T WORRY, WE WEREN'T TALKING ABOUT YOU.

MUCH...

'THAT'S NO COMET...'

BY ANASTASIA'S BONES!

VALENTINE...

IT'S SO *NICE* TO PAY MY RESPECTS TO THE FAMILY ONE *LAST* TIME.

ARE YOU ALL WELL? ARE YOU ALL STILL GOOD LITTLE CHILDREN?

FORGIVE MY *MELODRAMATIC* ENTRANCE.

I'VE SPENT SO MUCH OF MY LIFE IMMERSED IN ESPIONAGE AND SUBTERFUGE THAT I FIND RISING ABOVE IT ALL ESPECIALLY LIBERATING.

PERHAPS THAT'S WHY I'M DEVELOPING A TASTE FOR *GRANDILOQUENT* GESTURES...

THE DARKSTAR IS TARGETED UPON IMPERIAL EARTH.

WHEN IT FIRES, DANTE AND THE LADY JENA WILL BE AT THE *HEART* OF THE SINGULARITY WHICH TURNS EARTH INTO A *BLACK HOLE*.

MADNESS!

MADNESS THAT *YOU* CREATED, *FATHER!*

YOU BONDED ME WITH AN IMPERFECT WEAPONS CREST, SENT ME INTO *EXILE* WHEN IT DISFIGURED ME, ABANDONED ME TO *KILL* OR *BE KILLED.*

WE'VE PLAYED THE GREAT GAME FOR CENTURIES — *NO MORE!* TODAY I *END* THE GAME. *FOREVER!*

DANTE, YOU SURE KNOW HOW TO SHOW A GIRL A GOOD TIME!

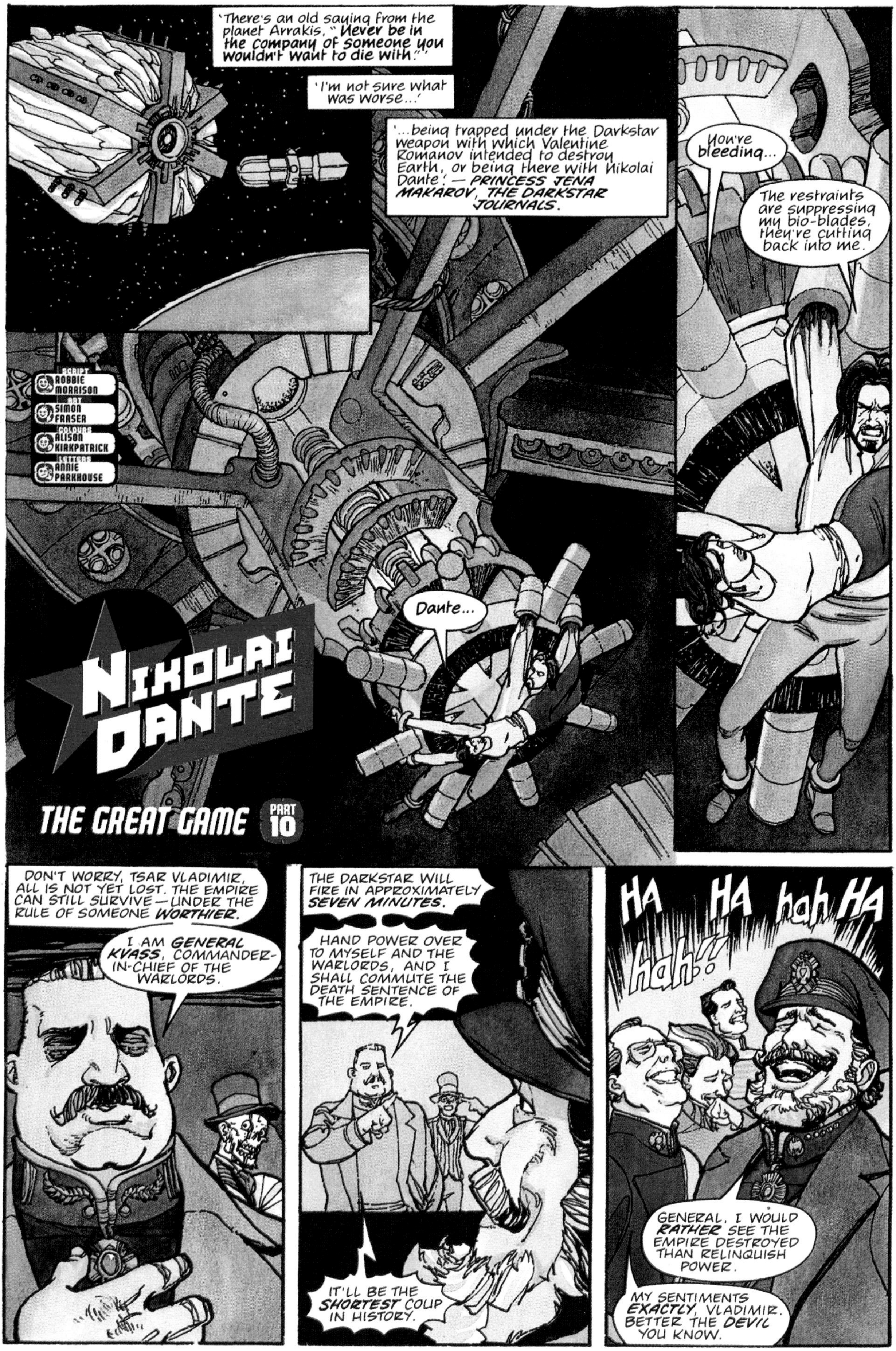
'There's an old saying from the planet Arrakis, "Never be in the company of someone you wouldn't want to die with."'
'I'm not sure what was worse...'
'...being trapped under the Darkstar weapon with which Valentine Romanov intended to destroy Earth, or being there with Nikolai Dante.' — PRINCESS JENA MAKAROV, THE DARKSTAR JOURNALS.
You're bleeding...
The restraints are suppressing my bio-blades, they're cutting back into me.
SCRIPT ROBBIE MORRISON
ART SIMON FRASER
COLOURS ALISON KIRKPATRICK
LETTERS ANNIE PARKHOUSE
Dante...
NIKOLAI DANTE
THE GREAT GAME PART 10
DON'T WORRY, TSAR VLADIMIR, ALL IS NOT YET LOST. THE EMPIRE CAN STILL SURVIVE — UNDER THE RULE OF SOMEONE WORTHIER.
I AM GENERAL KVASS, COMMANDER-IN-CHIEF OF THE WARLORDS.
THE DARKSTAR WILL FIRE IN APPROXIMATELY SEVEN MINUTES.
HAND POWER OVER TO MYSELF AND THE WARLORDS, AND I SHALL COMMUTE THE DEATH SENTENCE OF THE EMPIRE.
IT'LL BE THE SHORTEST COUP IN HISTORY.
HA HA hah HA hah!!
GENERAL, I WOULD RATHER SEE THE EMPIRE DESTROYED THAN RELINQUISH POWER.
MY SENTIMENTS EXACTLY, VLADIMIR. BETTER THE DEVIL YOU KNOW.

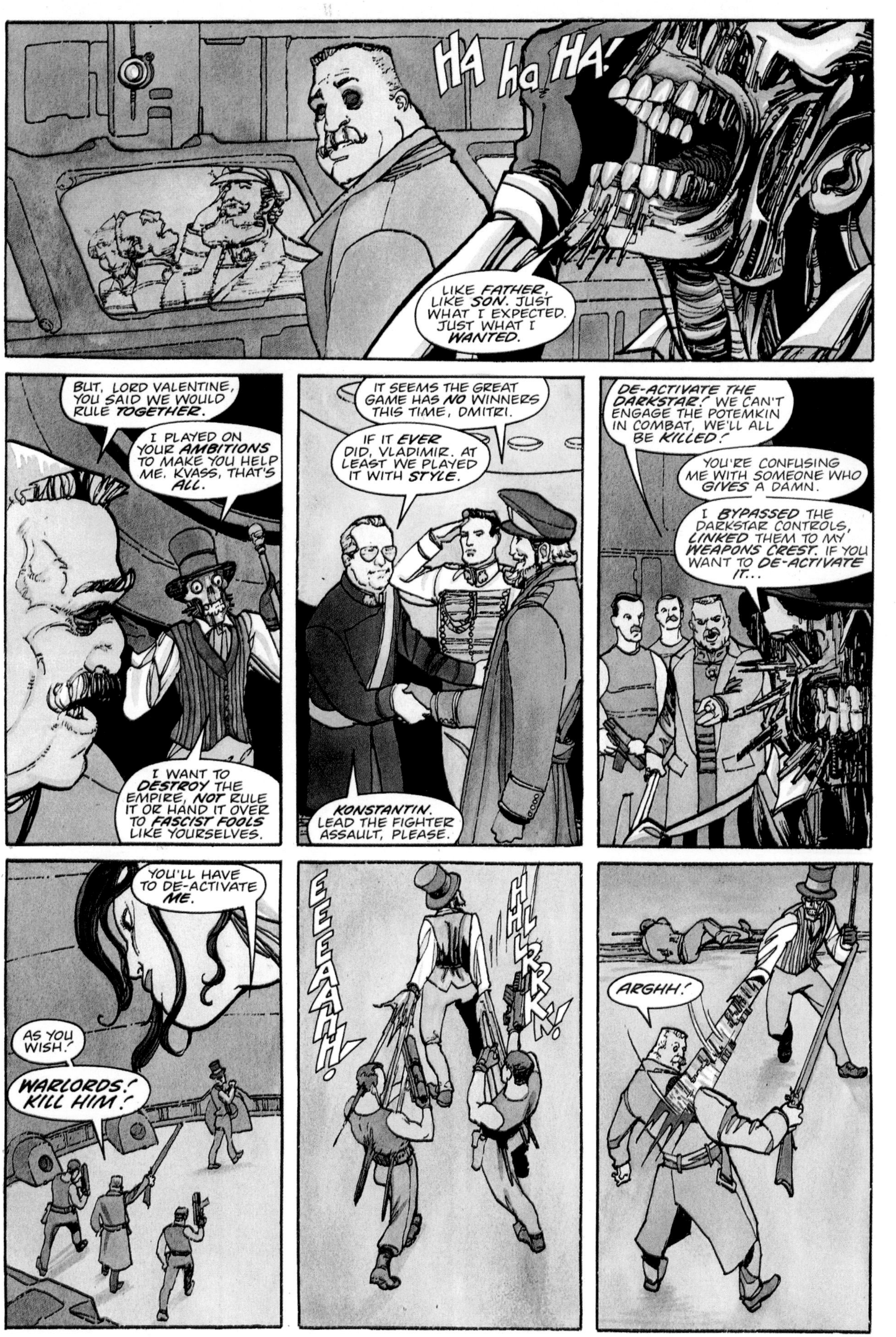
HA ha HA!
LIKE FATHER, LIKE SON. JUST WHAT I EXPECTED. JUST WHAT I WANTED.
BUT, LORD VALENTINE, YOU SAID WE WOULD RULE TOGETHER.
I PLAYED ON YOUR AMBITIONS TO MAKE YOU HELP ME, KVASS, THAT'S ALL.
I WANT TO DESTROY THE EMPIRE, NOT RULE IT OR HAND IT OVER TO FASCIST FOOLS LIKE YOURSELVES.
IT SEEMS THE GREAT GAME HAS NO WINNERS THIS TIME, DMITRI.
IF IT EVER DID, VLADIMIR. AT LEAST WE PLAYED IT WITH STYLE.
KONSTANTIN. LEAD THE FIGHTER ASSAULT, PLEASE.
DE-ACTIVATE THE DARKSTAR! WE CAN'T ENGAGE THE POTEMKIN IN COMBAT, WE'LL ALL BE KILLED!
YOU'RE CONFUSING ME WITH SOMEONE WHO GIVES A DAMN.
I BYPASSED THE DARKSTAR CONTROLS, LINKED THEM TO MY WEAPONS CREST. IF YOU WANT TO DE-ACTIVATE IT...
YOU'LL HAVE TO DE-ACTIVATE ME.
AS YOU WISH!
WARLORDS! KILL HIM!
EEEAAAHH!
HHLRRKK!
ARGHH!

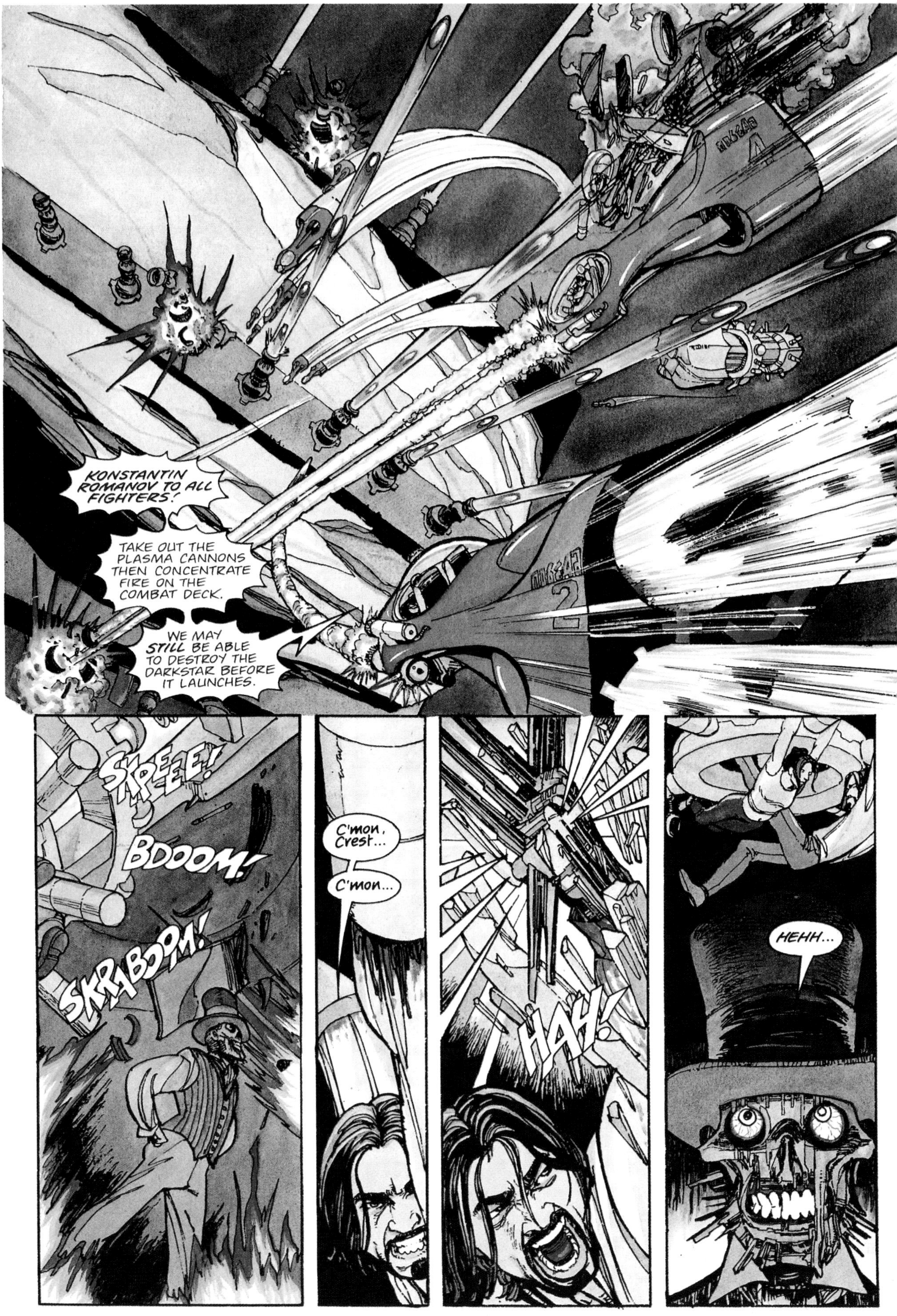
KONSTANTIN ROMANOV TO ALL FIGHTERS!
TAKE OUT THE PLASMA CANNONS THEN CONCENTRATE FIRE ON THE COMBAT DECK.
WE MAY STILL BE ABLE TO DESTROY THE DARKSTAR BEFORE IT LAUNCHES.
SKREEEE!
BDOOM!
SKRABOOM!
C'mon, Crest...
C'mon...
HAY!
HEHH...

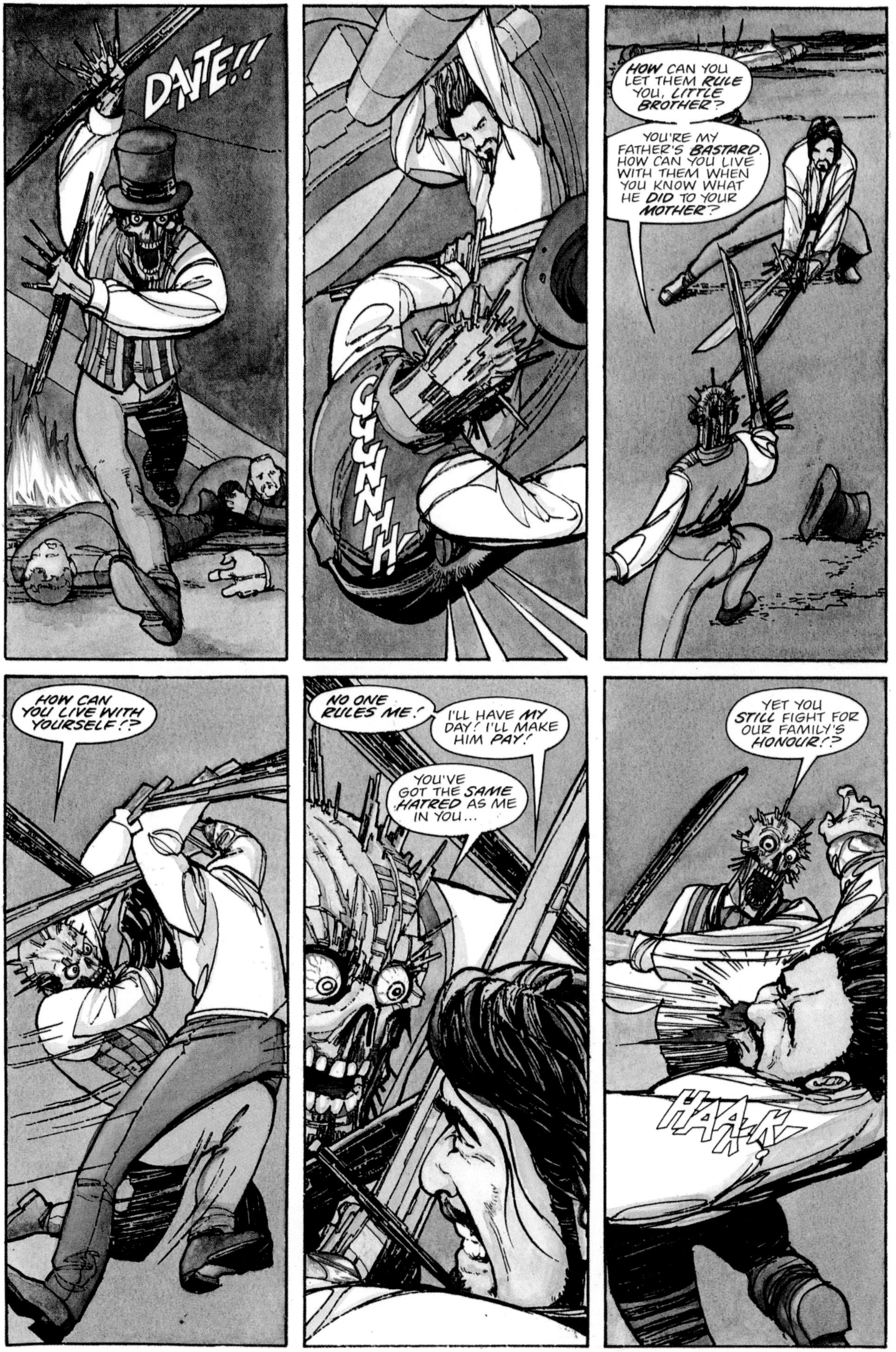
DANTE!!
GUNNH!
HOW CAN YOU LET THEM RULE YOU, LITTLE BROTHER?
YOU'RE MY FATHER'S BASTARD. HOW CAN YOU LIVE WITH THEM WHEN YOU KNOW WHAT HE DID TO YOUR MOTHER?
HOW CAN YOU LIVE WITH YOURSELF!?
NO ONE RULES ME!
I'LL HAVE MY DAY! I'LL MAKE HIM PAY!
YOU'VE GOT THE SAME HATRED AS ME IN YOU...
YET YOU STILL FIGHT FOR OUR FAMILY'S HONOUR!?
HAAK!

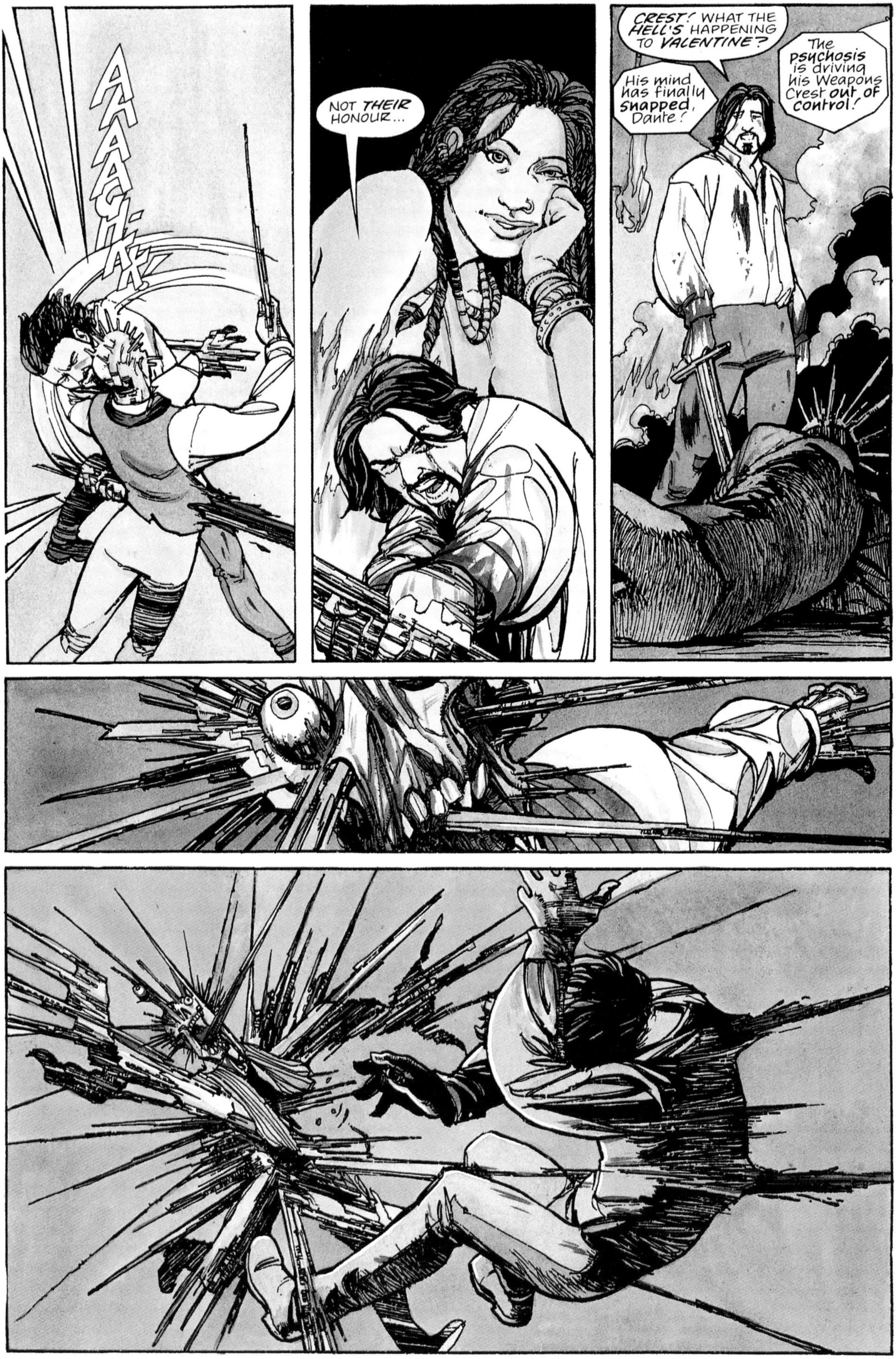

AAAAGH-AAA
NOT THEIR HONOUR...
CREST! WHAT THE HELL'S HAPPENING TO VALENTINE?
His mind has finally snapped, Dante!
The psychosis is driving his Weapons Crest out of control!

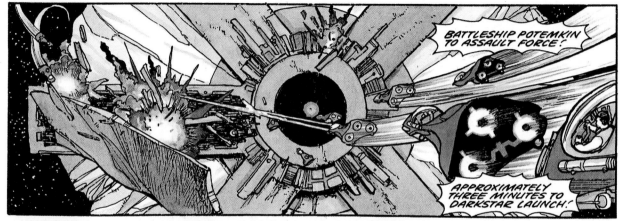

BATTLESHIP POTEMKIN TO ASSAULT FORCE!

APPROXIMATELY THREE MINUTES TO DARKSTAR LAUNCH!

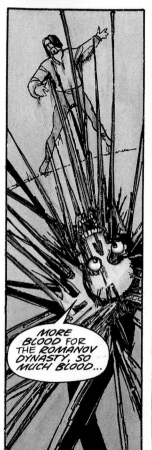

MORE BLOOD FOR THE ROMANOV DYNASTY, SO MUCH BLOOD...

D-Dante...

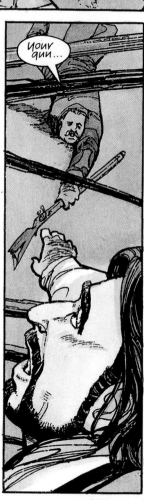

Your gun...

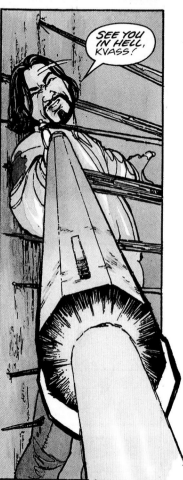

SEE YOU IN HELL, KVASS!

VALENTINE!

JENA!

DANTE!

HURRY UP! WE'VE ONLY GOT *SECONDS* BEFORE THE DARKSTAR FIRES!

YEAH, YEAH.

I'M HERE, I'M HERE.

'LEAST I THINK *MOST* OF ME IS.

Stay with the Romanovs and you'll *become like them*, boy.

Better to die now...

NIKOLAI! THE DARKSTAR!

THIS IS FOR *ELOISE!*

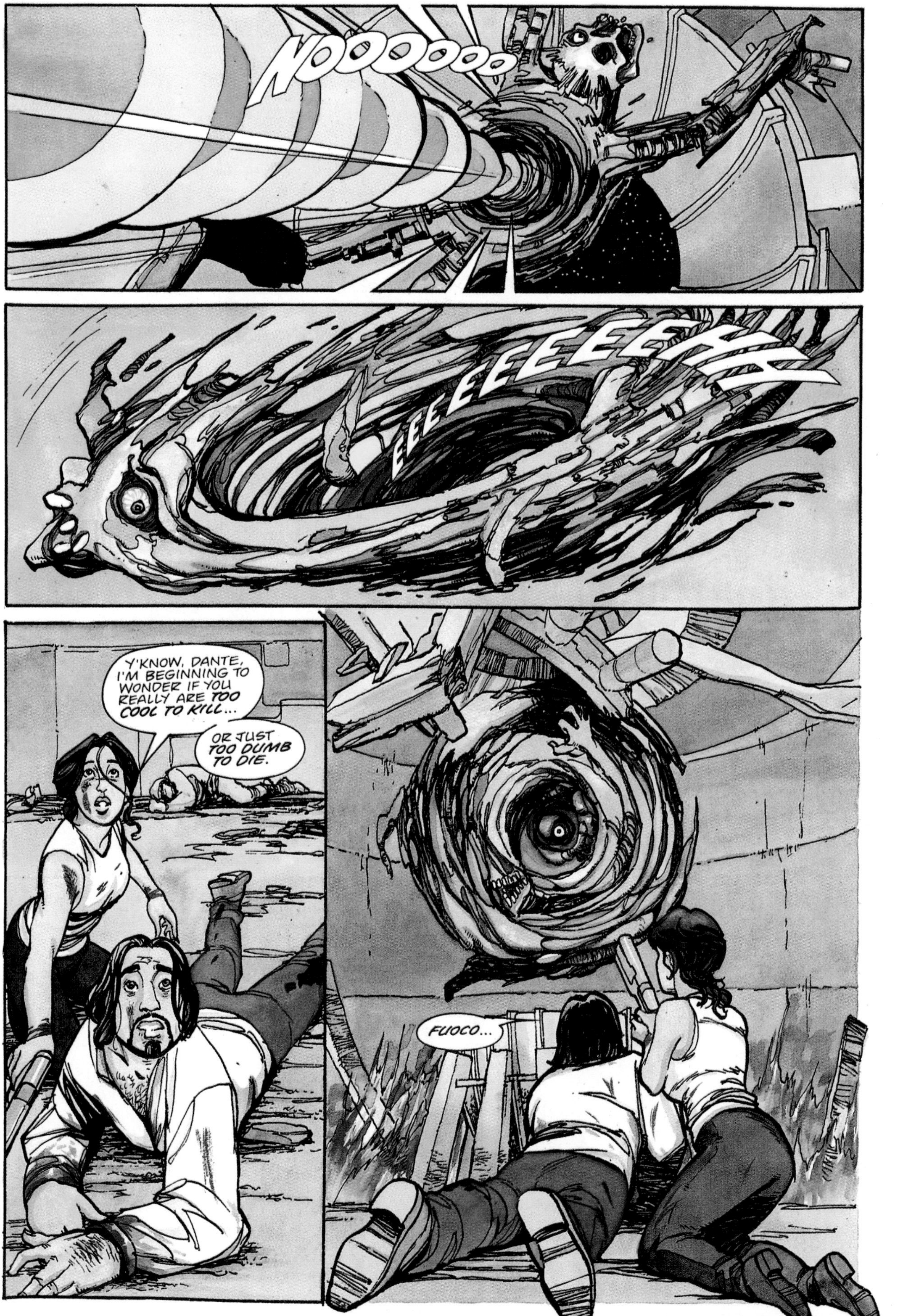
NOOOOOOO
EEEEEEEEEEEEEH
Y'KNOW, DANTE, I'M BEGINNING TO WONDER IF YOU REALLY ARE TOO COOL TO KILL...
OR JUST TOO DUMB TO DIE.
FUOCO...

VALENTINE *CONTROLLED* THE DARKSTAR THROUGH THE BIOTECHNOLOGY OF HIS WEAPONS CREST.

THE CREST STARTED *DISASSEMBLING* WHEN IT INADVERTENTLY BECAME THE WEAPON'S *TARGET*...

...STOPPING THE CHAIN REACTION THAT WOULD'VE DESTROYED US ALL AND TURNING *VALENTINE* HIMSELF INTO THE *DARKSTAR SINGULARITY*.

HE'LL TAKE PRIDE OF PLACE IN THE WINTER PALACE *MUSEUM* — A UNIQUE TOURIST ATTRACTION AND A TESTAMENT TO ROMANOV *VENGEANCE*.

THE *VALENTINE SINGULARITY*!

YOU'RE SUCH A *LOVING FATHER*, DMITRI.

I CLAIM THE DARKSTAR FOR THE HOUSE OF *MAKAROV*. UNDER THE CONTRACT I HAVE WITH ITS DRAGUTIN MANUFACTURERS, IT'S ONLY RIGHT--

AFTER WHAT'S HAPPENED TODAY, IT'S ONLY *RIGHT* THAT THE DARKSTAR BECOMES THE POSSESSION OF THE *ROMANOV* DYNASTY.

ANYTHING ELSE WILL MEAN *WAR*--

BY *ANASTASIA'S BONES!*

IT'S CALLED *DETENTE*...

A TIME-HONOURED TRADITION OF THE GREAT GAME.

WE DON'T HAVE IT.

AND *WE* DON'T HAVE IT.

LATER, ON THE BATTLESHIP POTEMKIN.

DANTE.

THE CELEBRATIONS ARE IN FULL SWING. PEOPLE ARE ASKING FOR YOU.

NEVER ATTEND A PARTY THAT HAS *ME* AS THE GUEST OF HONOUR, JENA.

YOU DID *SAVE* THE EMPIRE, DANTE.

MAYBE EVEN THE *UNIVERSE*...

YEAH, AND I'M GOING TO KEEP KNOCKING BACK VODKA 'TIL I'M *DRUNK ENOUGH* TO THINK IT WAS *WORTH* SAVING.

MIND IF I *JOIN* YOU?

I'M A *DANGEROUS* MAN TO GET DRUNK WITH, MILADY.

NOT MY FAULT, THINGS JUST SEEM TO *HAPPEN* TO ME...

HMMM, I'M SURE THEY DO.

HERE'S TO LIVING DANGEROUSLY...

KLINK

THE END

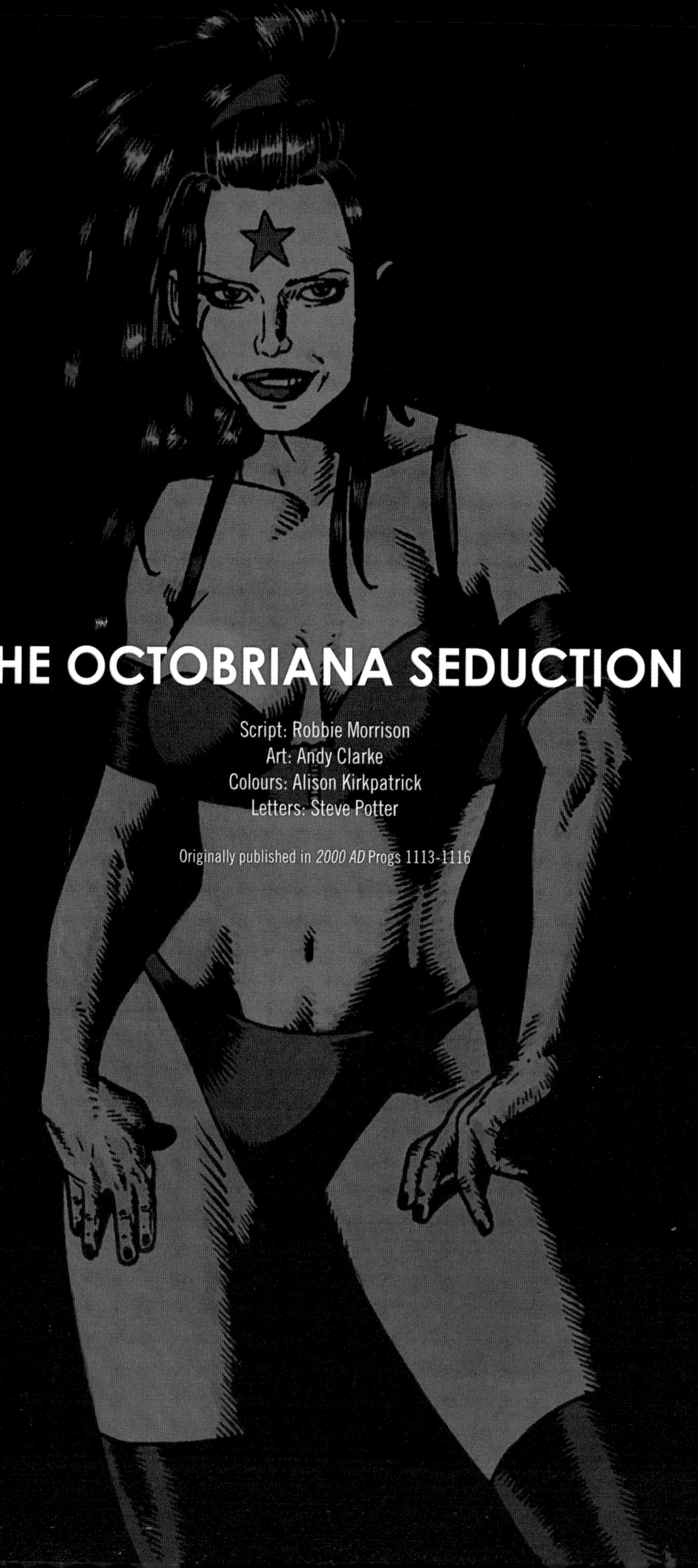

THE OCTOBRIANA SEDUCTION

Script: Robbie Morrison
Art: Andy Clarke
Colours: Alison Kirkpatrick
Letters: Steve Potter

Originally published in *2000 AD* Progs 1113-1116

SCRIPT
ROBBIE
MORRISON

ART
ANDY
CLARKE

COLOUR
ALISON
KIRKPATRICK

LETTERS
STEVE
POTTER

THE YEAR OF THE TSAR 2667.

THE WINTER PALACE OF THE ROMANOV DYNASTY.

ONLY IF YOU DON'T LOOK *DOWN*, CREST...

Awesome view.

Quite inspirational, Dante, no?

You've climbed out of so many ladies' bedchambers after robbing them that I imagined you would have been used to heights by now.

HEY, I'M *HAPPY* TO RISK MY LIFE FOR *LOVE* AND *MONEY*, BUT *THIS* IS —

Bojemoi...

Uh, *VIKTOR?*

SORRY TO DISTURB WHAT, *uh, WHATEVER* YOU'RE DOING, BUT WE'VE BEEN ORDERED TO REPORT TO DMITRI IMMEDIATELY.

THOUGH IT *MIGHT* BE AN IDEA IF YOU PUT SOME *PANTS* ON FIRST.

ALLOW ME TO INTRODUCE *HENRI STASHINSKY*, OUR MAN IN *PARIS*. *DEAD MAN*, THAT IS. AN UNMARKED HOV-DRONE DELIVERED THE BODY AN HOUR AGO.

AS I'M SURE YOU KNOW, PARIS IS GOVERNED BY *CARDINAL ROSTAND* AND HIS *CABINET NOIRE* — UNDER THE SUPERVISION OF THE TSAR.

STASHINSKY RAN OUR PARISIAN SPY NETWORK, ONE OF THE MOST SUCCESSFUL IN THE EMPIRE. YOU MAY RECOGNISE THE WORD BURNED INTO HIS BODY...

SMERSH, AN ACRONYM COINED BY STALIN CENTURIES AGO FROM THE SLOGAN *'SMERT SHPIONAM'* – *'DEATH TO SPIES'*.

THE *CABINET NOIRE* ARE SENDING US A MESSAGE, GENTLEMEN. IT WOULD BE *RUDE* NOT TO RESPOND IN *KIND*.

STASHINSKYS LIST OF OPERATIVES IS MISSING, HE MAY HAVE GIVEN IT TO ANOTHER AGENT FOR SAFEKEEPING.

IF THE CABINET NOIRE HAD IT, THEY'D HAVE SENT US MORE THAN ONE BODY. FIND IT BEFORE THEY DO, DANTE...

AND *KILL* WHOEVER DID THIS TO STASHINSKY.

VIKTOR WILL ACCOMPANY YOU. CALL ME *SENTIMENTAL* IF YOU WILL, BUT *PARIS* IS THE CITY IN WHICH HE WAS CONCEIVED.

YEAH?

I ALWAYS THOUGHT HE HAD A CERTAIN *GALLIC* CHARM...

Ahh, *PARIS BY MOONLIGHT*, eh, VIKTOR...

THE LAST RELIABLE SIGHTING OF STASHINSKY WAS IN AN ENTERTAINMENTS COMPLEX ON THE *MONTMARTRE*...

THE *THEATRE BEAUJOLAIS!* PARIS'S PREMIERE NIGHTSPOT FOR ALMOST A *MILLENNIUM!*

PATRONISED OVER THE AGES BY FRANCE'S GREATEST HEROES AND ARTISTS— *D'ARTAGNAN, CYRANO, LAUTREC, PIAF, LA BAKER, TATI, DENEUVE, RENO!*

WHERE, IN THE TRUE SPIRIT OF OUR SOCIALIST PAST, A *SCUMBAG'S* MONEY IS AS WELCOME AS AN *ARISTOCRAT'S.*

WHICH IS WHY IT'S THE BEST PLACE FOR ME, *CESAR NOIRET*, THE GREATEST PICKPOCKET IN ALL OF FRANCE, TO BEGIN YOUR LESSONS IN THE NOBLE ART OF PILFERING.

PICKING POCKETS IS A GOOD PROFESSION FOR AMBITIOUS YOUNG ROGUES LIKE YOURSELVES. YOU MADE THE RIGHT DECISION IN --

ZUT ALORS!

BUMP!

PARDONNEZ MOI, MONSIÉUR.

RUSSIAN OAFS! ACT AS IF THEY RULE THE WORLD. I MEAN, *THEY DO,* BUT...

ANYWAY, YOU'RE DOING THE RIGHT THING, PAYING ME TO ACT AS YOUR TUTOR. JUST LOOK *HOW MUCH* I'VE STOLEN SINCE WE GOT HERE...

Remember, Dante, you're on an espionage mission in a hostile city-state, you could become the target of assassination at any moment. Treat everyone as an enemy.

THANKS FOR THE ADVICE, CREST.

THE NAMES DANTE! NIKOLAI DANTE!

AND I CAN DRINK ANY MAN OR WOMAN UNDER THE TABLE!

MY MONEY POUCH — IT — IT'S GONE! SOMEBODY PICKED MY POCKET! I'VE BEEN ROBBED!

THE DRINKS ARE ON ME!

HEY! DIDN'T ANYONE HEAR ME?

IT'LL TAKE MORE THAN THE OFFER OF A FREE DRINK TO GET THROUGH TO THEM, STRANGER, THE SHOW'S ABOUT TO BEGIN.

HELL, A BOMB WOULDN'T GET THROUGH TO THEM ONCE OUR STAR ATTRACTION STARTS STRUTTING HER STUFF.

LADIES AND GENTLEMEN, PLEASE SHOW YOUR APPRECIATION FOR THE GODDESS OF LOVE, THE QUEEN OF SEDUCTION...

THE BEAUTIFUL, THE VOLUPTUOUS, THE REVOLUTIONARY...

OCTOBRIANA!!

WHOA! NOW THERE'S A LADY WORTH DYING FOR...

I do wish you'd stop using these prophetic phrases, Dante.

'When Nikolai Dante and Viktor Romanov arrived in Paris to investigate the death of their spy, Stashinsky, we followed them to the Theatre Beaujolais...

'It's not our fault we lost them there, I mean, you train us to be voyeurs. Who could possibly take their eyes off Octobriana?' – CABINET NOIRE SURVEILLANCE SECTION.

NIKOLAI DANTE

SCRIPT
ROBBIE MORRISON
ART
ANDY CLARKE
COLOURS
ALISON KIRKPATRICK
LETTERS
STEVE POTTER

♪ Rogues do it, Thieves do it, Even Saints and Sinners do it... ♪

the octobriana seduction pt. 2

♪ Ooohhhhh... ♪

♪ Let's do it! ♪

♪ Ooohhhhh... ♪

♪ Let's fall in love! ♪

LET'S DO IT NOW, MY *SEXY LITTLE KITTEN!*

I'M THE BEAST OF THE *BEDCHAMBER*, AND I'LL MAKE YOU MY *TIGRESS!*

MMMNNPH!

THE RUSSIAN *FREAK* ATTACKED PHILIPPE! TOOK HIM OUT WITH A SINGLE BLOW!

WHUMPFFH!

TO ATTACK *ONE* OF US IS TO ATTACK THE *ENTIRE* TEAM!

Perhaps your brother is spending too much time in your company. This fight is a move of *Dantesque* recklessness. I recognise his opponents from my databanks — the Olympic Savate Team.

SAVATE?

A French form of boxing that involves striking with the feet as well as the fists.

ALL FOR ONE AND ONE FOR ALL!

SPLATTT!

Dante, have you ever entered a drinking establishment and not ended up in a brawl?

ONCE, IN A LITTLE CANTINA DOWN ACAPULCO WAY.

THE *MARIACHI BAND* AND I TOOK OUR FIGHT OUTSIDE AS A FAVOUR TO THE BARMAID.

COME TO THINK OF IT, THE FIGHT WAS *OVER HER*, ANYWAY...

SKRUNKK!

HANG ON, VIKTOR! I'LL--

--help you?

ARE YOU BOYS FINISHED *PLAYING* WITH YOURSELVES? *GOOD.*

NOW, SHOULD I BE *OUTRAGED* THAT YOU NEARLY UPSTAGED ME, OR *FLATTERED* YOU DEFENDED MY *HONOUR* AGAINST THESE BRUTES?

THEY VIEW MY SHOW AS LITTLE MORE THAN AN ELABORATE *STRIPTEASE.*

IS THAT HOW *YOU* SEE ME, *SIR?* AS A *SEXUAL PLAYTHING*, AN OBJECT OF MERE *TITILLATION?*

TIT-TIT-TITILLATION? NO. IT, IT'S *ARTISTIC.* YOU'RE A *LIVING* WORK OF ART.

IT WAS MY BROTHER WHO WAS DEFENDING YOUR HONOUR — I JUST WENT ALONG FOR THE *RIDE*.

DON'T BE MODEST, *ARROGANCE* IS FAR MORE ATTRACTIVE.

I'D BE DISAPPOINTED IF THE *HERO OF RUDINSHTEIN* SUCKED UP TO ME LIKE SOME WEAK-WILLED ROMANTIC FOOL.

YOU'VE *HEARD* OF RUDINSHTEIN?

NO. I'VE HEARD OF *YOU*.

I CHOOSE ONLY THE GREATEST HEROES OF THE AGE AS MY LOVERS, MEN WHO CAN... *MOVE THE EARTH*.

I THINK *YOU'RE* ONE OF THEM, NIKOLAI DANTE.

AND I THINK YOU'RE A GOOD JUDGE OF CHARACTER.

SHALL WE GO TO YOUR DRESSING ROOM, OR JUST *SLIP UNDER* ONE OF THESE TABLES?

Ohh, I'M MORE OF A *CHALLENGE* THAN THAT.

I HOLD *INTELLECT* IN AS HIGH A REGARD AS PHYSICAL APPEARANCE, NIKOLAI. I WANT TO BE *DAZZLED* BY YOUR WIT, *SEDUCED* BY YOUR *SILVER* TONGUE.

YOU WON'T BE DISAPPOINTED, MILADY.

NO ONE SAYS THINGS THEY *DON'T* MEAN WITH MORE *SINCERITY* THAN ME.

MY ADDRESS.

CALL UPON ME. IF YOU FEEL *MAN* ENOUGH.

THE LADY OCTOBRIANA
69 RUE St. DENIS, PARIS

THE *CITY OF LOVERS* SURE KNOWS HOW TO KEEP UP ITS REPUTATION, EH, VIK?

VIKTOR?

Ahh, *FUOCO*. You *FANCY* her...

LISTEN, I WAS ONLY FOOLING AROUND. SHE'S NOT MY TYPE, *REALLY*. GO AFTER HER, HIT HER WITH THAT *ROMANOV* CHARM.

C'MON, VIKTOR, SOMETIMES YOU JUST HAVE TO *GO* FOR IT, SOMETIMES YOU'VE GOT *NOTHING* TO LOSE.

AND SOMETIMES WHEN YOU'VE GOT *EVERYTHING* TO LOSE, THAT'S WHEN YOU HAVE TO GO FOR IT *MOST*.

BROTHERLY LOVE.

HOW *TOUCHING*.

Whoa... Who ate all the pies?

ALLOW US TO INTRODUCE OURSELVES. *INQUISITOR ABAKUMOV*, HEAD OF SECULAR SECURITY, AND...

...ST. JOAN DELACROIX, MOTHER SUPERIOR OF THE RIGHTEOUS SISTERS.

WE FRENCH TAKE INSULTS AGAINST OUR CULTURE VERY SERIOUSLY. YOU'VE WRECKED THE THEATRE BEAUJOLAIS AND PROBABLY SHATTERED OUR HOPES OF OLYMPIC SUCCESS.

OUI. I'M AFRAID WE MAY HAVE TO CUT SHORT YOUR VISIT TO OUR CITY – WITH *THE GUILLOTINE*.

THINGS MIGHT LOOK BAD, VIK, BUT DON'T WORRY, I'LL GET *US* OUT OF THIS, AND *YOU* IN WITH OCTOBRIANA.

TRUST ME...

DESPITE THE GRAVITY OF THE CHARGES LAID AGAINST YOU, *ST. JOAN* AND I ARE WILLING TO DROP THEM ON THE CONDITION THAT YOU *LEAVE* PARIS BY NOON TOMORROW.

CALL IT AN ACT OF *DIPLOMATIC COURTESY*...

SCRIPT
ROBBIE MORRISON

ART
ANDY CLARKE

COLOURS
ALISON KIRKPATRICK

LETTERS
STEVE POTTER

CALL IT *BLACKMAIL*, LARDASS.

YOU COULD'VE JUST SAID THIS TOWN ISN'T *BIG* ENOUGH FOR *BOTH* OF US. THERE'S *NO WAY* I COULD ARGUE WITH THAT!

FOR ONCE, I'M LESS *FORGIVING* THAN INQUISITOR ABAKUMOV, I THINK WE REQUIRE AN ACT OF *PENANCE* FROM YOU.

I SOMETIMES HOLD *CONFESSION* IN *NOTRE DAME CATHEDRAL* FOR THE PARISIAN ELITE.

PERHAPS YOU'D CARE TO ATTEND, *UNBURDEN* YOURSELF.

CONFESSION *IS* GOOD FOR THE SOUL.

I'M SAVING *MY* CONFESSIONS FOR MY *MEMOIRS*. BESIDES, THEY INVOLVE A LOT OF *SEX* AND *VIOLENCE*. MIGHT BE A LITTLE *RISQUE* FOR YOU, *SISTER*.

THE DEVIL'S *STRONG* IN YOU, BOY, BUT I'VE CONVERTED GREATER SINNERS IN THE PAST.

I'D BE GRATEFUL FOR THE OPPORTUNITY TO *EXORCISE* YOUR DEMONS.

WELL, A LITTLE *EXERCISE* NEVER HURT ANYONE. YOU'VE GOT YOURSELF A DATE, SISTER.

YOU CAN TRY *CONVERTING* ME, I'LL TRY *CORRUPTING* YOU...

UNTIL THEN, NIKOLAI DANTE, I'LL *PRAY* FOR YOU...

COOL. MAKES A CHANGE FROM EVERYBODY *CURSING* ME...

WOMEN ARE *ALL* CRAZY, VIKTOR. TO STOP THEM GETTING *DANGEROUS* AND CRAZY, YOU'VE GOT TO TELL THEM WHAT THEY *WANT* TO HEAR.

BUT DON'T WORRY, I'LL DO THE TALKING.

NUMBER 69. THERE *SHE* IS.

RIGHT, GRAB HER ATTENTION, VIKTOR. A COUPLE OF PEBBLES THROWN GENTLY AGAINST THE WINDOW USUALLY GETS THEM CURIOUS.

SKRASH!

WHAT?!

Nice one, Viktor!

I'm trying to play *Cupid*, and you're trying to make us look *stupid!*

WHO'S THERE!?

NIKOLAI!? NIKOLAI DANTE!?

Ohh, IT'S YOU...

HAVE YOU BROUGHT A MESSAGE FROM DANTE?

WHERE ARE YOU GOING? STEP BACK INTO THE *LIGHT*.

MILADY, WHAT I HAVE TO SAY TO YOU CAN ONLY COME FROM THE *SHADOWS,* FOR IF I WERE TO STAND IN THE *LIGHT* OF YOUR *BEAUTY,* I WOULD SURELY BE STRUCK *SPEECHLESS.*

I KNOW MY BROTHER SEEMS *IRRESISTIBLE* – WITTY, CHARMING, *DEVILISHLY* HANDSOME – BUT HE'S A *ROGUE,* AN *ADVENTURER.*

HE'LL LOVE YOU AND LEAVE YOU BY THE DAWNING OF THE NEW DAY. HE'S NOT WORTHY TO LICK YOUR *FEET,* LET ALONE ANYTHING ELSE.

THANKS FOR YOUR CONCERN, BUT I *WASN'T* GOING TO RESPECT HIM IN THE MORNING. ALL I'M AFTER IS A LITTLE *FUN,* ONE NIGHT OF PASSION.

ONE NIGHT OF *TRUE* PASSION WOULD BE WORTH A *LIFETIME* OF CASUAL EMBRACES WITH *NIKOLAI DANTE.*

HE'S NOT *WORTHY* OF YOU, MILADY. *NO* MAN IS.

Least of all... Viktor Romanov...

THE MEREST GLANCE FROM YOU. THE SMALLEST WORD HAS THE POWER TO *BREAK* MY HEART.

YOU'RE AN *ANGEL,* LADY OCTOBRIANA, A *GODDESS,* TOO BEAUTIFUL FOR THIS *CRUEL, UGLY* WORLD...

YOUR HAIR, *GLOWING* IN THE MOONLIGHT, YOUR *SOULFUL, SULTRY* EYES, YOUR *SWEET, SWEET* LIPS, YOUR *VOLUPTUOUS, BODICE-RIPPING* BOSOM, YOUR *LONG, GRACEFUL* LEGS, THE *CURVE* OF YOUR *THIGHS...*

AND YOUR *BRAINS* AND *PERSONALITY* AND ALL THAT *DEEP* CHARACTER STUFF – THEY'RE *GREAT* TOO.

I WOULD *FIGHT* ALL THE FORCES OF THE EMPIRE JUST TO HOLD YOU IN MY ARMS, TO *WHISPER* YOUR NAME LIKE A *DREAMER* WHO'S SCARED THE DREAM MIGHT *END*...

AND I WOULD *DIE* HAPPY TO HEAR *YOU* WHISPER *MY* NAME.

Viktor...

YOU'VE SET *FIRES* WITHIN ME THAT I THOUGHT *NO* MAN WOULD *EVER* LIGHT AGAIN.

I *WANT* YOU VIKTOR. I WANT YOU *NOW.*

COME TO ME. *ENTER* MY CHAMBER OF *PLEASURES*...

Yesss!

I'm in there!

S-SORRY, VIK, FORGOT MYSELF. I-I MEAN *YOU'RE* IN THERE. GO FOR IT.

JUST RELAX AND HAVE *FUN,* eh?

?

You know, Dante, for all your lies and boasts and cheap bravado, I do believe you're developing a romantic streak.

YEAH, *WELL, MAYBE,* BUT DON'T TELL ANYONE, *CREST,* I'VE GOT A *REPUTATION* TO KEEP UP.

SPEAKING OF WHICH, WE'VE GOT A DATE WITH A *NUN.*

YOU'RE THE STRONG, *SILENT TYPE*, AGAIN, eh, VIKTOR? NO *MORE* WORDS, NO MORE *POETRY*...

Ohh, WELL, THEY DO SAY IT'S THE *QUIET* ONES YOU HAVE TO *WATCH*...

Notre Dame is one of the oldest religious institutions in Europe, Dante. Please show a little respect, even if you don't subscribe to the beliefs it represents.

RESPECT? DON'T WORRY, CREST, I'M WEARING MY *GOD-FEARING PANTS* TONIGHT.

BLESS ME, MAMA, FOR I HAVE SINNED!

THEN YOU'VE COME TO THE RIGHT PLACE TO BE *PUNISHED*, NIKOLAI DANTE.

I ONLY PRAY YOU SCREAM AS *SWEETLY* AS OUR *FALLEN SAINT* HERE...

NIKOLAI DANTE

SMERSH

SMERSH. DEATH TO SPIES.

QUITE *FITTING* IN THE CIRCUMSTANCES, NO?

SCRIPT
ROBBIE MORRISON

ART
ANDY CLARKE

COLOURS
ALISON KIRKPATRICK

LETTERS
STEVE POTTER

WHEN WE EXECUTED YOUR SPY *STASHINSKY*, WE EXPECTED THE ROMANOV DYNASTY TO SEND SOMEONE TO RECOVER HIS HIDDEN DATABASE OF OPERATIVES.

WE'VE HAD YOU AND VIKTOR UNDER SURVEILLANCE SINCE YOU ARRIVED IN PARIS, PRAYING THAT YOU WOULD LEAD US TO THE DATABASE OR YOUR OTHER AGENTS.

OUR PRAYERS HAVE BEEN ANSWERED, FOR YOU'VE DONE *BOTH* – THOUGH WE NEVER EXPECTED TO UNCOVER SUCH A *HIGH*-RANKING TRAITOR.

I BECAME SUSPICIOUS OF *ST.JOAN* WHEN SHE INSISTED UPON MEETING WITH YOU AGAIN.

the octobriana seduction pt. 4

CONFESSION IS *ONLY* GOOD FOR THE SOUL WHEN ACCOMPANIED BY A LITTLE LIGHT *TORTURE*. SHE SOON REVEALED *EVERYTHING*.

THE DATA YOU'RE AFTER IS STORED ON A *NANO-DISC* CONCEALED IN HER CRUCIFIX.

YOUR ESPIONAGE SUCCESSES AGAINST US WERE SO DAMAGING THAT WE FINALLY EMPLOYED SPECIALIST HELP TO HUNT DOWN STASHINSKY.

FUNNY, I EXPECTED *YOU* TO FALL FOR HER CHARMS, NOT YOUR *RETARD* BROTHER...

OCTOBRIANA?

YES, BOY, THE *LADY* OCTOBRIANA.

THE GODDESS OF LOVE, THE QUEEN OF SEDUCTION.

'POSSIBLY THE DEADLIEST ASSASSIN I'VE COME ACROSS IN A LIFETIME OF STATE TERROR.'

SORRY, VIKTOR! A GIRL CAN ONLY *FAKE* IT FOR SO LONG!

WITH *DANTE*, I COULD'VE MIXED A LITTLE BUSINESS AND PLEASURE, BUT *YOU?* EVEN THE *TSAR* COULDN'T PAY ME *THAT* MUCH...

YOU'RE AN *EMBARRASSMENT* TO YOUR DYNASTY, THE INBRED IDIOT IN THE ATTIC.

YOU SHOULD'VE HEARD YOURSELF UNDER THE BALCONY, TALKING ABOUT *LOVE* AND *BEAUTY* AND THE *PURITY* OF IT ALL.

IT'S THE YEAR OF THE TSAR *2667* — *EVERYBODY'S* GOT AN *ULTERIOR* MOTIVE. NO ONE BELIEVES IN ALL THAT POETIC, IDEALISTIC *GARBAGE.*

ROMANCE IS DEAD, VIKTOR.

Ohh, A LITTLE *TEAR.*

MAYBE I WAS WRONG, MAYBE YOU'RE A GENUINE *INNOCENT.* MAYBE ROMANCE ISN'T *QUITE* DEAD YET.

BUT IT WILL BE WHEN I BLOW YOUR BRAINS ALL THE WAY BACK TO RUSSIA!

FROM THE FILES OF THE IMPERIAL RAVEN CORPS...

'Viktor Romanov: The lone wolf of the Romanov Dynasty.'

'Dwells in isolation, shunning or being shunned by his siblings.'

'Weapons Crest Capabilities: Unknown.'

'No Imperial agent has ever dared investigate him.'

EEEEEEEEEEEAAAHHH!!

SUBDUE HIM! AND *NO* SHOOTING – YOU MIGHT DAMAGE SOMETHING!

THIS IS A *HOUSE OF GOD!* THE FURNISHINGS ARE WORTH A *FORTUNE!*

The odds are against you, Dante.

Bearing in mind our location, I don't wish to sound ironic, but it may take a *miracle* to extricate us from this predicament...

ONE MIRACLE COMING UP, CREST!

YOU DESTROYED MY *ANTI-GRAV* HARNESS!

RUN!

NASTY!

I JOINED THE CABINET NOIRE TO SERVE *GOD*, AND FOUND THAT THEY ONLY SERVED *THEMSELVES*.

SO YOU TRANSFERRED YOUR LOYALTIES TO THE *ROMANOVS*.

THINK *THEY'RE* ANY BETTER?

YES. *YOU'RE* ONE OF THEM.

I'VE NEVER BEEN KISSED BY A *SAINT* BEFORE.

AND I'VE NEVER KISSED A *SINNER*. MAYBE YOU'RE NOT AS BAD AS THEY SAY.

MAYBE, MAYBE NOT, YOU STILL HAVEN'T HEARD MY CONFESSION. WE BETTER HURRY.

'I DON'T THINK CARDINAL ROSTAND AND THE TSAR WILL APPRECIATE THE MESSAGE I'VE LEFT THEM.'

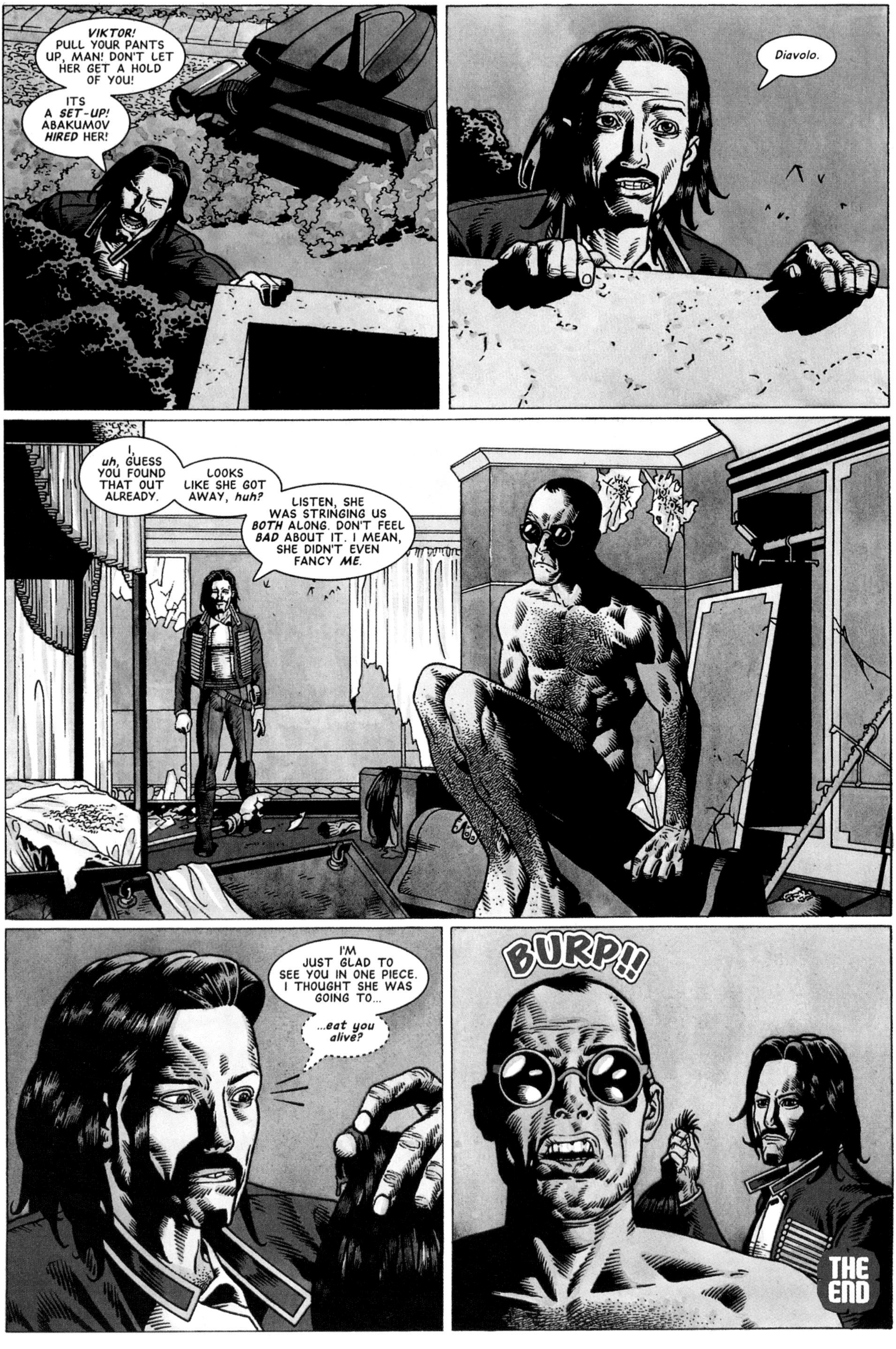
VIKTOR! PULL YOUR PANTS UP, MAN! DON'T LET HER GET A HOLD OF YOU!
ITS A SET-UP! ABAKUMOV HIRED HER!
Diavolo.
I, uh, GUESS YOU FOUND THAT OUT ALREADY.
LOOKS LIKE SHE GOT AWAY, huh?
LISTEN, SHE WAS STRINGING US BOTH ALONG. DON'T FEEL BAD ABOUT IT. I MEAN, SHE DIDN'T EVEN FANCY ME.
I'M JUST GLAD TO SEE YOU IN ONE PIECE. I THOUGHT SHE WAS GOING TO...
...eat you alive?
BURP!!
THE END

THE MASQUE OF DANTE

Script: Robbie Morrison
Art: Charlie Adlard
Colours: Alison Kirkpatrick
Letters: Annie Parkhouse

Originally published in *2000 AD* Progs 1125-1127

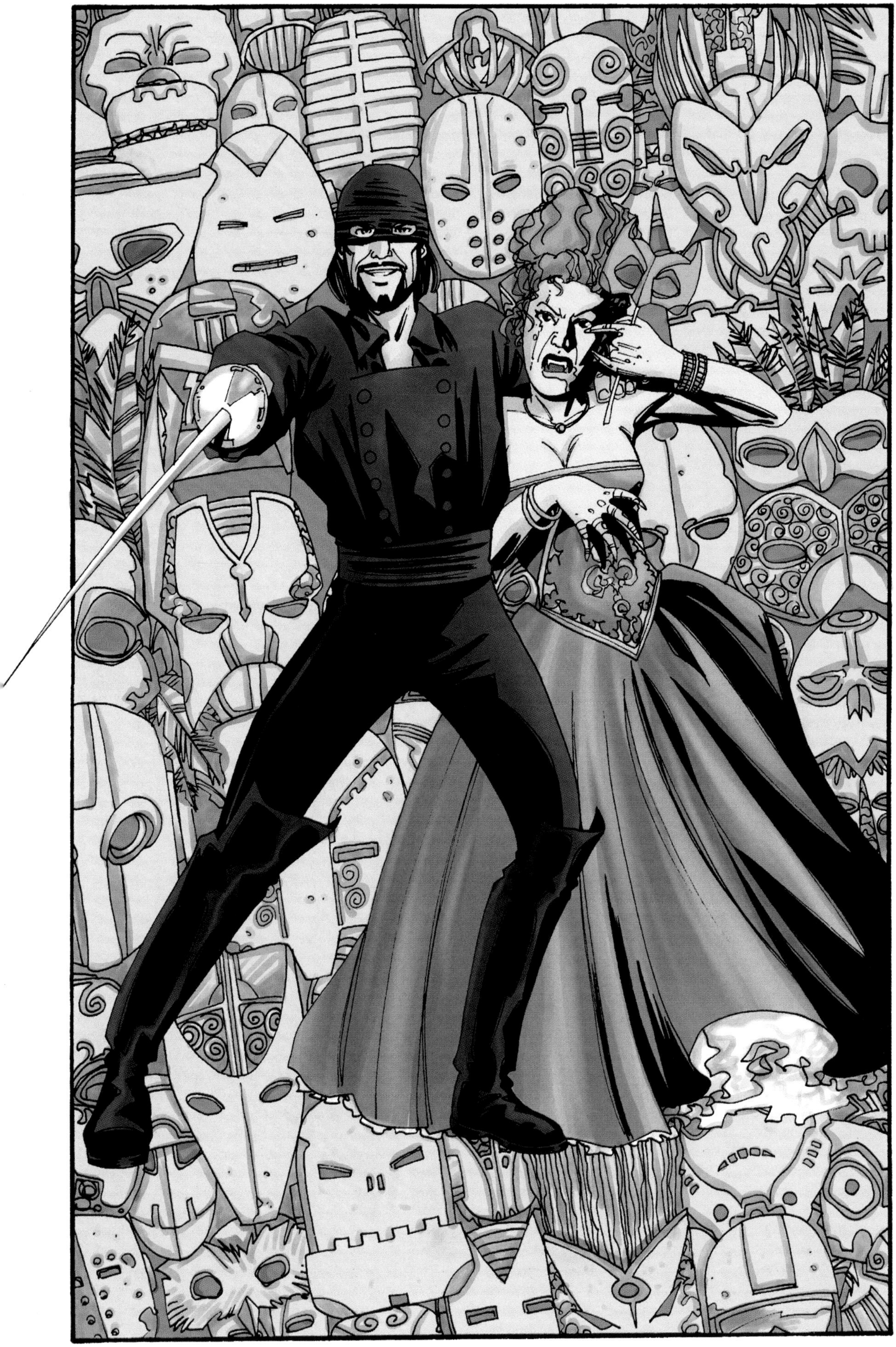

THE YEAR OF THE TSAR 2668.

KRONSTADT MANOR, KALINGRAD.

MARIA BERIA, CHANNEL GORKY, LIVE AND EXCLUSIVE FROM A SOCIAL EVENT THAT RIVALS NIKOLAI DANTE'S EPIC PARTY AT THE HOTEL YALTA...

A MASQUERADE BALL TO CELEBRATE THE ENGAGEMENT OF TOMAS KRONSTADT, RUSSIA'S MOST ELIGIBLE BACHELOR, TO THE WOMAN WHO FINALLY STOLE HIS HEART, LADY CONSTANCE BOVARY.

EVERYONE WHO'S ANYONE IS HERE, THEIR IDENTITIES CONCEALED BEHIND EXOTIC MASQUES.

SO IF YOU THINK YOU'RE SOMEONE AND YOU'RE SOMEPLACE ELSE WITHOUT AN INVITATION, YOU BETTER THINK AGAIN.

YOUR EX HAS A THING ABOUT MASKS, NASTASIA.

NEVER TRUST A MAN IN A MASK UNLESS HE'S TRYING TO ROB YOU— 'LEAST THEN YOU KNOW WHAT HIS MOTIVES ARE.

YOU FOLLOWED ME, LITTLE BROTHER?

DON'T YOU REMEMBER WHAT I SAID I'D DO TO ANYONE WHO TRIED TO STOP ME?

YEAH. BUT OUR FATHER THREATENED ME WITH PRETTY MUCH THE SAME THING IF I DIDN'T STOP YOU.

THE WINTER PALACE OF THE ROMANOV DYNASTY. SIX HOURS AGO...

WE CAUGHT UP WITH TOMAS KRONSTADT AFTER THE *SHOCK* ANNOUNCEMENT OF HIS ENGAGEMENT.

DOES THIS MEAN YOUR ROMANCE WITH *NASTASIA ROMANOV* IS OVER?

ONE DOESN'T HAVE *ROMANCES* WITH THE LIKES OF NASTASIA, ONLY *CASUAL AFFAIRS* AND *BRIEF ENCOUNTERS.*

SHE'S A *FEMME FATALE*, NOT *BRIDE-TO-BE* MATERIAL...

BBZZZTT!

LYING, SCHEMING, TWO-FACED, TWO-TIMING, TWO-BIT, NARCISSISTIC THESPIAN SCUMBAG!

THERE, THERE, IT'S *ALRIGHT*, I'M *HERE*. LET IT ALL OUT.

NIKOLAI, WHAT DO YOU THINK YOU'RE DOING?

UH, COMFORTING YOU?

Y'*KNOW*, LIKE BROTHERS AND SISTERS AND FAMILIES ARE MEANT TO DO FOR EACH OTHER.

NIKOLAI, NEVER IN A MILLION YEARS WILL I THINK OF YOU AS A *REAL* BROTHER, SO GET YOUR HANDS *OFF* ME OR I'LL TORTURE *YOU* WORSE THAN I'M GOING TO TORTURE KRONSTADT!

I DIDN'T KNOW YOU *CARED* ABOUT HIM THAT MUCH.

I *DON'T!* KRONSTADT WAS THE MOST *BORING* LOVER I'VE EVER HAD! HE LOVED *HIMSELF* MORE THAN *ME!*

I WAS GOING TO *DUMP* HIM IN THE *CRUELEST,* MOST *HUMILIATING* WAY I COULD THINK OF.

WELL, NOW YOU DON'T HAVE TO.

NO! BECAUSE HE DUMPED ME *FIRST! LIVE* ON CHANNEL GORKY! BEFORE THE *ENTIRE* EMPIRE!

NOBODY DUMPS ME, NIKOLAI!

SO, UH, WHAT'RE YOU GOING TO DO?

I'M GOING TO *KILL* HIM! I'M GOING TO *KILL* HER! AND I'M GOING TO KILL *ANYONE* WHO GETS IN MY WAY!

BE MY GUEST. I DON'T EVEN KNOW THE HAPPY COUPLE.

UNHAPPY, NIKOLAI. THEY'RE GOING TO BE *VERY* UNHAPPY.

THREE HOURS AGO...

AND *YOU* JUST LET HER *GO?*

LET HER WANDER ON OUT OF HERE WITH *MURDER* ON HER MIND?

TOMAS KRONSTADT IS BEST KNOWN AS A MEDIA CELEBRITY—*ACTOR, SINGER, DANCER.* ESSENTIALLY *TALENTLESS*, BUT HIS *LOOKS* MAKE HIM POPULAR WITH LITTLE GIRLS AND OLD LADIES.

HOWEVER, HE ALSO OWNS A CONTROLLING INTEREST IN *GORKY COMMUNICATIONS.*

WE'RE LOSING OUR *PROPAGANDA WAR* WITH THE TSAR BECAUSE OF HIS ALLIANCE WITH THE *HOUSE OF BOLSHOI*, THE MEDIA DYNASTY.

KRONSTADT HAS AGREED TO SELL US HIS SHARE OF GORKY COMM, THUS GIVING US A MEDIA PLATFORM TO PROMOTE OUR OWN INTERESTS.

THE DEAL ISN'T FINALISED UNTIL *TOMORROW.* IT'S *IMPERATIVE* THAT KRONSTADT REMAINS ALIVE UNTIL THEN.

YOU WILL *PURSUE* NASTASIA AND *STOP* HER FROM KILLING HIM.

SHE MIGHT NOT BE TOO *HAPPY* ABOUT THAT...

WHO ARE YOU *MORE* SCARED OF, NIKOLAI? *HER?*

OR *ME?*

EITHER WAY YOU DIE. WHAT A SHAME.

AND HOW DO YOU PROPOSE TO TAKE ME HOME? WITH THAT LITTLE BIO-BLADE?

ACTUALLY, IT'S A PRETTY BIG BIO-BLADE AND I'M GETTING PRETTY DAMN GOOD WITH IT.

SO, AS YOU CAN SEE, I'M IN KIND OF A CATCH-22 SITUATION HERE.

PPTUUUH!

FROM THE FILES OF THE IMPERIAL RAVEN CORPS...

Nastasia Romanov: The Romanov Bitch. Narcissistic and murderously coquetish. A habitual killer of anyone less admiring of her looks than she is herself.

Weapons Crest Capabilities: The transmutation of bodily fluids into venomous or acidic substances brutally delivered by fang and claw.

HHHSSSS!

TAKE IT EASY, NASTASIA, I DON'T WANT TO HAVE TO GET *TOUGH* WITH YOU.

TOUGH WITH ME?

I'LL *SKIN* YOU *ALIVE! TEAR* OFF YOUR *TESTICLES* AND *TOAST* THEM LIKE *MARSHMALLOWS!*

Avoid her claws, Dante! Nastasia's venom is the deadliest poison in the Empire.

RIGHT, CREST!

AS IF THE FACT THAT THEY CAN *SLIT* MY THROAT OR *SPILL* MY GUTS OVER THE ROOFTOP ISN'T BAD *ENOUGH!*

GGGNNHH!

GGRRRAAAHHH!

Dante!

Block her assault with your bio-blades!

THIS IS *CRAZY—WE'RE FAMILY!*

She's beyond reason, Dante, caught in the throes of a berserker fury.

Her tantrums are legendary. Lovers, friends, aquaintances, total strangers— she's killed them all for lesser offences than yours.

WHOA!

KRSHHY...

Do you think Tomas Kronstadt will be annoyed to find us attending his engagement party **without** an invitation?

DON'T WORRY, CREST...

I'M THE KING OF THE GATECRASHERS.

NO ONE MAKES AN ENTRANCE LIKE ME!

YEEOON!

WHO?

NIKOLAI DANTE!? COUNTESSA DE WINTER!?

WE *REALLY* HAVE TO STOP MEETING LIKE THIS, KOLYA.

YEAH, IT MUST BE AWKWARD BUMPING INTO PEOPLE YOU'VE *RIPPED OFF*.

WHERE'S MY *MONEY*? YOU STOLE A *FORTUNE* FROM ME IN THE HOTEL YALTA.

ARE WE GOING TO LET SOMETHING AS *PETTY* AS MONEY COME BETWEEN US?

IN OTHER WORDS, YOU'VE *SPENT* IT.

OF COURSE. BESIDES, YOU STOLE IT FROM OTHER PEOPLE BEFORE I STOLE IT FROM YOU.

THAT'S *NOT* THE POINT...

WHAT'RE YOU DOING HERE? I DIDN'T KNOW YOU WERE A FRIEND OF KRONSTADT'S.

NEITHER DOES HE. I'M HERE TO SAVE HIS ASS— AND HIS BRIDE-TO-BE'S, WHOEVER THE HELL *SHE* IS...

LADY CONSTANCE! THERE'S AN *INTRUDER* ON THE—

BY VLADIMIR'S BEARD! THERE HE IS!

ANIMAL! IF YOU'VE HURT MY FIANCÉE...

FIANCÉE? YOU'RE HIS..? YOU'RE GOING TO MARRY *HER*? BEST OF LUCK, JUST WATCH YOUR *BACK*.

BY THE WAY, FOR THE *MARRIAGE CERTIFICATE*, HER NAME'S NOT *BOVARY*, IT'S—

DOOOOPH!

WHO IS THIS *FOOL*, CONSTANCE?

NIKOLAI DANTE. I HAD THE *BAD* LUCK TO MEET HIM IN THE HOTEL YALTA LAST YEAR. HE'S BEEN *SPYING* ON ME, *STALKING* ME EVER SINCE.

AND NOW HE'S MADE ME SMASH THE *LAST* BOTTLE OF MY *FAVOURITE* PERFUME!

DON'T LISTEN TO HER, SHE'S JUST AFTER YOUR MONEY.

I'M TRYING TO STOP NASTASIA ROMANOV FROM *KILLING* YOU. YOU DITCHED HER FOR 'CONSTANCE' HERE AND NOW SHE'S COMING AFTER YOU.

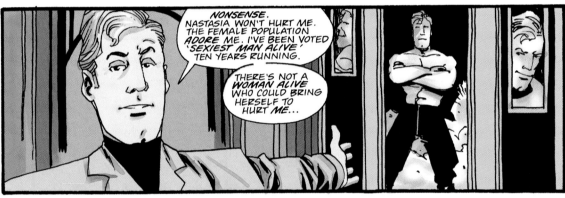

NONSENSE. NASTASIA WON'T HURT ME. THE FEMALE POPULATION *ADORE* ME. I'VE BEEN VOTED 'SEXIEST MAN ALIVE' TEN YEARS RUNNING.

THERE'S NOT A *WOMAN ALIVE* WHO COULD BRING HERSELF TO HURT *ME*...

WHOA! EARTH CALLING KRONSTADT!

THAT'S WHAT WOMEN ARE *HERE* FOR—TO *HURT* US AND MAKE OUR LIVES *HELL*.

NO, *BOY*. THAT'S WHAT MY *ENFORCERS* ARE FOR.

BEAT HIM TO WITHIN AN INCH OF HIS LIFE, MEN, THEN TOSS HIM INTO THE *SEWERS*.

CONSTANCE, MY *LOVE*, I BELIEVE IT'S TIME WE HONOURED OUR GUESTS WITH OUR PRESENCE.

THEY'RE SIMPLY *DYING* TO MEET YOU.

BYE BYE, NIKOLAI!

MMMNNPH!

CHITTOVSKY TO SECURITY COMMAND! BACK-UP REQUIRED IN LADY CONSTANCE'S BEDCHAMBER! TELL THEM TO COME ARMED!

THLLRRH!

AHH, FUOCO...

THE INTRUDER! HE'S TAKEN OUT CHITTOVSKY AND HARDONSKY!

OUFFF! ARGH!

ON YOUR FEET, HE'S GETTING AWAY!

DON'T LET HIM OUT OF YOUR SIGHT!

GLOGOVAC TO SECURITY COMMAND. INFORM LORD KRONSTADT THAT DANTE'S ESCAPED.

HE JUST DISAPPEARED. LIKE—LIKE A PHANTOM...

It's fortunate that you insist on carrying your Gentleman Thief mask with you wherever you go...

OLD HABITS DIE HARD, CREST.

YOU NEVER KNOW WHEN YOU MIGHT HAVE TO DO A LITTLE THIEVING.

COMMUNICATIONS CHAMBER. KRONSTADT MANOR.

WE WERE INTERRUPTED BEFORE I COULD PROPERLY CONGRATULATE YOU ON YOUR ENGAGEMENT TO THE 'SEXIEST MAN ALIVE,' COUNTESSA.

OR SHOULD THAT BE LADY CONSTANCE BOVARY?

NEITHER OF THEM.

AND, PLEASE, DON'T BOTHER ASKING MY REAL NAME. THE ONLY WAY TO SURVIVE THE EMPIRE IS TO NOT GET CLOSE TO ANYONE.

STRANGE ADVICE FROM SOMEONE ABOUT TO GET MARRIED...

WHAT'S THE GAME? KILL HIM ON THE HONEYMOON AND STEAL HIS FORTUNE?

NOTHING SO *CRUDE*, KOLYA. WHAT *DO* YOU THINK I AM?

KRONSTADT IS SELLING HIS HOLDINGS IN NUMEROUS COMPANIES —NOTABLY *GORKY COMMUNICATIONS* — TO FINANCE THE CREATION OF A *RELIGION* DEVOTED ENTIRELY TO *HIMSELF*.

CONTRACTUAL TERMS ARE AGREED, BUT THE ACTUAL SALES AREN'T FINALISED 'TIL *NOON TOMORROW*, WHICH I ASSUME IS WHY YOU'RE TRYING TO STOP NASTASIA KILLING KRONSTADT...

THE ROMANOV DYNASTY ARE BUYING HIS SHARE OF GORKY COMM, AND HIS DEATH COULD JEOPARDISE THE SALE.

BEFORE YOU ARRIVED, I STOLE THE SECURITY CODES FOR THE TRANSACTIONS AND BROUGHT THE SALES FORWARD TO *MIDNIGHT TONIGHT*.

NOW I'M INTERCEPTING THE COMPUTERISED TRANSFER OF THE FUNDS AND RE-DIRECTING THEM INTO MY OWN OFFWORLD ACCOUNTS INSTEAD OF KRONSTADT'S.

USUALLY, I PREFER *HANDS-ON-HEISTS* TO *TECHNOLOGICAL FRAUD*, BUT KRONSTADT'S SO *REPULSIVE* THAT I --

ARE YOU *LISTENING* TO ME?

NO... I PRETTY MUCH *LOST IT* WHEN YOU ASKED ME WHAT I THOUGHT OF YOU.

ENJOYING YOURSELVES?

WHO!?

DANTE— DON'T YOU RECOGNISE YOUR HALF-SISTER?

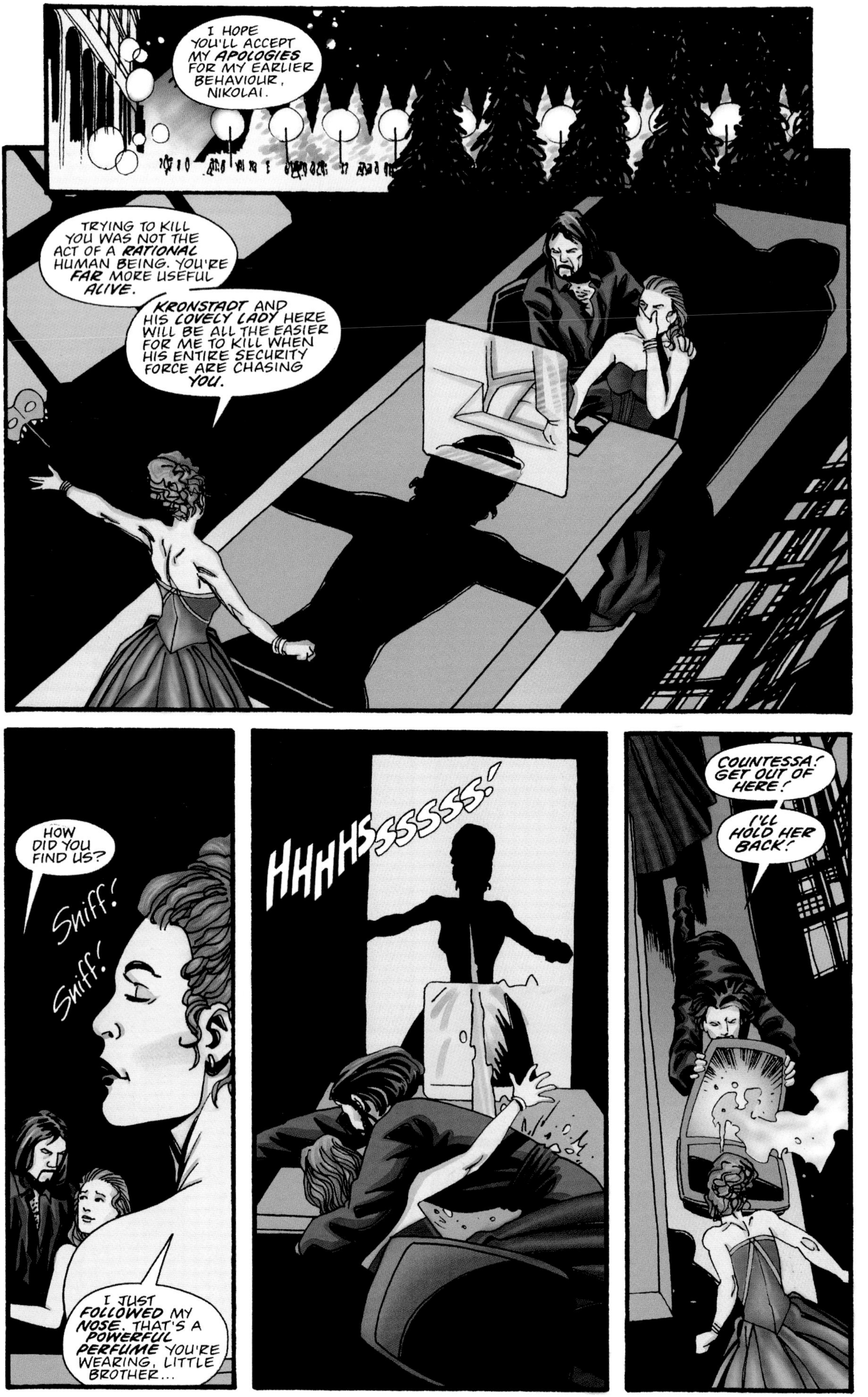
I HOPE YOU'LL ACCEPT MY APOLOGIES FOR MY EARLIER BEHAVIOUR, NIKOLAI.
TRYING TO KILL YOU WAS NOT THE ACT OF A RATIONAL HUMAN BEING. YOU'RE FAR MORE USEFUL ALIVE.
KRONSTADT AND HIS LOVELY LADY HERE WILL BE ALL THE EASIER FOR ME TO KILL WHEN HIS ENTIRE SECURITY FORCE ARE CHASING YOU.
HOW DID YOU FIND US?
Sniff!
Sniff!
I JUST FOLLOWED MY NOSE. THAT'S A POWERFUL PERFUME YOU'RE WEARING, LITTLE BROTHER...
HHHHSSSSSSS!
COUNTESSA! GET OUT OF HERE!
I'LL HOLD HER BACK!

HELP! THE INTRUDER! HE'S BACK THERE! HE TRIED TO *KIDNAP* ME!

DANTE!?

DON'T WORRY, MY DEAR, I'LL HAVE HIM *STUFFED* AND *MOUNTED* AS A WEDDING PRESENT FOR--

NASTASIA!?

ENFORCERS! RESTRAIN HER! PROTECT ME!

DANTE, *MY FRIEND,* YOU SPOKE THE TRUTH. CAN YOU EVER FORGIVE ME FOR DOUBTING..?

FORGIVE YOU? *FORGIVE YOU!?*

YOU ORDERED YOUR ENFORCERS TO *BEAT HELL* OUT OF ME! YOU MADE ME GATECRASH THIS POSING PRETENTIOUS EXCUSE FOR A PARTY!

STOP *NASTASIA* FROM KILLING YOU?

UUNNGH!

I'M GOING TO KILL YOU MYSELF!!

HOW ABOUT SOME HELP HERE, 'TASIA, NOW THAT WE'RE *ROMANOVS* TOGETHER AGAIN.

OH, DON'T CONCERN YOURSELF WITH *THEM,* KOLYA...

I *SPIKED* THE MANOR'S *WATER SUPPLY* BEFORE I JOINED THE PARTY.

NOTHING *TOO TOXIC*...

RRRLF! BARRRF! BOAK!

JUST ENOUGH TO *TURN* THEIR *STOMACHS*.

AND JUST TO MAKE SURE THE CELEBRATIONS WERE WELL AND TRULY *SPOILED*, I ADDED A LITTLE *EXTRA FLAVOURING* TO THE GUESTS' FOOD AND DRINK AS WELL.

YUM YUM!

NASTASIA, YOU DID *ALL THIS* JUST TO WIN ME BACK. I NEVER KNEW YOU LOVED ME SO MUCH.

YOU'VE PROVED ONCE AND FOR ALL THAT YOU, AND *ONLY* YOU, ARE WORTHY ENOUGH FOR ME TO LOVE.

I'LL MAKE YOU MINE ONCE AGAIN, NASTASIA. THE *AGONY* OF HAVING TO LIVE *WITHOUT ME* IS OVER.

COME HERE, FALL INTO MY ARMS BEFORE YOU *FAINT* WITH *RAPTURE*.

OHH, *TOMAS*...

WHAT'RE YOU DOING? HE'S A *LYING, CHEATING SCUMBAG* — BELIEVE ME, IT TAKES *ONE* TO *KNOW* ONE!

IT'S A WOMAN'S PREROGATIVE TO *CHANGE* HER MIND. BESIDES, WHO COULD RESIST THE *'SEXIEST MAN ALIVE'*?

OKAY! DON'T LISTEN TO ME! *RUIN* YOUR LIFE!

I'M ONLY YOUR *HALF-BROTHER*, WHY SHOULD I EVEN *HALF-CARE*?

MMMPH!

HHHSSSSS!

AAAGH·KK!

WHOA—KILLER KISS!

I DIDN'T FALL FOR HIS DUBIOUS CHARMS FIRST TIME AROUND, KOLYA. WHAT MADE YOU THINK I WOULD *THIS* TIME?

NOW ALL I HAVE TO DO IS PAY MY RESPECTS TO HIS FIANCEE.

SOMEHOW I THINK SHE ALREADY KNOWS THE ENGAGEMENT'S *OFF.*

A ROMANOVA EAGLE, EN ROUTE FROM KRONSTADT MANOR TO THE WINTER PALACE OF THE ROMANOV DYNASTY.

I MUST ADMIT, BOY, I'M IMPRESSED BY YOUR... *BUSINESS ACUMEN.*

HACKING INTO THE FINANCIAL MARKETS TO BRING FORWARD THE SALE OF GORKY COMMUNICATIONS— THUS NEGATING THE NEED TO KEEP KRONSTADT ALIVE— WAS A STROKE OF *GENIUS.*

I AGREE. LET'S DRINK TO YOUR *CRIMINAL GENIUS.*

THOUGH I DO HOPE TOMAS'S RUNAWAY FIANCEE DIDN'T HELP YOU IN ANY WAY—YOU LOOKED QUITE *COSY* TOGETHER...

I don't wish to be **alarmist**, Dante, but bearing in mind Nastasia's vindictive reputation, the wine could be poisoned.

BOJEMOI!

LOOK AT THAT *MAGNIFICENT* SCENERY! MAKES YOU *PROUD* TO BE *RUSSIAN!*

YOU DIDN'T *SWITCH GLASSES* THERE, DID YOU? SURELY YOU *TRUST* ME, KOLYA.

YEAH! 'COURSE I TRUST YOU...

NOT THAT IT WOULD DO YOU ANY GOOD. AS AN EXPERIENCED *POISONER*, I WOULD FORSEE YOU SWITCHING GLASSES AND PUT THE VENOM INTO *MINE* INSTEAD OF *YOURS*.

IF I WANTED TO POISON YOU, THAT IS.

LOOK! ISN'T THAT *ALFREDO MARCONI AND HIS ACROBATIC ELEPHANTS!?*

ANYWAY... CHEERS.

THEN AGAIN, AS I'M *IMMUNE* TO MY OWN VENOM, I'D BE AS WELL POISONING *BOTH* GLASSES...

THE MOVEABLE FEAST

Script: Robbie Morrison
Art: Simon Fraser
Colours: Alison Kirkpatrick
Letters: Annie Parkhouse

Originally published in *2000 AD* Progs 1128-1130

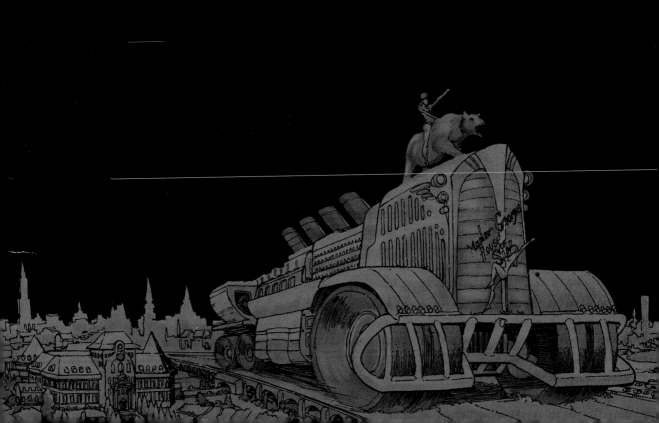

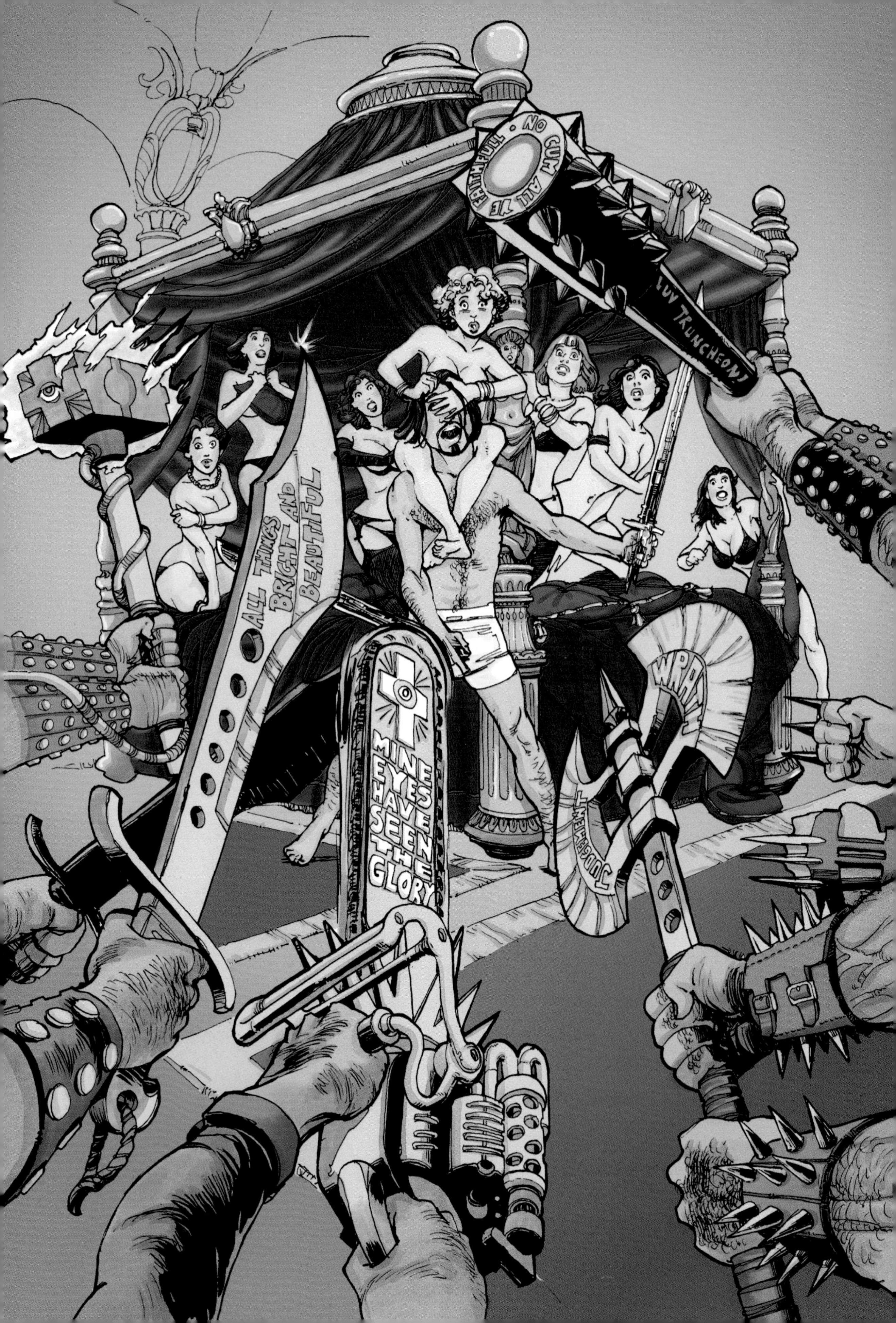

NO CUM ALL YE FAITHFULL
LUV TRUNCHEON!
ALL THINGS BRIGHT AND BEAUTIFUL
MINE EYES HAVE SEEN THE GLORY
JUDGEMENT

'The legendary Madame Di Giorgi's House of Sin is by far the most profitable criminal enterprise legalised by the Tsar in the early days of his reign.'

'The House of Sin brings new meaning to the term "pleasure cruise" as it travels the globe on a rollercoaster ride to paradise. Accommodation is available on a daily, weekly or monthly basis, dependent on spending power and staying power. Decadence and discretion are guaranteed.'

'Debate still rages over which is the oldest profession in the Empire, thievery or—to put it politely—seduction for the purposes of financial gain...

'...though many aristocrats who board the House of Sin wealthy in St. Petersburg and disembark destitute on the other side of the world might argue that they're one and the same.'— THE IMPERIAL TIMES TRAVELOGUE, 2661.

THANKS FOR VOLUNTEERING ME FOR THIS MISSION, ANDREAS.

AN ALL-EXPENSES-PAID WEEKEND IN THE HOUSE OF SIN. SOME GUYS HAVE ALL THE LUCK.

DON'T GET TOO CARRIED AWAY, KOLYA. I SPENT A COUPLE OF YEARS ONBOARD WHEN I WAS YOUR AGE, AND I'M STILL PAYING THE BILL...

SINNERS! FORNICATORS!

SOUNDS LIKE SOMEONE'S SHOUTING ON US...

TURN BACK AND EMBRACE THE TEACHINGS OF THE SKOPTZY IF YOU WISH TO SAVE YOUR IMMORTAL SOULS!

BOARD THAT SHIP OF SLEAZE AND SCANDAL AND YOU SHALL BE IMPALED UPON A RED-HOT POKER AND SENTENCED TO BURN IN HELL FOR ALL ETERNITY!

THE HOUSE OF SIN DESTROYS ALL WHO ENTER HER! YOUR ONLY SALVATION IS TO ABSTAIN FROM THE PLEASURES OF THE FLESH!

TURN YOUR BACK ON SIN! JUST SAY NO!

CREST? WHO?

The Sect of the Skoptzy and their leader Arnheim Ivanov. A religious cult who believe that promiscuity is the key to Hell.

Many of them resort to self-castration in their quest for saintliness—

YEOW!

GET A LIFE, IVANOV! IT'S A FREE WORLD! MORE OR LESS...

DO I HANG ABOUT YOUR TEMPLES DOING A STRIPTEASE WHEN YOU'RE PREACHING NONSENSE AND RELIEVING YOUR CONGREGATION OF DONATIONS?

MADAME DI GIORGI!

IT WOULD BE OF LITTLE CONSEQUENCE IF YOU DID, HARLOT—THE SKOPTZY ARE IMMUNE TO YOUR DEMONIC CHARMS.

OUR REPRESSOR-ROBES CONDITION US TO RESIST TEMPTATION BY ADMINISTERING ELECTRO-SHOCKS AT THE SLIGHTEST IMPURE THOUGHT OR STIMULATION.

IS THAT A FACT?

GIVE 'EM AN EYEFUL, GIRLS! WE'LL SEE HOW PURE THEY ARE!

STEADY, MEN. HOLD HARD.

I-I THINK THAT'S THE *P-PROBLEM*, CHIEF...

DAMN! Forgive my language, Lord...

OOOHH!

FWOARGH!

SHOCKING BEHAVIOUR FROM MEN OF GOD!

EASY CREDIT TERMS

YEAH... YOU JUST CAN'T GET *DEDICATED FANATICS*, THESE DAYS.

Sorry, Chief. Spirit's willing, but the flesh's weak...

Ssshhh! Stay where you are!

Maybe we can fool them into thinking we're praying...

'The House Of Sin circumnavigates the Earth every 80 days, frequently stopping at sites of great natural beauty or cultural and historical significance.'

'Not that the clientele seem especially interested in that kind of sightseeing.'

MY **PLAYBOY** DAYS ARE OVER, MARIA.

I'M ENTERING A NEW PHASE OF **MATURITY** AND **RESPONSIBILITY**, CONCENTRATING ON MORE ADMIRABLE PURSUITS, SUCH AS BUILDING A CAREER...

YOU'RE BREAKING MY HEART—AND MY **ACCOUNTANT'S**.

ANDREAS ROMANOV, UNDISPUTED KING OF THE **HELLRAISERS**, **ACTUALLY** CAME HERE ON DYNASTIC BUSINESS?

I'D LIKE TO BUY SHARES IN THIS HOUSE OF ILL-REPUTE, BECOME YOUR **SLEEPING PARTNER**. YOU **KNOW** I HAVE THE RIGHT EXPERIENCE.

AND THEN YOU'LL **SPY** ON THE TSARIST OFFICIALS WE SERVICE AND MANIPULATE THEIR **COMPROMISING POSITIONS** TO THE BENEFIT OF THE ROMANOV DYNASTY?

DISCRETION GUARANTEED, ANDREAS. **YOU** OF ALL PEOPLE SHOULD BE GRATEFUL FOR THAT.

TRUE, THERE'RE ENOUGH STORIES ABOUT ME AROUND ALREADY. BUT THOSE WILD DAYS ARE **GONE**.

YOU'RE NOT EVEN CONVINCING **YOURSELF**, ANDREAS.

I THINK WATCHING THE BOY BEHAVE LIKE AN **ARROGANT, MISOGYNISTIC PIG** IS MAKING YOU WONDER IF THAT'S ALL THE EMPIRE THINKS OF **YOU**...

BOY!?

THE NAME'S **DANTE**, MA'AM. **NIKOLAI DANTE**. **THE HERO OF RUDINSHTEIN!**

AND I CAN **OUT-DRINK, OUT-FIGHT** AND **OUT-LOVE** ANY MAN, WOMAN OR ALIEN IN THE EMPIRE!

HOW HAVE I MANAGED TO WORK WITH MEN FOR SO LONG **WITHOUT** BEING DRIVEN INSANE?

A **DEAL**, ANDREAS. YOU CAN BECOME MY **PARTNER**—SLEEPING OR OTHERWISE—IF THE **BOY** SURVIVES **THE HELLRAISER GAUNTLET**.

THE **WHAT**?

A GAUNTLET OF PURE UNADULTERATED **PLEASURE**. A TRIAL OF **MALE ENDURANCE** SO DRAINING, SO ARDUOUS THAT ONLY **ONE MAN** HAS EVER COMPLETED IT.

YES. AND IT AGED ME **TEN YEARS**.

HEY, IF **ANDREAS** CAN DO IT, **I** CAN DO IT.

WE'RE **HELLRAISERS EXTRAORDINAIRE**—IT RUNS IN THE FAMILY.

YOU'RE EITHER VERY **BRAVE** OR VERY **STUPID**, BOY.

SOME OF MY **SEDUCTRESSES** ARE SO **BEAUTIFUL** THEY MAKE MEN **CRY**, OTHERS SO **WICKED** THEY MAKE THEM **SCREAM**...

WHAT THE HELL!

THE HERO OF RUDINSHTEIN **NEVER** RUNS FROM A BATTLE...

ESPECIALLY NOT A BATTLE OF **THE SEXES!**

'One thing Nikolai Dante can never be accused of is good timing.'

'Who else could choose to run *The Hellraiser Gauntlet*, a titanic sexual endeavour which reduced most men to snivelling wrecks within minutes...

BOJEMOI...

AND *THIS* IS JUST FOR *STARTERS*.

WITHIN FIRING RANGE NOW, *MINISTER IVANOV.*

GOOD.

READY THE *ATTACK-ANGELS* AND PREPARE TO PENETRATE HER DEFENCES.

'...on the very same day the Skoptzy Sect decided to blast the modern-day Sodom and Gomorrah that is the House Of Sin off the face of the Earth?'

'A major case of coitus interruptus, to say the least.' — 'BRIGANDS OF THE EMPIRE' BY MARIA BERIA.

IS IT *ME?*

OR DID THE *EARTH* JUST MOVE?

THE DAY OF JUDGEMENT HAS COME!

PURGE THE HOUSE OF SIN!

LOOK AT THEM, THE *CREAM* OF IMPERIAL SOCIETY. *POLITICIANS*, *ARISTOCRATS*, *CELEBRITIES*, ALL CAUGHT—forgive my crude phraseology, Lord—WITH THEIR *PANTS DOWN*...

YOU HAVE *ONE* CHANCE, *SINNERS!*

RENOUNCE *SATAN* AND *ALL* HIS EVILS AND CONVERT TO *SKOPTZYISM* OR BE *EXCOMMUNICATED* FROM THIS *MORTAL PLANE!*

ORAL
ANAL
DIGGLE

THE LORD *SMILES* UPON US, *ESAU.*

WE'VE SURPRISED A TRULY *PRODIGIOUS* SINNER IN THE VERY *MIDST* OF COMMITTING HIS *VILE* ACTS!

CAN'T A GUY EVEN HAVE AN *ORGY* IN PEACE, THESE DAYS?

DIAVOLO!

CAREFUL, ESAU, HE LOOKS A *DESPERATE* ONE. SOME SINNERS ARE SAID TO POSSESS THE STRENGTH OF *DEMONS!*

FEAR NOT, ISAAC, NO *DEMON* CAN STAND AGAINST *MY* RIGHTEOUS FURY!

MY BODY IS A *TEMPLE*. I TRAIN EVERY DAY TO *STEEL* MYSELF FOR THE *BATTLE* AGAINST EVIL--

YEAH, BUT I FIGHT *DIRTY!*

ULG!

Focus Dante, keep your head. In an inebriated state, you've more prone to reckless brawling than precision swordsmanship.

KIND OF *HARD* TO CONCENTRATE WHEN YOU'VE GOT A PAIR OF *WARM THIGHS* WRAPPED AROUND YOUR NECK, CREST...

AND EVERY BONE IN YOUR BODY'S SCREAMING FOR YOU TO TURN YOUR HEAD ROUND THE *OTHER* WAY!

HHKKK!

NOW, WHERE WERE WE, YOU *SEXY LITTLE KITTEN*?

OHH, I RATHER THOUGHT YOU WERE GOING TO CONTINUE BEING *CHIVALROUS* AND PROTECT US FROM FURTHER ATTACK.

UHH, YEAH. RIGHT, OF COURSE...

HAPPILY CONVERT...

ASHAMED OF OUR WICKED, WICKED WAYS...

SPLENDID! HOWEVER, IN ADDITION TO *VOWS* OF *VIRTUE*, WE REQUIRE A LITTLE *SACRIFICE* AS A SIGN OF YOUR SINCERITY.

CASTRATION— THEREBY REMOVING THE ROOT OF ALL YOUR PROBLEMS.

PERSONALLY, I'D RATHER BE *DEAD* THAN LIVE WITHOUT THE *FAMILY JEWELS*...

WHO!?

HIS NAME'S *DANTE!* NIKOLAI *DANTE!* THE HERO OF RUDINSHTEIN!

AND YOU SKOPTZY BETTER START SAYING YOUR *PRAYERS*, 'CAUSE THE HERO OF RUDINSHTEIN *NEVER* RUNS FROM A FIGHT!

WHOA, LADIES, LADIES, LADIES! THERE'S A LOT MORE OF *THEM* THAN THERE IS OF *ME*...

NIKOLAI DANTE? NIKOLAI *DANTE!*

THE ALMIGHTY HAS DELIVERED UNTO US ONE OF THE *GREATEST SINNERS* IN *ALL* THE EMPIRE! LET YOUR GUNFIRE *SING* THE LORD'S PRAISES!

Dante!

Evasive action!

Evasive action means dodge the bullets, not dive straight into them!

NO CHOICE, CREST...

THERE ARE *LADIES* PRESENT, AND MY *REPUTATION'S* ON THE LINE.

I'VE *GOT* TO TRY AND *IMPRESS* THEM!

LOOK AT HIS *EYES*, THAT *SMILE*— TRULY THE *DEVIL* IS STRONG WITHIN HIM.

FLAGELLATOR! PUNISH HIM! *FLAY* HIM ALIVE AND CONSIGN HIS SOUL TO THE *DARKEST DEPTHS* OF HELL!

AAAHHH!

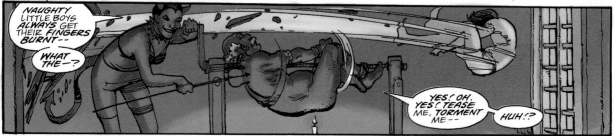

NAUGHTY LITTLE BOYS *ALWAYS* GET THEIR *FINGERS* BURNT--

WHAT THE--?

YES! OH. YES! TEASE ME, *TORMENT* ME--

HUH!?

GGNNPHH!

ANDREAS...?

NIKOLAI!

BY THE VIRGIN'S VIRTUE!

IS THERE NO END TO THE INFAMY WITHIN THESE WALLS?

SHOCKING, ISN'T IT?

Excellent strategy, Dante—bringing the electro-whip into contact with his Repressor-Robes to cause a terminal overload...

THIS IS YOUR NEW PHASE OF MATURITY AND RESPONSIBILITY!?

ROMPING AROUND WITH THE MADAME OF THE HOUSE OF SIN WHILE I'M GETTING MY ASS WHIPPED BY A SKOPTZY COMMANDO SQUAD!?

YOUR ANGER'S PERFECTLY JUSTIFIED, NIKOLAI. I CAN ONLY APOLOGISE FOR MY POOR PERFORMANCE AS A ROLE MODEL...

I'VE TRIED TO BE A GENTLEMAN, TRIED TO LIVE ABOVE MYSELF, TO RESIST TEMPTATION. BUT THE HARDER I TRY, THE WORSE I GET. SO WHAT THE HELL...

SOME OF US ARE JUST BORN TO BE BAD, AND THE WORLD'D BE A DAMNED SIGHT POORER WITHOUT US.

THAT'S MORE LIKE IT, ANDREAS. YOU CAN'T KEEP A GOOD MAN DOWN!

MADAME, LIE THERE AND AMUSE YOURSELF 'TIL I RETURN.

THIS WON'T TAKE LONG.

YOU WANT TO BE A HELLRAISER, KOLYA?

I'LL SHOW YOU HOW TO RAISE HELL!

'The Skoptzy Sect regarded the presence of Nikolai Dante and Andreas Romanov as an extra blessing when they began their assault on the House of Sin...

THERE THEY ARE! TAUNTING US WITH THEIR DEPRAVITY, FLAUNTING THEIR SINFULNESS!

PUNISH THEM IN THE NAME OF THE LORD! LET THEM FEEL THE WRATH OF GOD!

'...though they soon learned that there's sometimes a very fine line between a blessing and a curse' — 'NIKOLAI DANTE : A CHARACTER ASSASSINATION' — VARIOUS CONTRIBUTORS.

LOOKS LIKE THE KNIVES ARE OUT FOR THE ROMANOV BROTHERS.

AGAIN.

KNIVES, KOLYA?

THOSE AREN'T KNIVES...

THIS IS A KNIFE!

FROM THE FILES OF THE IMPERIAL RAVEN CORPS:

Andreas Romanov: Reckless adventurer, incorrigible playboy and philandering seducer of wealthy widows and heiresses.

Weapons Crest Capabilities: Bioblades which generate a lethal energy-field the size of which is directly variable to the scale of the target.

Rumoured to have once decapitated 27 men with a single blade.

Yeughh...

NICE SHOT.

I'VE THROWN BETTER. HOW MANY DO YOU MAKE IT?

UHH, TWELVE, THIRTEEN MAYBE...

KIND OF HARD TO TELL WHEN THEY'RE ALL IN PIECES.

Hmph.

NOWHERE NEAR MY RECORD.

ABOMINATIONS! THE HOUSE OF SIN ITSELF SHALL BE THE ENGINE OF YOUR DESTRUCTION!

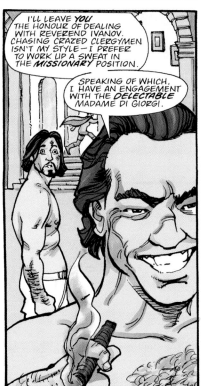

I'LL LEAVE YOU THE HONOUR OF DEALING WITH REVEREND IVANOV. CHASING CRAZED CLERGYMEN ISN'T MY STYLE— I PREFER TO WORK UP A SWEAT IN THE MISSIONARY POSITION.

SPEAKING OF WHICH, I HAVE AN ENGAGEMENT WITH THE DELECTABLE MADAME DI GIORGI.

He's heading for the cockpit, Dante!

I believe he intends to sabotage the guidance system and cause this behemoth to crash.

IVANOV! DESTROY THOSE CONTROLS AND YOU'LL KILL YOURSELF AS WELL AS EVERYONE ELSE!

I'LL DIE HAPPY— THE LORD LOVES A MARTYR AS MUCH AS HE HATES A SINNER.

THEN HE'S AS CRAZY AS YOU ARE...

BLASPHEMER!
YEAH, AND PROUD OF IT.
COME AHEAD, REVEREND. CONVERT ME...
UNGH!
BEG YOUR PARDON, MILADY!
Heh!
AS YOUR SOUL PLUMMETS INTO HELL, BOY, I SHALL RISE TO THE HEAVENS!
YEAH?
GRAVITY MIGHT HAVE SOMETHING TO SAY ABOUT THAT!

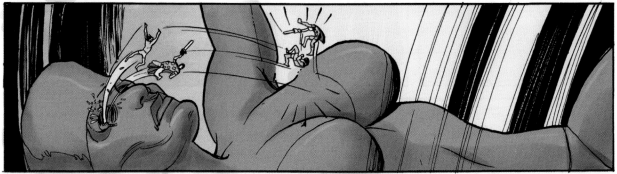

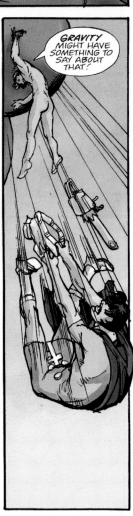

Ouch.

Y'KNOW, CREST. I NEVER THOUGHT I'D BE HAPPY TO DROP MY *PANTS* FOR SOMEONE AS *UGLY* AS THAT...

...MOUNTAINOUS MAMMARIES...

I'M TELLING YOU, ANDREAS, GETTING BACK UP HERE WAS LIKE CLIMBING THE HIMALAYAS. LUCKY WE'VE GOT THE REST OF THE WEEKEND TO RECOVER...

RECOVER? SURELY YOU HAVEN'T FORGOTTEN OUR CHALLENGE, NIKOLAI?

YOU HAVEN'T EVEN COMPLETED THE *FIRST STAGE* OF *THE HELLRAISER GAUNTLET.*

AND NOW MY SEDUCTRESSES ARE *JUST DYING* TO THANK YOU FOR SAVING THE HOUSE OF SIN.

TAKE *ME* FIRST, NIKOLAI...

LOVE YOU LONG TIME...

I TRIED TO WARN YOU, KOLYA.

YOU CAN GET *TOO MUCH* OF A *GOOD THING.*

Ulp...

'And so, Nikolai Dante became only the second man to survive the Hellraiser Gauntlet, albeit by the narrowest of margins. His response to Madame Di Giorgi's suggestion that they try for 'best out of three' remains unprintable.'—*SMIRNOFF BOOK OF RECORDS, 2668.*

DIAVOLO...

I FEEL AS THOUGH I'VE BEEN THROUGH EVERY *WORLD WAR* SINCE HISTORY BEGAN.

YOU'RE HOLDING UP BETTER THAN I DID. AT LEAST YOU CAN STILL *WALK*...

THOUGH I DO HOPE YOU TOOK *PRECAUTIONS*.

HEY! I *ALWAYS* PRACTISE *SAFE SEX*.

I MEANT *SECURITY PRECAUTIONS*—THERE MAY HAVE BEEN *TSARIST AGENTS* AMONGST THE SEDUCTRESSES.

THE HELLRAISER GAUNTLET IS COMPOSED *ENTIRELY* OF COMPROMISING SITUATIONS, AND THE TSAR WOULD LOVE TO GET HIS HANDS ON INCRIMINATING EVIDENCE WHICH COULD *EMBARRASS* OUR FAMILY.

COME ON, ANDREAS...

HOW CAN I *POSSIBLY* EMBARRASS THE FAMILY ANY MORE THAN I *ALREADY* DO?

TOUR OF DUTY

Script: Robbie Morrison
Art: Charlie Adlard
Colours: D'Israeli
Letters: Annie Parkhouse

Originally published in *2000 AD* Progs 1131-1133

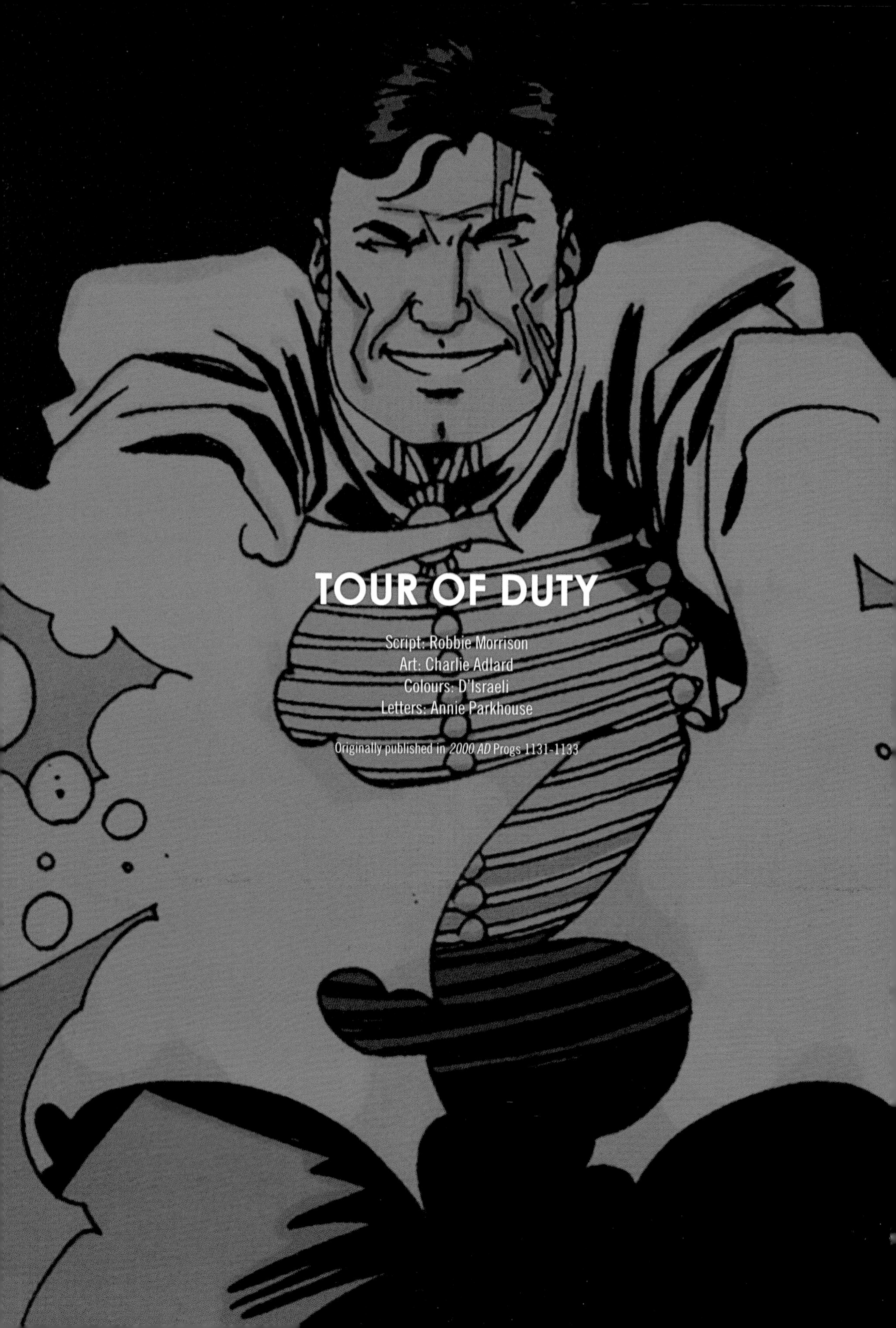

SCRIPT
ROBBIE MORRISON
ART
CHARLIE ADLARD
COLOURS
D'ISRAELI
LETTERS
ANNIE PARKHOUSE

THE YEAR OF THE TSAR 2668. ST PETERSBURG.

'No one writes letters anymore, Mama.

'We've let holo-communications and the Imperial Net take over, banished letters, banished writing to a graveyard of ancient texts, pulp fiction and historical romances...

'But can there really be any more powerful and lasting expression of what's in your heart than something written in your own hand?'

'Maybe that's why writing to you now, to tell you the man I love—the man I think loves me—seems so fitting, so right.'

QUENTIN! QUENTIN!

'I can hardly believe something so good grew out of the Empire. He's the most caring, considerate, gentle, sensitive, tender, unassuming and romantic lover I've ever had.'

'Romance...

'It almost seems too good to be true!'

INGRID! OVER HERE!

THIS IS WHERE WE MET. REMEMBER, QUENTIN? IN THIS HOTEL, IN THIS ELEVATOR...

UH, YEAH.

I WAS HERE WITH *LADY JULIANNA* AND YOU WERE MEETING A GROUP OF CHILEAN WINE MERCHANTS.

THAT'S WHY IT'S THE RIGHT PLACE TO TELL YOU SOMETHING I HOPE YOU *ALREADY* KNOW...

I LOVE YOU, QUENTIN OURWARD. I'LL LOVE YOU TIL THE DAY I DIE.

FUOCO...

I CAN'T GO THROUGH WITH THIS.

WITH WHAT?

WE'VE DONE *EVERY* THING THERE IS TO DO ALREADY...

INGRID, I'M *NOT* WHO YOU THINK I AM.

I'M NO *WINE IMPORTER*— THE ONLY WINE *I* IMPORT GOES STRAIGHT DOWN MY THROAT AND INTO MY BELLY!

BUT YOU *DON'T* DRINK--

OH, BUT I *DO*, AND I'LL PROBABLY DRINK A *LOT* MORE TO FORGET *THIS*!

IT'S *ALL LIES*, INGRID, EVERYTHING I'VE TOLD YOU...

GOOD AFTERNOON!

It's all lies.

INGRID WAGNER? ALLOW US TO INTRODUCE OURSELVES. I AM *KONSTANTIN ROMANOV, PALADIN* OF THE ROMANOV DYNASTY, AND THIS IS...

TELL HER YOUR *REAL* NAME, LITTLE BROTHER. YOU USUALLY SAY IT WITH SUCH *FLAIR* AND *ARROGANCE*.

Dante. Nikolai Dante.

WE SEEM TO HAVE SOMETHING OF A *DELICATE* SITUATION ON OUR HANDS.

YOU'RE THE *LADY-IN-WAITING* TO *JULIANNA MAKAROV*, THE *TSAR'S* YOUNGEST DAUGHTER, AND NIKOLAI IS A *ROMANOV*, ONE OF THE TSAR'S GREATEST ENEMIES.

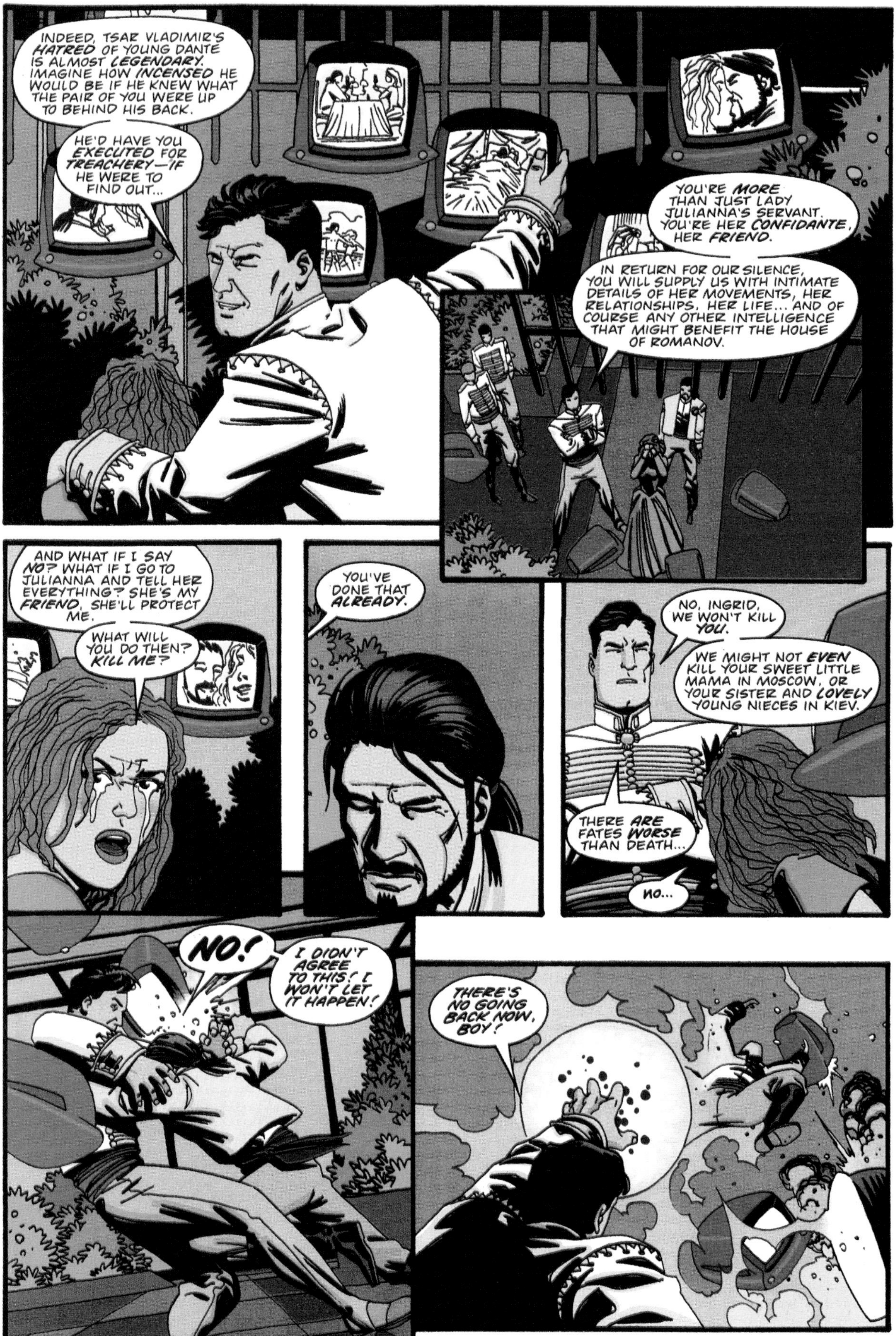

INDEED, TSAR VLADIMIR'S HATRED OF YOUNG DANTE IS ALMOST LEGENDARY. IMAGINE HOW INCENSED HE WOULD BE IF HE KNEW WHAT THE PAIR OF YOU WERE UP TO BEHIND HIS BACK.
HE'D HAVE YOU EXECUTED FOR TREACHERY—IF HE WERE TO FIND OUT...
YOU'RE MORE THAN JUST LADY JULIANNA'S SERVANT. YOU'RE HER CONFIDANTE, HER FRIEND.
IN RETURN FOR OUR SILENCE, YOU WILL SUPPLY US WITH INTIMATE DETAILS OF HER MOVEMENTS, HER RELATIONSHIPS, HER LIFE... AND OF COURSE ANY OTHER INTELLIGENCE THAT MIGHT BENEFIT THE HOUSE OF ROMANOV.
AND WHAT IF I SAY NO? WHAT IF I GO TO JULIANNA AND TELL HER EVERYTHING? SHE'S MY FRIEND, SHE'LL PROTECT ME.
WHAT WILL YOU DO THEN? KILL ME?
YOU'VE DONE THAT ALREADY.
NO, INGRID, WE WON'T KILL YOU.
WE MIGHT NOT EVEN KILL YOUR SWEET LITTLE MAMA IN MOSCOW, OR YOUR SISTER AND LOVELY YOUNG NIECES IN KIEV.
THERE ARE FATES WORSE THAN DEATH...
NO...
NO!
I DIDN'T AGREE TO THIS! I WON'T LET IT HAPPEN!
THERE'S NO GOING BACK NOW, BOY!

YOUR PART IN THIS IS *OVER*. YOU... KEPT YOUR *END* UP.

IT'S A LITTLE *LATE* TO START DEVELOPING A *CONSCIENCE*.

I ALREADY *KNOW* YOUR ANSWER, BUT MAKING YOU SAY IT YOURSELF WILL DRAIN THE LAST BIT OF *DEFIANCE* FROM YOU.

WILL YOU *SPY* FOR US, GIRL?

YES...

THESE *CHARMING* MEN ARE YOUR *CONTROLLERS*. GO WITH THEM. THEY'LL BEGIN YOUR *TRAINING* IMMEDIATELY.

INGRID... I-I'M SORRY...

DON'T *INSULT* ME BY PRETENDING THERE WAS *EVER* ANYTHING BETWEEN US.

YOU'RE *WORSE* THAN *HE* IS. HOW CAN YOU *USE* PEOPLE LIKE THAT? HOW COULD YOU USE *ME* LIKE THAT?

I OPENED *MYSELF* UP TO YOU, AND YOU SLID IN A *KNIFE*.

I'LL HATE YOU 'TIL THE DAY I DIE, NIKOLAI DANTE.

PROPER LITTLE *HEARTBREAKER*, AREN'T YOU, NIKOLAI.

THE END

THE YEAR OF THE TSAR 2668. GENETICO RESEARCH SATELLITE, ORBITING IMPERIAL EARTH.

'Gene Prospecting is the science of pinpointing the specific genes that predispose sentient beings throughout the Empire to disease.'

SCRIPT
ROBBIE MORRISON
ART
CHARLIE ADLARD
COLOURS
D'ISRAELI
LETTERS
ANNIE PARKHOUSE

'Tightly inbred populations have limited pools of genes which make it easier for scientists to locate DNA associated with ailments such as multiple sclerosis, schizophrenia, cancer and alcoholism.

'The abnormal proteins that these genes are responsible for producing are isolated, studied, and patented. Drugs and medicines are then manufactured to counter their debilitating effects.'

'Gene Prospecting has been labelled the ultimate exploitation...

THE GENETICO GENEPOOL, THE STORE OF LIVING DNA FROM WHICH WE CONDUCT OUR RESEARCH.

NIKOLAI DANTE

TOUR OF DUTY PART 2

'...ruthlessly acquiring the DNA of the Empire's more primitive indigenous peoples for the profit of companies such as GenetiCo and its founder Raoul Sequanna'— IMPERIAL TIMES, SCIENCE SECTION.

THE HEART, OR PERHAPS MORE ACCURATELY, THE WOMB OF OUR OPERATIONS.

COSY...

WE APPRECIATE THE TOUR, DR. SEQUANNA, BUT OUR PROPOSITION HAS LITTLE TO DO WITH GENETICO, AND EVERYTHING TO DO WITH YOU.

THEN PERHAPS IT WOULD BE WISER TO DISCUSS IT IN PRIVATE, *LORD KONSTANTIN...*

ONCE MY *OTHER* HONOURED GUEST OF TODAY HAS COMPLETED HIS BUSINESS AND DEPARTED.

GENTLEMEN, MY DAUGHTER, *LUISA.*

AND I'M SURE YOU'RE ALREADY ACQUAINTED WITH THE TSAR'S LORD PROTECTOR, *COUNT PYRE.*

A PLEASURE AS *ALWAYS,* DANTE...

PYRE! MAKE ONE MOVE AGAINST ME, AND I'LL--

KONSTANTIN, PLEASE INFORM YOUR *BASTARD BROTHER* THAT THE ENMITY BETWEEN US IS PURELY *PERSONAL,* AND SHOULD NOT BECOME AN ISSUE WHEN WE ARE ALL ON WHAT I ASSUME IS *OFFICIAL* BUSINESS.

THE SHAPESHIFTER'S RIGHT, NIKOLAI. CONDUCT YOURSELF WITH DIGNITY OR I'LL BE FORCED TO TAKE ACTION AGAINST *YOU.*

COUNT PYRE IS THE IMPERIAL LIAISON BETWEEN GENETICO AND THE RULING HOUSE OF MAKAROV, RESPONSIBLE FOR APPROVING THE *GENE-PATENTS* WE APPLY FOR.

HE JUST WANTS TO BE *FIRST* IN LINE WHEN THEY FIND THE GENE FOR *UGLINESS* AND MAKE A *CURE* FOR IT...

A RAPIER *WIT,* DANTE.

DR. SEQUANNA, I'LL BE IN TOUCH WHEN *TSAR VLADIMIR* DECIDES WHAT HIS *PERCENTAGE SPLIT* OF YOUR NEW PATENTS WILL BE.

VERY GOOD, COUNT PYRE. *DR. ZAMEL* WILL ESCORT YOU TO YOUR SHIP.

AS YOU MAY BE AWARE, DOCTOR, WE ROMANOVS ARE THE PRODUCT OF A BREEDING PROGRAMME INTENDED TO PROMOTE THE GENETIC PURITY OF OUR BLOODLINE.

MY FATHER WISHES YOU TO SUPERVISE THE CREATION OF A *ROMANOV GENEPOOL* NOT DISSIMILAR TO WHAT YOU HAVE HERE.

THIS WILL ALLOW US TO WIPE OUT THE FEW REMAINING FLAWS AND WEAKNESSES IN OUR PHYSICAL AND PSYCHOLOGICAL MAKE-UP, AND AVOID FURTHER *SURPRISES* SUCH AS *DANTE.*

AMONGST *OTHERS*...

YOU AND PYRE DON'T *LIKE* EACH OTHER VERY MUCH, DO YOU?

TO PUT IT *MILDLY*...

A FEW MONTHS BACK, HIS LOVER *MARALIS* TRIED TO ASSASSINATE ME.

I'M STILL HERE, AND SHE'S *NOT.*

'AND PYRE ISN'T EXACTLY THE *FORGIVING* TYPE!'

I *told* you, boy...

...that a part of *Maralis* lives on within me...

...and that one day that part would claim your life.

SOUNDS AS THOUGH YOU LEAD AN *EXCITING* LIFE.

I'M GLAD *SOMEONE* DOES—FATHER AND I HAVEN'T LEFT THIS SATELLITE IN AS LONG AS I CAN REMEMBER.

BOJEMOI...

WHAT ABOUT YOUR *MOTHER*?

GENETICO IS MY FAMILY, NIKOLAI.

I'M *HONOURED* BY YOUR *PROPOSITION*, BUT I'M AFRAID I CAN'T *POSSIBLY* ACCEPT.

TO AID THE HOUSE OF ROMANOV WOULD JEOPARDISE THE INDEPENDENCE AND NEUTRALITY OF GENETICO IN THE EYES OF THE TSAR.

THE EMPIRE'S *CHANGING*, SEQUANNA.

SOON, *EVERYONE* WILL HAVE TO CHOOSE SIDES...

NOW...

DO I HAVE TO MAKE YOU AN OFFER YOU *CAN'T* REFUSE?

WHY NOT COME BACK WITH ME FOR A WHILE—THERE'S *NO ONE* BETTER QUALIFIED TO EDUCATE YOU IN THE WAYS OF THE WORLD.

I'LL INTRODUCE YOU TO MY LITTLE BROTHER *ARKADY*—SOMEONE ELSE WHO NEEDS TO GET *OUT* MORE.

YOU'RE VERY *KIND*, SIR, BUT—

WHAT CAN I SAY, I'M A *NICE GUY*...

IT'S IN MY *GENES*.

CONGRATULATIONS, LITTLE BROTHER...

EVEN OUT HERE, YOU MANAGE TO GET US INTO TROUBLE.

ME!?

WHAT THE HELL DID I DO?

DR. SEQUANNA BELIEVES YOUR FRIEND COUNT PYRE INFECTED THE GENEPOOL WITH HIS OWN SHAPESHIFTING GENES TO CAUSE THIS MUTATION.

PYRE...

SO MUCH FOR KEEPING BUSINESS AND PLEASURE SEPARATE. YOU SHOULD'VE LET ME RUN HIM THROUGH WHEN WE HAD THE CHANCE.

FATHER, WE HAVE TO ACTIVATE THE EXTINCTION CODE. IT'S THE ONLY CHANCE.

NO, LUISA! YOU KNOW WHAT'LL HAPPEN IF WE DO THAT!

YES! AND I KNOW WHAT'LL HAPPEN IF WE DON'T—YOU'LL ALL DIE!

LUISA!

NO... PLEASE...

THE DNA IN THE POOL IS ENCODED WITH AN EXTINCTION GENE INTENDED FOR USE IN THE EVENT OF A RIVAL GENETICS CORP RAIDING OUR FACILITIES.

ACCESSING THE GENETICO MAINFRAME WITH THIS KEY WILL AUTOMATICALLY ACTIVATE THE CODE. ALL WE HAVE TO DO IS FIND A TERMINAL.

THEN LEAD THE WAY, GIRL. IT'S STARTING AGAIN.

THERE! THE MONITOR OUTPOST!

IF WE CAN REACH IT...

QUICKLY! THEY'RE COMING! PULL ME UP!

ALL IN GOOD TIME, DOCTOR.

PERHAPS NOW YOU'D CARE TO RECONSIDER MY EARLIER PROPOSITION TO HEAD THE ROMANOV GENEPOOL PROJECT...

FATHER!

KONSTANTIN, WHAT THE HELL ARE YOU DOING?

MAKING THE GOOD DOCTOR AN OFFER HE CAN'T REFUSE.

JOIN US, SEQUANNA.

SWEAR ALLEGIANCE TO THE ROMANOV DYNASTY OR I'LL INTRODUCE THOSE BEASTS BELOW TO THEIR CREATOR.

I...I...

LORD KONSTANTIN! PLEASE! I'LL DO IT!

FATHER TAUGHT ME EVERYTHING HE KNOWS. I'LL DO IT. ANYTHING! WHATEVER YOU WANT!

THAT'S THE SPIRIT, GIRL!

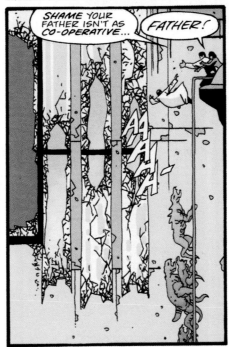

SHAME YOUR FATHER ISN'T AS CO-OPERATIVE...

FATHER!

AAA-

AAAGHKKK!

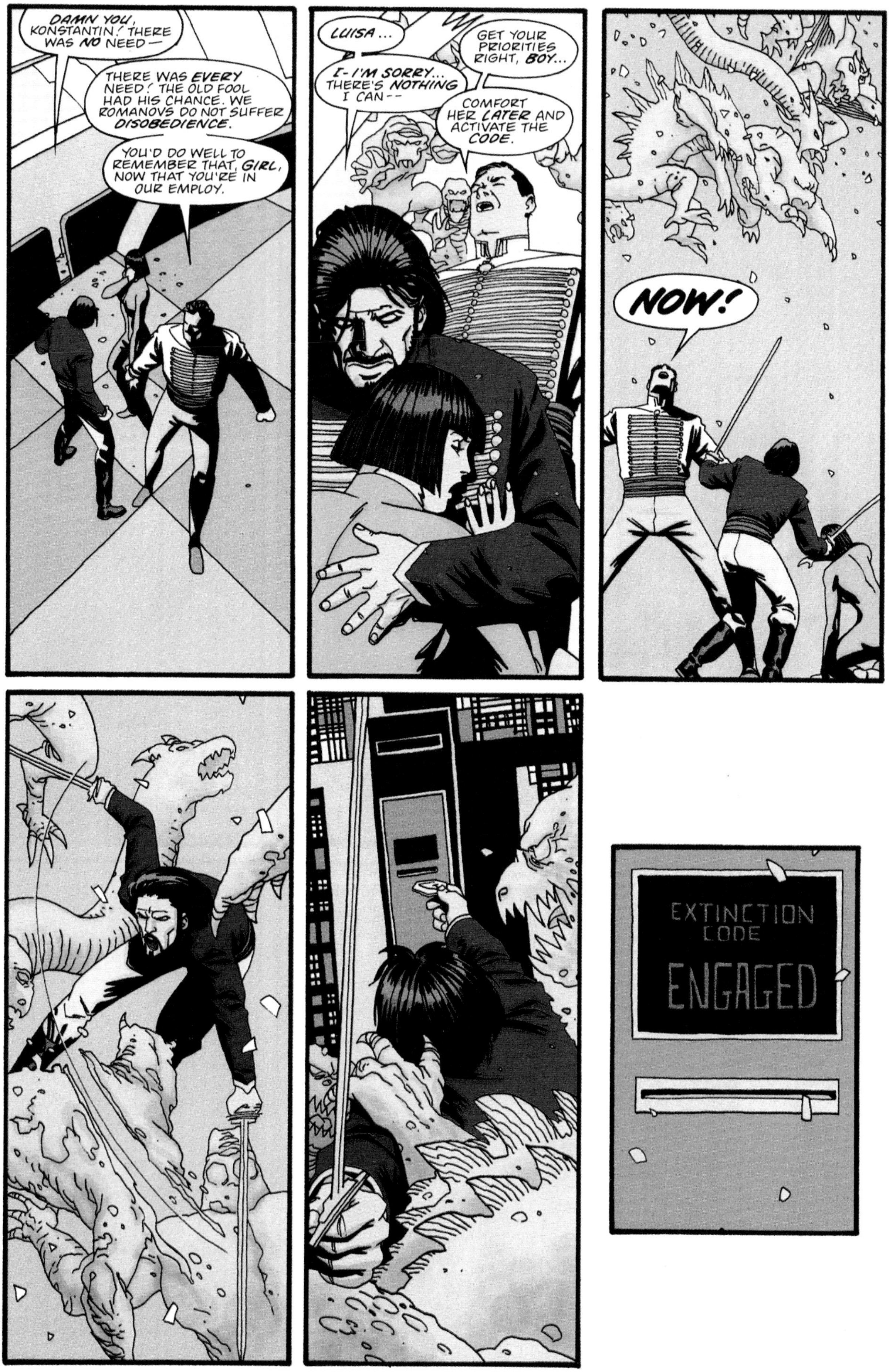
DAMN YOU, KONSTANTIN! THERE WAS NO NEED—
THERE WAS EVERY NEED! THE OLD FOOL HAD HIS CHANCE. WE ROMANOVS DO NOT SUFFER DISOBEDIENCE.
YOU'D DO WELL TO REMEMBER THAT, GIRL, NOW THAT YOU'RE IN OUR EMPLOY.
LUISA...
I-I'M SORRY... THERE'S NOTHING I CAN--
GET YOUR PRIORITIES RIGHT, BOY...
COMFORT HER LATER AND ACTIVATE THE CODE.
NOW!
EXTINCTION CODE
ENGAGED

ABOUT TIME, LITTLE BROTHER...

I WAS BEGINNING TO THINK I WAS GOING TO HAVE TO GET MY HANDS *BLOODY*...

UNNH...

LUISA!

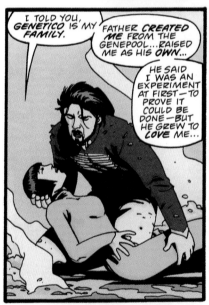

I TOLD YOU, GENETICO IS MY FAMILY.

FATHER *CREATED* ME FROM THE GENEPOOL...RAISED ME AS HIS *OWN*...

HE SAID I WAS AN EXPERIMENT AT FIRST—TO PROVE IT COULD BE DONE—BUT HE GREW TO *LOVE* ME...

DON'T BE *SAD* FOR ME, NIKOLAI DANTE. BE *HAPPY*.

YOU TAUGHT ME *ENOUGH* ABOUT YOUR WORLD TO MAKE ME KNOW I *NEVER* WANTED TO BE PART OF IT...

Yeah...

You've not the only one, Luisa.

THE END

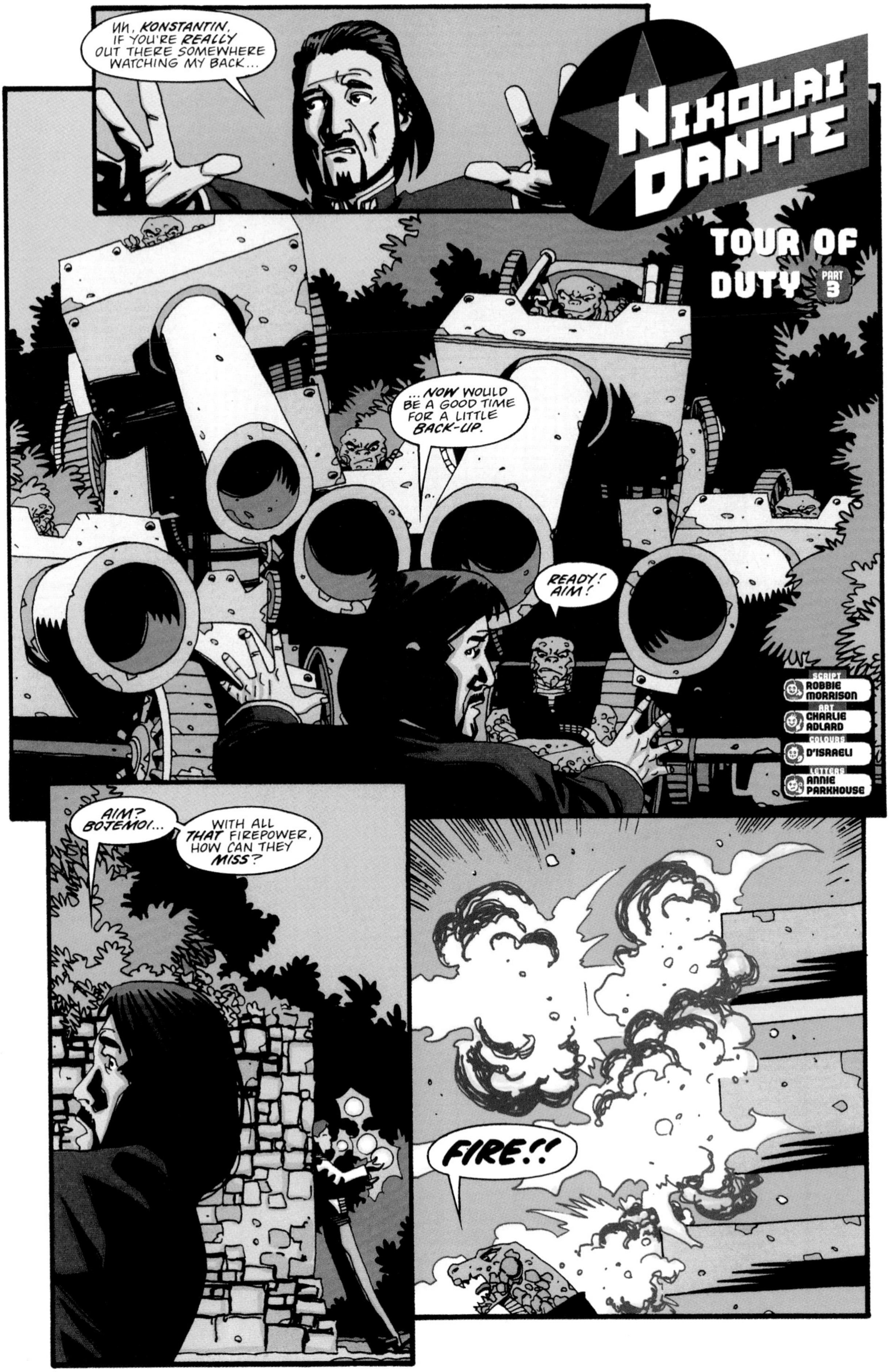
UH, KONSTANTIN, IF YOU'RE REALLY OUT THERE SOMEWHERE WATCHING MY BACK...
NIKOLAI DANTE
TOUR OF DUTY PART 3
...NOW WOULD BE A GOOD TIME FOR A LITTLE BACK-UP.
READY! AIM!
SCRIPT ROBBIE MORRISON
ART CHARLIE ADLARD
COLOURS D'ISRAELI
LETTERS ANNIE PARKHOUSE
AIM? BOJEMOI...
WITH ALL THAT FIREPOWER, HOW CAN THEY MISS?
FIRE?!

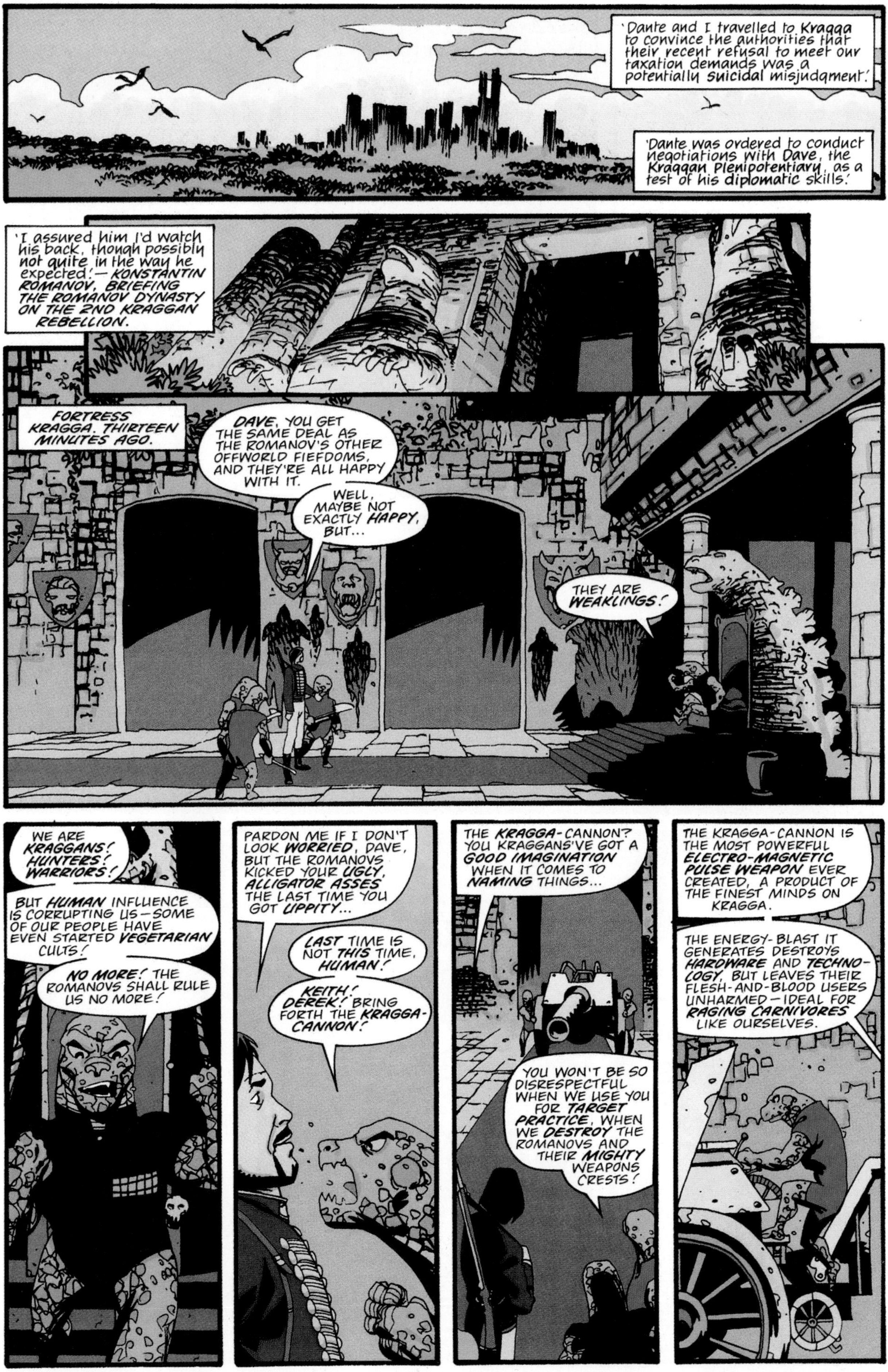

'Dante and I travelled to Kragga to convince the authorities that their recent refusal to meet our taxation demands was a potentially suicidal misjudgment.'
'Dante was ordered to conduct negotiations with Dave, the Kraggan Plenipotentiary, as a test of his diplomatic skills.'
'I assured him I'd watch his back, though possibly not quite in the way he expected.' — KONSTANTIN ROMANOV, BRIEFING THE ROMANOV DYNASTY ON THE 2ND KRAGGAN REBELLION.
FORTRESS KRAGGA. THIRTEEN MINUTES AGO.
DAVE, YOU GET THE SAME DEAL AS THE ROMANOV'S OTHER OFFWORLD FIEFDOMS, AND THEY'RE ALL HAPPY WITH IT.
WELL, MAYBE NOT EXACTLY HAPPY, BUT...
THEY ARE WEAKLINGS!
WE ARE KRAGGANS! HUNTERS! WARRIORS!
BUT HUMAN INFLUENCE IS CORRUPTING US — SOME OF OUR PEOPLE HAVE EVEN STARTED VEGETARIAN CULTS!
NO MORE! THE ROMANOVS SHALL RULE US NO MORE!
PARDON ME IF I DON'T LOOK WORRIED, DAVE, BUT THE ROMANOVS KICKED YOUR UGLY, ALLIGATOR ASSES THE LAST TIME YOU GOT UPPITY...
LAST TIME IS NOT THIS TIME, HUMAN!
KEITH! DEREK! BRING FORTH THE KRAGGA-CANNON!
THE KRAGGA-CANNON? YOU KRAGGANS'VE GOT A GOOD IMAGINATION WHEN IT COMES TO NAMING THINGS...
YOU WON'T BE SO DISRESPECTFUL WHEN WE USE YOU FOR TARGET PRACTICE, WHEN WE DESTROY THE ROMANOVS AND THEIR MIGHTY WEAPONS CRESTS!
THE KRAGGA-CANNON IS THE MOST POWERFUL ELECTRO-MAGNETIC PULSE WEAPON EVER CREATED, A PRODUCT OF THE FINEST MINDS ON KRAGGA.
THE ENERGY-BLAST IT GENERATES DESTROYS HARDWARE AND TECHNOLOGY, BUT LEAVES THEIR FLESH-AND-BLOOD USERS UNHARMED — IDEAL FOR RAGING CARNIVORES LIKE OURSELVES.

UNFORTUNATELY, YOU ROMANOVS ARE *SYMBIOTICALLY BONDED* WITH THE TECHNOLOGY OF YOUR WEAPONS CRESTS.

OUR SCIENTISTS ARE *98% CERTAIN* THAT THE CANNON'LL BLOW YOU APART AS SURELY AS IF WE'D DROPPED A *FRAG-GRENADE* DOWN YOUR THROAT.

GOOD ENOUGH *ODDS* FOR US! WHAT DO YOU SAY TO THAT?!

THAT YOU SHOULD'VE *SHUT UP* AND *SHOT* ME IN THE *BACK* 'STEAD OF TELLING ME ALL ABOUT YOUR SECRET WEAPON.

GNURGH!

SKRAKK!

BOOMM!

CREST!

PLOT ME THE QUICKEST COURSE BACK TO THE *STRIKEHAWK!* WE'VE GOT TO WARN *KONSTANTIN* ABOUT THIS.

The fact that Konstantin remained behind and let you enter the lizards' den alone may mean he's already aware of the threat.

BOJEMOI! AND THEY CALL *ME* THE BASTARD OF THE FAMILY!

'LEAST THE KRAGGANS DON'T SEEM TO HAVE...

...any other cannons.

YOU WERE *DISAPPOINTING* PREY, DANTE!

KRAGGANS! WE *FIRE* ON MY COMMAND!

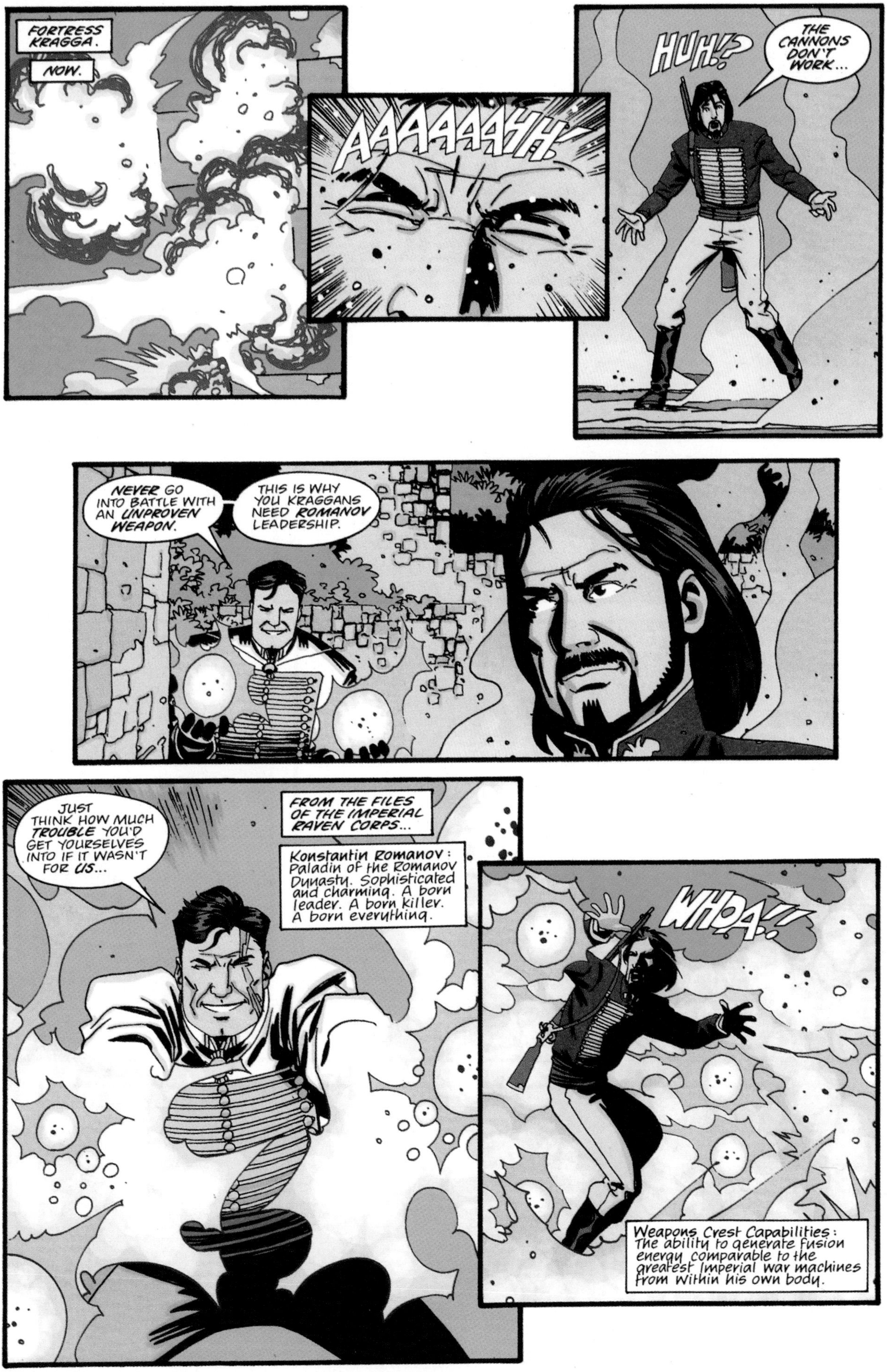
FORTRESS KRAGGA.
NOW.
AAAAAAAYH!
HUH!?
THE CANNONS DON'T WORK...
NEVER GO INTO BATTLE WITH AN UNPROVEN WEAPON.
THIS IS WHY YOU KRAGGANS NEED ROMANOV LEADERSHIP.
JUST THINK HOW MUCH TROUBLE YOU'D GET YOURSELVES INTO IF IT WASN'T FOR US...
FROM THE FILES OF THE IMPERIAL RAVEN CORPS...
Konstantin Romanov: Paladin of the Romanov Dynasty. Sophisticated and charming. A born leader. A born killer. A born everything.
WHOA!!
Weapons Crest Capabilities: The ability to generate fusion energy comparable to the greatest Imperial war machines from within his own body.

BOOM! **KA-DOOM!**

LETTING ME GET OUT OF THE WAY WOULD'VE BEEN NICE!

NO ONE EVER ACCUSED *ME* OF BEING *NICE*.

DAVE. THIS YEAR, KRAGGA WILL PAY AN EXTRA 10% IN TAX AS *PUNISHMENT* FOR TODAY'S OFFENCE.

YESSIR, LORD KONSTANTIN! AND I'LL ADD ANOTHER 5% ON TOP OF THAT AS A SIGN OF OUR *DEEPEST* REGRET...

MAKE IT 10. IF YOU'RE GOING TO BE *OBSEQUIOUS*, GO FOR *BROKE*.

YOU KNEW ABOUT THE CANNONS, DIDN'T YOU?

OF COURSE. WE JUST WEREN'T SURE HOW EFFECTIVE THEY WOULD BE TARGETED UPON OUR WEAPONS CRESTS.

SO YOU *SET* ME UP!?

TURNED ME INTO A *HUMAN TARGET*!?

YOU HAD TO BE *USEFUL* FOR *SOMETHING*, LITTLE BROTHER.

THE END

THE CADRE INFERNALE

Script: Robbie Morrison
Art: Simon Fraser
Colours: Gary Caldwell
Letters: Annie Parkhouse

Originally published in *2000 AD* Progs 1134-1137

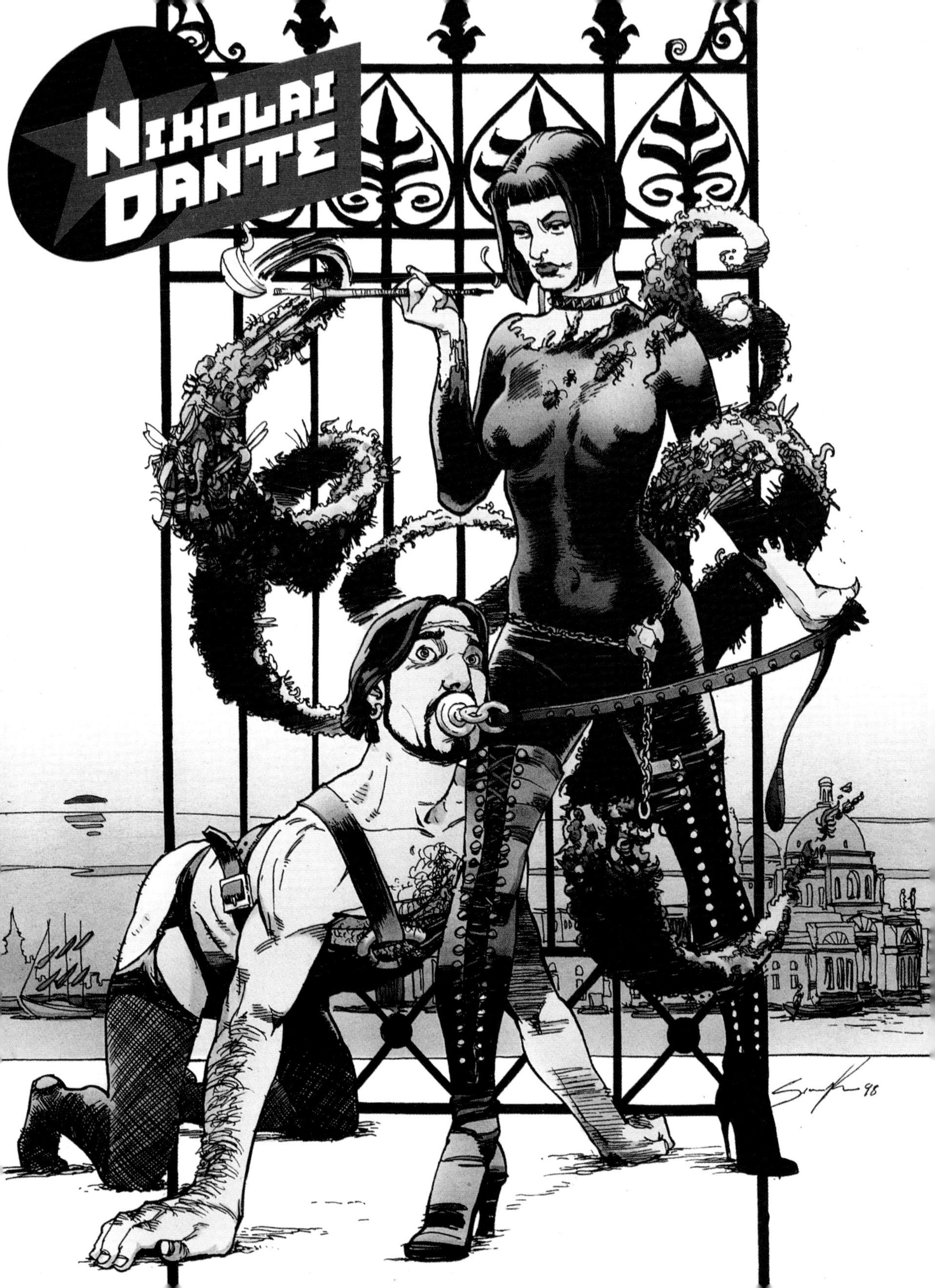
NIKOLAI
DANTE

LULU! ARKADY SAID YOU WANTED TO SEE ME URGENTLY.

BOJEMOI...

CLOSE THE DOOR, NIKOLAI.

IF THE SERVANTS SEE ME LIKE THIS, THEY'LL HAVE A HEART ATTACK.

THEY'RE NOT THE ONLY ONES...

LIQUID LATEX, KOLYA. IT HARDENS TO FORM A HYPO-ALLERGENIC SECOND SKIN THAT LEAVES LITTLE TO THE IMAGINATION AND PEELS OFF AS EASILY AS UNZIPPING A BANANA.

THOUGH IT MIGHT NOT BE TOO KIND TO A BODY AS HAIRY AS YOURS...

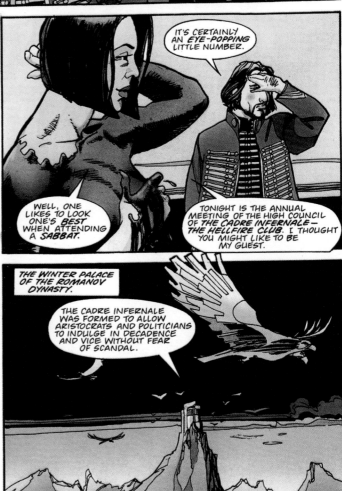

IT'S CERTAINLY AN EYE-POPPING LITTLE NUMBER.

WELL, ONE LIKES TO LOOK ONE'S BEST WHEN ATTENDING A SABBAT.

TONIGHT IS THE ANNUAL MEETING OF THE HIGH COUNCIL OF THE CADRE INFERNALE— THE HELLFIRE CLUB. I THOUGHT YOU MIGHT LIKE TO BE MY GUEST.

THE WINTER PALACE OF THE ROMANOV DYNASTY.

THE CADRE INFERNALE WAS FORMED TO ALLOW ARISTOCRATS AND POLITICIANS TO INDULGE IN DECADENCE AND VICE WITHOUT FEAR OF SCANDAL.

ISN'T THAT WHAT THEY USE THEIR POWER AND WEALTH FOR ANYWAY?

SUCH VENOM, NIKOLAI. YOU'RE AN ARISTOCRAT TOO, REMEMBER?

ACCEPT MY INVITATION, I PROMISE YOU AN UNFORGETTABLE EVENING OF ENTERTAINMENT.

OKAY, YOU TALKED ME INTO IT.

GOOD. I'VE BEEN CAMPAIGNING FOR A *BETTER CLASS* OF *DEVIANT* TO BE ALLOWED INTO THE RANKS OF THE CADRE, AND I DO BELIEVE *YOU* FIT THE BILL PERFECTLY.

THANKS FOR THE COMPLIMENT.

I THINK...

'In The Year Of The Tsar 2668, Venice, the ancient metropolis of the waterways, remains timeless.'

'The highlight of the Venetian year is the Carnival of Masques, when the ghosts of the past are said to rise from the depths and the entire population dons traditional costume and distinctive masques.'

'The resulting anonymity is perhaps what inspires the Cadre Infernale to hold nightly Sabbats over the course of the Carnival.'

TOP SHOW, GIRL!

THE *HUNT'S* AS GOOD AS THE *KILL!*

'While daylight hours are safe from the Cadre's nefarious activities, visitors — especially women of good virtue — are advised to stay indoors once nightfall descends...

'...for ghosts are notoriously unsympathetic to the plight of the living.' THE IMPERIAL TIMES TRAVELOGUE.

HELP ME! PLEASE...

WHOA! WHAT'S THE RUSH?

PLEASE, SIR...

THEY'RE AFTER ME...

THAT LITTLE *VIXEN'S* DUE A *SOUND THRASHING,* LAD. SHE'S GOT TO LEARN HER PLACE, SHE'S JUST A *SERVING WENCH.* SHE SHOULD BE *GRATEFUL* FOR OUR *ATTENTIONS,* NOT THROW WINE OVER US.

ABSOLUTELY. I WON'T BE SATISFIED TIL SHE *WASHES OUT* THE STAIN WITH HER *TONGUE.*

ARE YOU TWO *OLD FARTS* FOR REAL?

TAKE A HIKE OR I'LL KICK YOUR *FLABBY ASSES* ALL OVER THE ISLAND.

INSOLENT SWINE!

WE'LL MAKE YOU OUR *WHIPPING BOY,* TEACH YOU TO *RESPECT YOUR ELDERS!*

THE NAME'S *DANTE, NIKOLAI DANTE.*

AND I DON'T RESPECT MY ELDERS, MY JUNIORS...

...OR ANYONE ELSE IN BETWEEN.

WHOOAARRGH!

YOU JUST HUMILIATED THE *CREAM* OF BRITISH ARISTOCRACY, THIEF.

BETTER START *BEGGING* FOR THEIR *MERCY* WHILE YOU STILL CAN.

I'M NOT A *BEGGING MAN* OR AN *EASY TARGET*, SO MAYBE *YOU* BETTER START FIRING WHILE YOU STILL CAN.

GETTING INTO *TROUBLE* SEEMS TO BE YOUR *PARTY-PIECE*, LITTLE BROTHER, THOUGH SOMETIMES I DO WISH YOU'D WAIT UNTIL YOU ACTUALLY *ARRIVED* AT THE PARTY.

LADY LULU, IF THE BOY'S WITH YOU, THEN CONSIDER HIS INDISCRETION *FORGOTTEN*.

PLEASE ALLOW ME THE HONOUR OF *PROSTRATING* MYSELF BEFORE YOU.

WHAT *AGAIN*, CAPTAIN? PEOPLE WILL TALK!

NIKOLAI, MAY I PRESENT *CAPTAIN EMMANUEL*, HEAD OF BRITISH MILITARY INTELLIGENCE. AND THE *ENGLISH CONTINGENT* OF THE *CADRE INFERNALE.*

THEY'RE OUR *COMPANIONS* FOR TONIGHT'S *FESTIVITIES.*

THAT'S WHAT I LIKE ABOUT YOU, *KOLYA*...

YOUR ABILITY TO *MAKE FRIENDS* AND INFLUENCE PEOPLE.

NIKOLAI DANTE

The original Hellfire Club met in 18th century London. Its inner circle consisted of such luminaries as Benjamin Franklin, the Earl of Sandwich, the Prince of Wales and at least one Prime Minister of England.

It became known as the Cadre Infernale when it grew into a Pan-European network of societies, though its principal devotions—the worship of sex and extravagant public decadence—remain unchanged.

Frankly, Dante, I'm surprised they haven't asked you to join before now...

the cadre infernale: pt.2

SCRIPT
ROBBIE MORRISON

ART
SIMON FRASER

COLOURS
GARY CALDWELL

LETTERS
ANNIE PARKHOUSE

YEAH, WELL, YOU KNOW HOW IT IS, CREST. SOME PEOPLE JUST DON'T RECOGNISE *CLASS.*

Don't drink, Dante!

That isn't wine, it's blood!

PTUUHH!

DON'T SPIT IT OUT, *DRINK DEEPLY.* YOU MIGHT BE SURPRISED HOW *QUICKLY* YOU DEVELOP A TASTE.

AND DON'T WORRY ABOUT *HYGIENE,* I MAKE SURE MY DONORS UNDER-GO THE MOST *RIGOROUS* HEALTH CHECKS.

Yeugh...

WHO?

CAMILLA LE FANU, CHIEF MAGISTRATE OF VENICE AND HIGH PRIESTESS OF THE CADRE INFERNALE.

COUNTESS ELIZABETH DE BATHORY DISCOVERED THE REJUVENATING EFFECTS OF THE BLOODBATH CENTURIES AGO. HER MISTAKE WAS USING MURDER TO ACQUIRE DONORS.

THE YOUNG WOMEN OF VENICE ARE MY MAIN SOURCE OF SUPPLY.

IN RETURN, I EXEMPT THEM FROM TAXES THROUGHOUT THEIR WORKING LIVES. YOU'D BE SURPRISED HOW MANY PEOPLE WOULD RATHER LOSE BLOOD THAN PAY TAX.

THE FANGS ARE JUST FOR SHOW, THEN?

MOSTLY, THOUGH I HAVE TORN OUT THE THROATS OF A FEW YOUNG FOOLS WHO DISPLEASED ME.

WELL, I ALWAYS AIM TO PLEASE.

AND WHAT DO YOU MAKE OF OUR LITTLE... GET-TOGETHER?

TO BE HONEST, I THINK THEY'RE ALL TRYING A LITTLE TOO HARD TO SHOCK.

THEY SHOULD RELAX, LOOSEN THEIR LEATHERS, BE A BIT MORE NATURAL.

YOU THINK US INSINCERE? PRETENTIOUS? UNNATURAL IN OUR DESIRES AND PREFERENCES? SIR, YOU FORCE ME TO INTRODUCE YOU TO SOMEONE WHO'LL PROVE OTHERWISE.

COUNTESS MAGDA HOLLO, THE DOMINATRIX OF DÜSSELDORF.

WHEN WAS THE LAST TIME YOU CRIED, BOY?

HUH?

MY QUESTION DISTURBS YOU? GOOD. DOMINATION'S THE NAME OF MY GAME.

YOU'VE SHOWN NOTHING BUT DISRESPECT AND CONTEMPT FOR US SINCE YOU ARRIVED. YOU NEED TO BE DISCIPLINED.

WHOA...

COME, BOY!

TIME TO PLAY!

DON'T DO ANYTHING I WOULDN'T DO, NIKOLAI...

LOOK, I'M *REALLY* NOT INTO THIS.

DON'T WORRY, I'M A *PROFESSIONAL*. I HARDLY EVER LEAVE *VISIBLE* SCARS.

YOU'VE *NO* CHOICE. YOU MIGHT ONLY BE A GUEST, BUT YOU STILL HAVE TO ABIDE BY OUR RULES.

I USUALLY TRY TO MAINTAIN A *DETACHED, PROFESSIONAL* AIR, BUT IT'S BEEN A WHILE SINCE I ENCOUNTERED A FOUNT OF MALE ARROGANCE AS *DEEP* AS YOURS.

BY TORQUEMADA'S *THUMBSCREWS*, I'M GOING TO ENJOY DRAINING IT!

STOP *SQUIRMING*, BOY, I HAVEN'T EVEN *TOUCHED* YOU YET.

I'LL START WITH *LIT MATCHES* BETWEEN YOUR TOES, GRADUATE TO A LITTLE *WHIP-ACTION*, THEN TAKE THE *BRANDING IRONS* TO YOUR *BUTTOCKS*. WHAT DO YOU SAY TO THAT?

PASS.

WHAT? HOW?!?

ESCAPOLOGY'S THE NAME OF *MY* GAME, COUNTESS.

DON'T WORRY, JUST HANG *LOOSE*, I'LL COME *BACK* FOR YOU.

IN A COUPLE OF DAYS OV SO...

"The Countess must have unnerved you, Dante. You're leaving a party in which women, wine and wild orgies are available in shameful abundance?

"SOMETIMES ALL THAT SEEMS KIND OF POINTLESS..."

'Cadre Infernale Sabbats often only end when casualties start appearing, as aged hearts, livers and arteries explode with the effort the festivities demand'— *THE IMPERIAL TIMES TRAVELOGUE.*

"THERE HE IS!

"TRYING TO ESCAPE!"

"DON'T RESIST, DANTE, OR I'LL PUT A BULLET IN YOU THE WAY I SHOULD'VE DONE WHEN WE FIRST MET.

"IS THIS SOME SORT OF INITIATION CEREMONY OR SOMETHING, 'CAUSE FRANKLY, I DON'T WANT TO JOIN A CLUB THAT WANTS ME AS A MEMBER.

"BY GOD, YOU'RE A COOL ONE."

"WE'VE HAD... INCIDENTS BEFORE, BUT NOTHING LIKE THIS. WHAT KIND OF MONSTER ARE YOU?

"LOOK, IF THIS IS ABOUT THE COUNTESS, I DIDN'T MEAN ANYTHING. IT WAS JUST A BIT OF FUN.

"FUN!?"

DIAVOLO...

I DON'T SEE HER LAUGHING.

YOU WERE THE *LAST* PERSON SEEN WITH HER, THIEF.

CARE TO *ELABORATE*?

JUDGING FROM HER WOUND, I'D SAY SHE... *DISPLEASED* SOMEONE.

REALLY? I'D SAY YOU DISCOVERED A *DARK SIDE* TO YOURSELF, A *SADISTIC* STREAK, AND *POOR MAGDA* PAID THE PRICE FOR AWAKENING IT.

TAKE HIM TO THE DUNGEONS— OUR TORTURERS'LL *CUT* THE TRUTH OUT OF HIM.

NO!

LULU!

TORTURE'S *TOO GOOD* FOR MY LITTLE BROTHER...

HE DESERVES *FAR WORSE* THAN THAT.

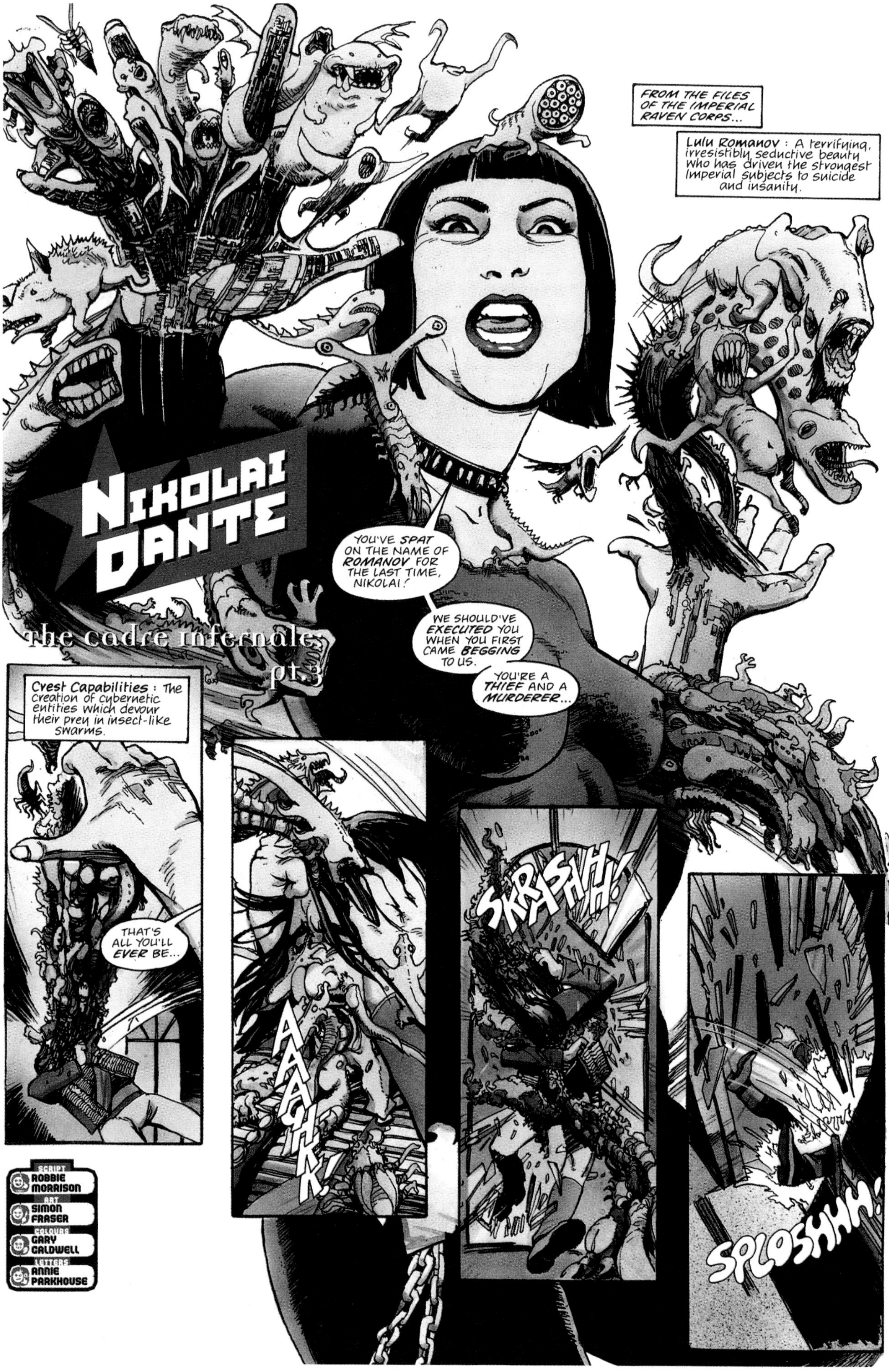
FROM THE FILES OF THE IMPERIAL RAVEN CORPS...
Lulu Romanov : A terrifying, irresistibly seductive beauty who has driven the strongest Imperial subjects to suicide and insanity.
NIKOLAI DANTE
the cadre infernale: pt.3
YOU'VE SPAT ON THE NAME OF ROMANOV FOR THE LAST TIME, NIKOLAI!
WE SHOULD'VE EXECUTED YOU WHEN YOU FIRST CAME BEGGING TO US.
YOU'RE A THIEF AND A MURDERER...
Crest Capabilities : The creation of cybernetic entities which devour their prey in insect-like swarms.
THAT'S ALL YOU'LL EVER BE...
AAAGHHK!
SKRASHHH!
SPLOSHHH!
SCRIPT ROBBIE MORRISON
ART SIMON FRASER
COLOURS GARY CALDWELL
LETTERS ANNIE PARKHOUSE

LAUNCH MY VAPORETTO FLEET. TELL THEM TO DREDGE FOR DANTE'S BODY.

TELL THEM NOT TO BOTHER.

THEY WON'T FIND ANYTHING.

'MY CYBER-SWARM ARE *HUNGRY* LITTLE DEVILS!'

I'M AFRAID YOU'LL HAVE TO EXCUSE ME.

KILLING ONE OF MY RELATIVES—EVEN IF HE WAS ONLY MY *FATHER'S BASTARD*—IS SOMETHING EVEN I CAN'T TAKE LIGHTLY.

OF COURSE, LULU, YOUR LOYALTY TO THE CADRE IS TO BE COMMENDED.

'It was a night unparalleled in the long, dark history of the Cadre Infernale.

'Magda Hollo, the Dominatrix from Dusseldorf, had been murdered, and the prime suspect, Nikolai Dante, ruthlessly executed by his own sister...

'... or so it seemed. Far worse was still to come.'— *INFERNAL MACHINATIONS : A HISTORY OF THE CADRE INFERNALE*, BY BARGO PARTRIDGE.

REALLY, NIKOLAI...

HUHH!?

I THOUGHT YOU'D HAVE BEEN MORE *REFRESHED* AFTER YOUR MOONLIGHT DIP.

BACK OFF, LULU! I DIDN'T KILL HER!

OF COURSE YOU DIDN'T. I KNOW THAT.

AND EVEN IF YOU HAD, I'D STAND BY *YOU* THE WAY I'D EXPECT YOU TO STAND BY *ME*. WE ARE *FAMILY*, AFTER ALL.

FAMILY?

YOU TRIED TO *KILL* ME!

NONSENSE.

IF I HAD WANTED YOU DEAD, YOUR SKELETON WOULD BE *PICKED CLEAN* AND RESTING AT THE BOTTOM OF THE *LAGOON*.

I JUST THOUGHT YOU MIGHT PREFER BEING *FREE* THAN BEING UNDER THE *TORTURER'S KNIFE* CONFESSING TO A CRIME YOU *DIDN'T* COMMIT.

NO. BUT *I* LEFT HER THERE, LULU. *ALONE*. AND SOMEBODY *BUTCHERED* HER.

WHAT*EVER* SHE WAS, SHE *DIDN'T* DESERVE THAT.

EVERYBODY THINKS I'M DEAD NOW— THAT SHOULD MAKE IT EASIER TO TRACK DOWN THE REAL KILLER.

OR PERHAPS GET YOURSELF *KILLED AGAIN*.

MAGDA HOLLO HAD *MANY* ENEMIES IN THE CADRE INFERNALE— SHE WAS EVEN LOBBYING SUPPORT TO *REPLACE* MAGISTRATE LE FANU AS HIGH PRIESTESS.

YOU'RE TRYING TO TELL ME IT COULD BE *ANY ONE* OF THEM?

OR *MORE* THAN ONE. *CONSPIRACIES* ARE COMMON AMONGST SECRET SOCIETIES.

STILL, IF YOU INSIST UPON PLAYING THE *AMATEUR DETECTIVE*...

'...WE BETTER RETURN YOU TO THE *SCENE* OF THE *CRIME*!'

SCAN FOR HIDDEN *SURVEILLANCE* EQUIPMENT, CREST.

THE PLEASURE CHAMBERS ARE SUPPOSED TO BE COMPLETELY PRIVATE, BUT I *DOUBT* THE HIGH PRIESTESS OF THE CADRE INFERNALE IS A WOMAN OF HER WORD.

Nano-Camera.

Concealed in the statue before you.

SUBTLE.

Tracing the signal...

It's linked to an underground surveillance system— adjacent to the palace dungeons.

CREST, HOW COME EVERY *PATH* I CHOOSE IN LIFE SEEMS TO BE A SHORTCUT TO A *DUNGEON* SOMEWHERE OR OTHER?

Fate?

DIAVOLO!

LOOKS LIKE WE JUST BROKE INTO THE CADRE INFERNALE'S *BLOOD BANK.*

Their life-signs are weak, but stable.

Le Fanu's milking them like cattle, keeping them barely alive and bleeding the nutrients she uses to maintain her youth from their bodies.

ACCESS THE SPY CAMERA AND FAST-FORWARD THE LAST TWO HOURS FOOTAGE— IT'S POSSIBLE THE KILLER MIGHT'VE BEEN *CAUGHT* ON FILM.

LE FANU!

Over-riding system controls.

RECORD THE FOOTAGE, CREST, WE CAN USE IT AS *EVIDENCE*.

AND START WORKING OUT SOME WAY TO *FREE* THESE WOMEN.

Dante, you're wanted for murder, and you're currently a **very** easy target in the **real** murderer's chamber of horrors. Escape is the best course of action...

SOMEONE'S *ALREADY* BEEN KILLED TONIGHT BECAUSE OF ME.

I'M *DAMNED* IF I'M GOING TO WATCH ANYONE ELSE DIE...

YOU'RE *DAMNED* ALREADY, BOY!

OOFF!

HHARK!

'The shock which greeted the news that Camilla Le Fanu had murdered Magda Hollo and tried to blame Nikolai Dante for the crime is astonishing in itself.'

'This, after all, was a woman who affected the air of a Gothic Vampire, bathed in blood to maintain her beauty...

NIKOLAI DANTE

the cadre infernale: pt.4

'...and was rumoured to have torn out the throats of seven lovers who had failed to satisfy her.'—'INFERNAL MACHINATIONS: A HISTORY OF THE CADRE INFERNALE' BY BARGO PARTRIDGE.

Dante! She's going for the jugular...

TELL ME SOMETHING I *DON'T* KNOW, CREST...

HOW DO I *TASTE?*

PRETTY GOOD?

FAINTLY ALCOHOLIC, ACTUALLY.

YOU HAVE A DRINK PROBLEM?

ONLY WHEN WOMEN LIKE *YOU* DRIVE ME TO IT.

SCRIPT
ROBBIE MORRISON

ART
SIMON FRASER

COLOURS
GARY CALDWELL

LETTERS
ANNIE PARKHOUSE

Don't goad her any further, Dante, she's too dangerous.

The **vampiric** manner in which she preys upon her victims also enhances her physical capabilities.

I THOUGHT YOU SAID THE YOUNG WOMEN OF VENICE *HAPPILY* DONATED THEIR BLOOD TO YOU IN RETURN FOR *TAX EXEMTIONS.*

ONLY THE *WORKING* POPULATION.

NONE OF *THESE* DONORS HAVE JOBS.

SUCKING THE LIFE OUT OF THEM'S A PRETTY EXTREME POLICY FOR DEALING WITH UNEMPLOYMENT.

IT KEEPS THEM OFF THE STREETS!

WHY'D YOU KILL THE *DOMINATRIX?*

BECAUSE SHE WANTED TO *REPLACE* YOU AS HIGH PRIESTESS?

YOU KILLED HER, BOY.

THE ONLY PERSON TRYING TO OUST ME FROM THE CADRE IS *YOUR SISTER.* I'VE KNOWN MAGDA SINCE FINISHING SCHOOL, SHE WAS MY *CLOSEST* FRIEND.

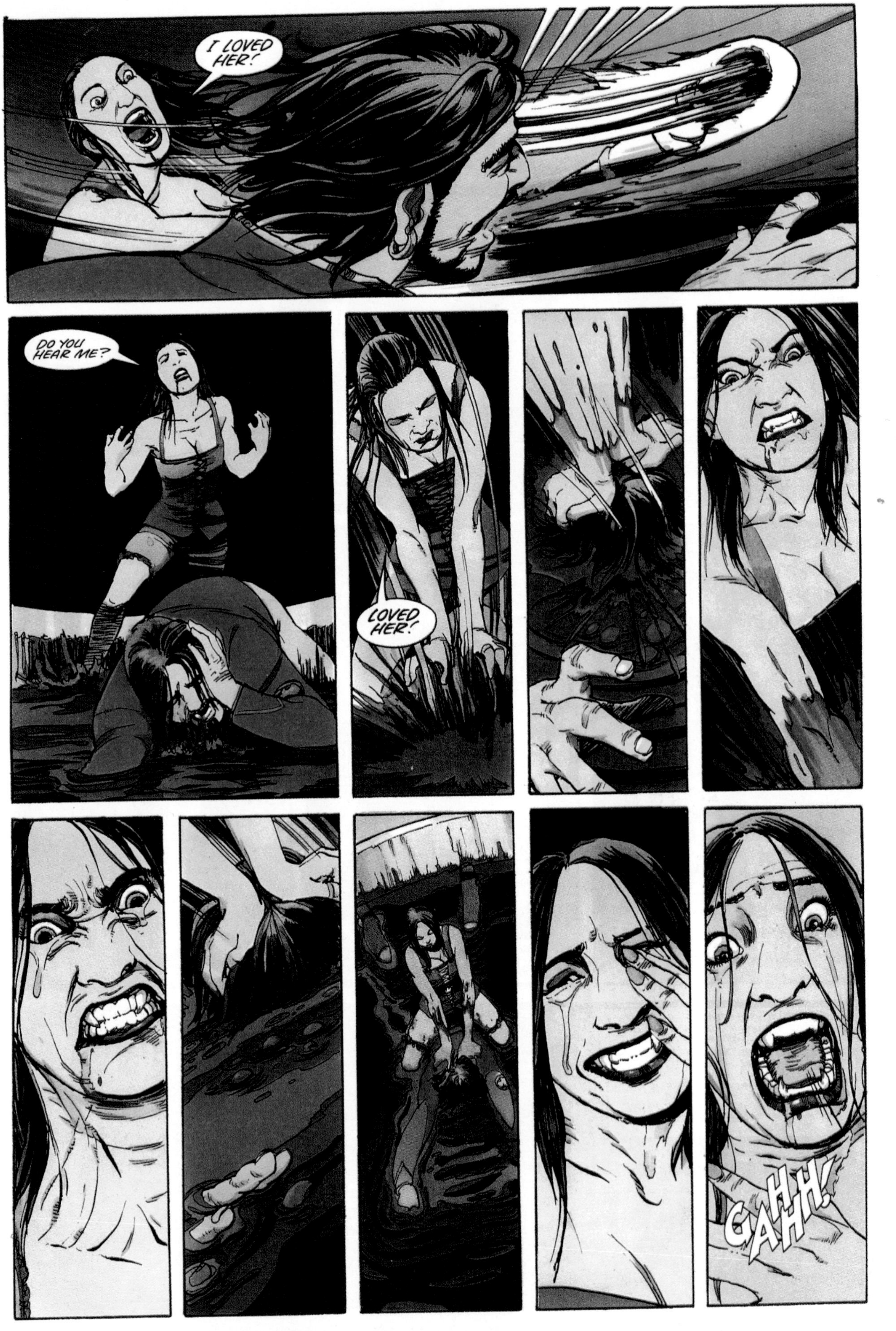
I LOVED HER!
DO YOU HEAR ME?
LOVED HER!
GAHHH!

HHHGGGLLLKK!

MAGNIFIQUE!

HURRAH!

Huh?

BRAVO!

GOOD SHOW, NIKOLAI.

WHILE YOU CONFRONTED CAMILLA, I SHOWED THE REST OF THE COUNCIL THE VID-EVIDENCE WE UNCOVERED— PROVING TO THEM BEYOND DOUBT THAT *SHE* WAS THE KILLER.

WHAT?

HOW DID *YOU* KNOW ABOUT THE...?

SHUSH, LITTLE BROTHER.

BEST WE TALK LATER.

LADIES AND GENTLEMEN OF THE COUNCIL, IN LIGHT OF RECENT CIRCUMSTANCES, I PROPOSE WE ELECT *LULU ROMANOV* AS *HIGH PRIESTESS* FORTHWITH.

'Lulu Romanov was named High Priestess of the Cadre Infernale on the final day of the Carnival of Masques.'

'The event was soured only by Nikolai Dante's refusal to accept the honorary life membership the Cadre wished to bestow upon him.' — 'INFERNAL MACHINATIONS: A HISTORY OF THE CADRE INFERNALE,' BY BARGO PARTRIDGE.

CONGRATULATIONS, LULU, YOU'VE BEEN CROWNED *QUEEN* OF A BUNCH OF ARISTOCRATIC OLD *PERVERTS.*

MAYBE, BUT PERVERTS WHO NEVERTHELESS HOLD POSITIONS OF GREAT *POWER* AND *INFLUENCE* THROUGHOUT THE EMPIRE...

AND WHO NOW OWE ALLEGIANCE TO *ME.*

YEAH. *SOME WORLD* WE'VE BUILT OURSELVES.

YOU'RE NOT *IMPRESSED?*

I'M *IMPRESSED* WITH *YOU,* LULU, THE WAY YOU *USED* ME.

JUST WISH I KNEW HOW YOU DID IT.

IT SEEMS I UNDERESTIMATED YOUR POWERS OF *DEDUCTION,* NIKOLAI — PERHAPS YOU SHOULD WEAR A *DEERSTALKER,* START SMOKING A *PIPE.*

HAVE YOU *RECOVERED* FROM BEING INTRODUCED TO MY *SWARM* YESTERDAY?

I ONCE SAW THEM DEVOUR THE FLESH OF AN *ENTIRE* REGIMENT IN UNDER TWO MINUTES, BUT THEY'RE ALSO USEFUL FOR *ESPIONAGE* PURPOSES.

AS *BUGS* FOR SPYING ON ENEMIES, OR AS WEAPONS OF *INFORMATION WARFARE.*

THEY CAN *INFILTRATE* SURVEILLANCE SYSTEMS, *ALTERING* RECORDED IMAGES, OR *CREATING* NEW ONES.

EVERYONE SAW WHAT I *WANTED* THEM TO SEE.

AMAZING WHAT YOU CAN DO WITH *EFFECTS* THESE DAYS.

I'M *GLAD* YOU'RE IMPRESSED, KOLYA. YOU *SHOULD* BE. AFTER ALL, I PROVED *TRUE* TO MY WORD.

I PROMISED YOU AN *UNFORGETTABLE* EVENING OF ENTERTAINMENT.

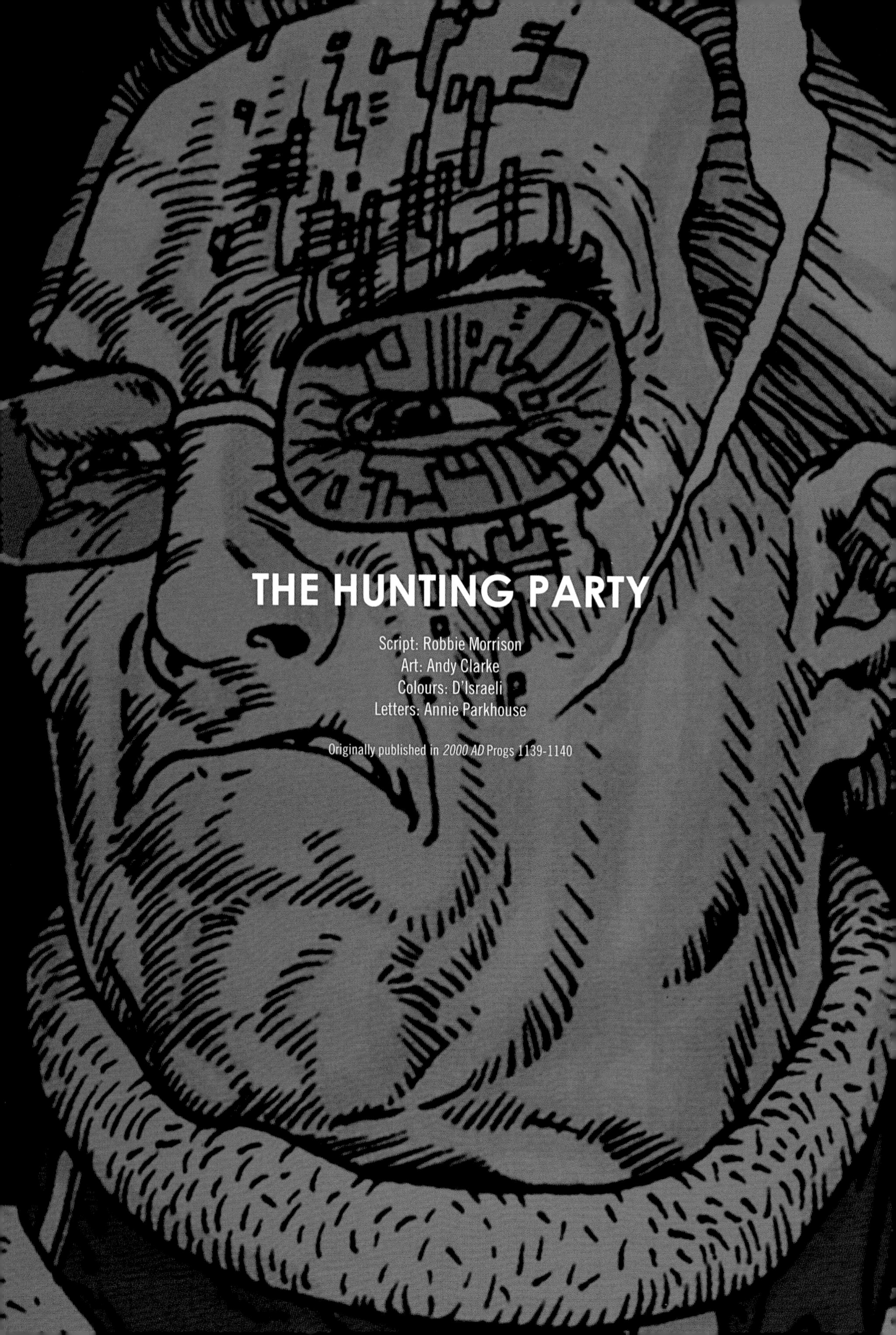

THE HUNTING PARTY

Script: Robbie Morrison
Art: Andy Clarke
Colours: D'Israeli
Letters: Annie Parkhouse

Originally published in *2000 AD* Progs 1139-1140

DMITRI

LULU

VIKTOR

ANDREAS

NIKOLAI DANTE

JOCASTA

KONSTANTIN

NASTASIA

ARKADY

SCRIPT
ROBBIE MORRISON
ART
ANDY CLARKE
COLOURS
D'ISRAELI
LETTERS
ANNIE PARKHOUSE

THE YEAR OF THE TSAR 2668.

THE STALKING GROUNDS OF THE ROMANOV DYNASTY.

PTT-CHOW!

SPAK

YOU MISSED, BOY.

YEAH.

SO I DID.

'It is a time-honoured tradition in Russian literature for aristocratic Hunting Parties to be portrayed as a microcosm of society, a metaphor for the cruel, predatory nature of humanity.'

'The annual hunt of the Family Romanov, however, is far more complex and disturbing, for it takes place near the Winter Palace, a tundra populated by some of the deadliest predators the Empire has to offer.'

'It is an environment in which the hunter can easily become the hunted, and is often credited with creating the ruthlessness of spirit and killer instincts which characterise the Romanovs.'
— *DYNASTY, BY MAXIM TURGENEV.*

WHO'S LEADING THE HUNT?

WHY, I DO BELIEVE I AM, *FATHER*. I'VE TERMINATED TWELVE TARGETS SO FAR—FIVE WITHOUT RECOURSE TO MY WEAPONS CREST.

OH, GET A LIFE *KONSTANTIN*. WE *LET* YOU WIN BECAUSE YOU'RE SUCH A *PAIN* TO LIVE WITH WHEN YOU LOSE.

THE REST OF US ARE JUST CULTURED ENOUGH TO APPRECIATE *SUBTLER* FORMS OF HUNTING. *INTELLIGENT PREY*, THAT'S THE CHALLENGE.

LULU'S RIGHT. GIVE A FOOL A BIG ENOUGH GUN AND HE'S SURE TO KILL SOMETHING. I PREFER TO *BREAK* MY PREY, *TAME* THEM LIKE THIS *LUCKY* BEAST.

THOUGH I AM CONSIDERING *SKINNING* HIM ALIVE TO MAKE A NEW OUTFIT FOR THE *SAVE-THE-WILDLIFE-FUND CHARITY BALL* NEXT WEEK.

WE'VE *ALL* RAISED OUR TARGET STATISTICS SINCE LAST YEAR.

I'VE PERSONALLY BAGGED TWO CASES OF *CHAMPAGNE*, A *BATHTUB* OF *BELUGA CAVIAR* AND THREE OF THE *SERVING WENCHES* BACK AT THE LODGE.

UH, SORRY, MOTHER.

I KNOW I PROMISED TO *BEHAVE*, BUT...

ANDREAS, IF YOU WISH TO *SQUANDER* YOUR LIFE AND FORTUNE *GAMBLING*, *CAROUSING* AND *CONTESTING PATERNITY SUITS*, THAT'S *YOUR* BUSINESS.

I NO LONGER *CARE*, YOU'RE THE *ONLY* THING IN THIS LIFE I'VE *EVER* GIVEN UP ON.

AND WHAT ABOUT YOU, VIKTOR?

BURRPP!

ON SECOND THOUGHTS, VIKTOR, I *REALLY* DON'T WANT TO KNOW WHAT YOU DO WITH YOUR KILLS.

EVEN *YOUNG* ARKADY'S BUILT HIMSELF A *RESPECTABLE* SCORE.

YEAH!

AND I'D'VE *OUTKILLED* YOU ALL IF *SOMEONE* HADN'T STOLEN MY WEAPONS CREST!

NIKOLAI'S THE ONLY ONE WHO'S YET TO RECORD A KILL. *IRONIC*—THE *WORST SHOT* AMONGST US HAS GOT THE *BEST FIREARM*.

HE'S *SAVED* MORE BEASTS THAN WE'VE KILLED—ALERTED THEM TO OUR PRESENCE WITH ALL HIS MISSED SHOTS AND BLUNDERING AROUND.

MAYBE I JUST DIDN'T HAVE A TARGET AS BIG AS YOUR MOUTH!

THIS ISN'T A *GAME*, BOY!

THE HUNT IS ONE OF OUR FAMILY'S OLDEST, MOST RESPECTED TRADITIONS, AND *YOUR* CONDUCT IS *SEVERELY UNBECOMING* AN ARISTOCRAT OF THE ROMANOV--

WOOAARGH!

COOL DOWN, KONSTANTIN. THE BOY'S ONLY TRYING TO INJECT A BIT OF FUN INTO WHAT COULD OTHERWISE BE DESCRIBED AS A COLD DAY IN HELL.

FUN, BIG BROTHER. JOCULARITY. DROLLERY. AMUSEMENT.

YOU REMEMBER, DON'T YOU?

YOU'VE BEEN SPENDING TOO MUCH TIME WITH DANTE.

DISCIPLINE IS VITAL, WE'RE PREPARING FOR *WAR*, WE HAVE TO MAINTAIN OUR KILLER EDGE.

HEY!

THE FAMILY THAT *PLAYS* TOGETHER *SLAYS* TOGETHER.

WHOOO!

WHO WOULD BELIEVE IT? THE FAMILY ROMANOV, THE MOST FEARED KILLERS IN THE EMPIRE, *PLAYING* LIKE THE CHILDREN THEY *NEVER* GOT A CHANCE TO BE.

THEY'VE STILL GOT SOMETHING OF *ME* IN THEM, *DMITRI*. YOU HAVEN'T BRED IT OUT OF THEM YET.

ENJOY IT WHILE YOU CAN, *JOCASTA*, IT WON'T LAST LONG, IT'S JUST A MATTER OF TIME.

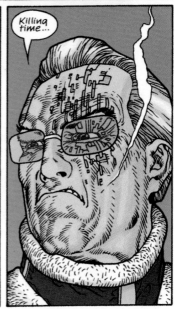

Killing time...

'When darkness falls, the Family Romanov retire to one of their many luxurious hunting lodges, where they warm themselves in the steam rooms, savour the finest foods and wines...

...and plan the following day's hunt with the meticulousness of a paranoid dictator planning a purge.' — 'DYNASTY', BY MAXIM TURGENEV.

I CAN'T PREDICT EXACTLY *WHEN*, BUT YOUR TARGET WILL LEAVE THE HUNTING PARTY TOMORROW, SO BE PREPARED TO STRIKE AT ANY TIME.

CAN'T SPEAK FOR OUR *BARBARIC COMPADRE*...

BUT ME AND SNAKE ARE THE BEST *GUNSLINGERS* MONEY CAN BUY.

WE WERE *BORN* READY, TO BE SURE.

FROM THE FILES OF THE IMPERIAL RAVEN CORPS...

Snake Lonnegan and Raoul Duke: Self-styled urban mercenaries. Never seen out of each other's company. No Tsarist affiliations.

Skua Khan : Former High Ruler of the Mongol Horde, turned assassin-for-hire to raise funds to stage a coup and reclaim his throne.

KILL ORDERS ARE USUALLY PLACED THROUGH THE IMPERIAL NET.

IT'S *HIGHLY IRREGULAR* FOR KILLER AND CLIENT TO EVER ACTUALLY MEET.

I *WANT* YOU TO KNOW WHO I AM.

KNOWING THAT MEANS YOU ALSO KNOW WHAT I'LL *DO* TO YOU IF YOU FAIL ME...

Wait till they're in range. Standard weaponry only. No Weapons Crests.

Give the beasts a sporting chance.

AAGOOO

BLAM BLAMM TOOM TOOM TOOM TOOM TOOM TOOM

Sporting chance.

IN ANCIENT TIMES, NIKOLAI, 'WOLF'S HEAD' WAS A NAME GIVEN TO THIEVES, BRIGANDS AND OUTLAWS.

PERHAPS THAT'S WHY YOU DIDN'T FIRE. PERHAPS YOU FEEL AN AFFINITY WITH THE BEASTS.

DON'T WORRY, THOUGH, WE'LL SOON CURE YOU OF ANY DISREPUTABLE QUALITIES.

LUCKY ME.

FATHER! WE MISSED ONE!

GET AFTER IT! EVERYONE! DON'T LET IT ESCAPE!

HEY, WHOA! IT'S JUST A CUB!

IT'S THE *PRINCIPLE*, BOY! NEVER LEAVE *ANYONE* ALIVE DURING WARFARE, EVEN IF THEY APPEAR TO POSE NO THREAT.

GENOCIDE MAY NOT BE *EASY* TO STOMACH, BUT IT SAVES YOU HAVING TO *WATCH* YOUR BACK.

BOJEMOI, YOU'RE ACTING LIKE IT WAS THE *TSAR* HIMSELF.

YOU'RE HARD TO STOMACH, DMITRI.

I'VE HAD MY FILL OF THIS BLOODTHIRSTY *FARCE*, AND--

AND YOU'RE GOING TO RETURN TO THE WINTER PALACE.

YOU'RE A CREATURE OF *HABIT*, JOCASTA.

ALLOW *ME* TO ESCORT YOU, *MOTHER*.

NO. *ME*. WE CAN HAVE A LOVELY *MOTHER/DAUGHTER* CHAT.

NIKOLAI...

I'D BE HONOURED IF *YOU'D* CHAPERONE ME BACK TO THE PALACE.

MY PLEASURE, MA'AM.

YOUR *HEART* DOESN'T SEEM TO BE IN THE HUNT, NIKOLAI.

SOMETHING TELLS ME YOU COULD *EASILY* HAVE MADE THE SHOTS YOU MISSED.

YEAH, WELL TERRORISING INNOCENT WOODLAND ANIMALS ISN'T EXACTLY MY IDEA OF *FUN*.

I'VE KILLED *MORE* THAN I EVER THOUGHT MYSELF *CAPABLE* OF—MORE THAN I EVER *WANTED* TO BE CAPABLE OF—SINCE I BECAME A ROMANOV.

BUT NEVER *ANYBODY* OR *ANYTHING* THAT DIDN'T GIVE ME *MORE* THAN ENOUGH REASON TO.

I SHOULD *HATE* YOU FOR WHAT YOU ARE, NIKOLAI—*DMITRI'S BASTARD SON*—BUT YOU HAVE NO IDEA HOW MUCH I'D LIKE TO HEAR MY OWN CHILDREN SPEAK LIKE THAT.

WATCHING HER CHILDREN INDULGE IN WHOLESALE *SLAUGHTER* IS SOMETHING *NO* MOTHER SHOULD SEE.

NO OFFENCE, MA'AM BUT MAYBE YOU SHOULD *VISIT* MORE OFTEN. YOU SAW THEM BACK THERE, THEY *MISS* YOU.

I *KNOW* WHAT THAT'S LIKE—MY MOTHER ABANDONED ME WHEN I WAS YOUNG.

I USED TO THINK ABANDONING THEM WOULD BE AN ACT OF *KINDNESS*.

GIVING BIRTH TO THEM WAS POSSIBLY THE *CRUELEST* THING I'VE EVER DONE.

I'M AS *RESPONSIBLE* AS MY BROTHER FOR TURNING THEM INTO THE *MONSTERS* THEY ARE...

YOUR BROTHER?

MY BROTHER.

YOUR FATHER.

DMITRI?

DMITRI'S YOUR...?

YES CHILD.

WHAT BETTER WAY TO MAINTAIN THE *PURITY* OF THE *ROMANOV BLOODLINE?*

DIAVOLO! I THINK I'M GOING TO BE *SICK...*

MAYBE *NOW* YOU UNDERSTAND WHY WE STAY APART.

THESE DAYS, I REALLY DO BELIEVE DMITRI WOULD DO ALMOST *ANYTHING* TO *RID* HIMSELF OF ME.

EEEEEEARGH!

BET HE NEVER SAW *THAT* COMING.

WIT, WISDOM AND *WONDROUS GUNPLAY,* COMPADRE. THAT'S WHAT I LIKE ABOUT YOU.

YOU'RE THE *OSCAR WILDE* OF THE WARRIOR SET.

HEY, D'YOU THINK THIS CRASH *ALONE* MIGHT HAVE *KILLED* THEM? THAT'D BE AN *ORIGINAL* LINE FOR OUR *ADVERTISING.*

YEAH... 'THE SINISTER SNAKE AND THE DANGEROUS DUKE— SO SHARP THEY DON'T EVEN NEED *BULLETS.*'

Our assailants are advancing upon us, Dante.

I'd advise *evasive action*— their best strategy would be to shoot our vehicles' fuel tanks and cause an explosion.

OK, CREST.

WE'RE GOING TO HAVE TO RUN A *GAUNTLET* TO REACH COVER, MA'AM. YOU GO *FIRST,* I'LL BRING UP THE *REAR.*

NOW!

REALLY:... THIS IS MOST *UNSEEMLY* FOR A WOMAN OF *MY* YEARS...

WE GOT A COUPLE OF *LIVE ONES,* SNAKE!

SHOOT YOUR LOAD!

THERE IT IS! FIRE!

BLAM BLAM BLAM

NIKOLAI DANTE

THE HUNTING PARTY PT. 2

'Over the years, a privileged few influential individuals have been invited to attend the annual hunt of the Romanov Dynasty.'

'The even-more-privileged few who survived the experience testify that the Romanovs pursue their prey with an almost psychotic zeal!'

SPAK SPAK SPAK SPAK

'Popular legend has it that during their hunting trips— and, by inference, in every other walk of life—nothing escapes the Romanovs...'

'...man or beast'— 'DYNASTY', BY MAXIM TURGENEV.

KEEP GOING, MA'AM!

HEAD FOR THE TREES AND DON'T LOOK BACK!

VIP

VISS

SCRIPT
ROBBIE MORRISON

ART
ANDY CLARKE

COLOURS
D'ISRAELI

LETTERS
ANNIE PARKHOUSE

PT-CHOW!

SKA-
BOOMM!

CARAMBA! FOR A MOMENT THERE, I THOUGHT *ROAST DUKE* WAS ON THE MENU.

HE SHOT OUT THE *FUEL TANKS.*

SURE, AND I TOLD YOU *WE* SHOULD'VE DONE THAT, BUT, NO, *YOU* HAD TO DO THE *BUTCH 'N' SUNDANCE CHARGE* AGAIN.

I'VE IDENTIFIED YOUR ATTACKERS FROM MY DATABANKS.

THE CAUCASIAN IS SNAKE LONNEGAN, HIS ACCOMPLICE *RAOUL DUKE.* TWO OF THE DEADLIEST KILLERS-FOR-HIRE IN THE ENTIRE EMPIRE.

ONLY THE *BEST* FOR ME, HUH?

TAR ☒
DT ☐

ZOOM+

IT'S *NOTHING* TO BE *FLATTERED* ABOUT, DANTE. THEY'VE CARRIED OUT SO MANY ASSASSINATIONS THAT THE AUTHORITIES WERE FORCED TO START A *SUPPORT CHARITY* FOR THE RELATIVES OF THEIR VICTIMS.

DUKE IS MARGINALLY MORE DANGEROUS— HIS CYBERVISION™ IMPLANTS ACT AS BOTH AN INFALLIBLE *TARGETING SYSTEM* AND DT-TV RECEIVERS.

SORRY ABOUT THIS, MA'AM.

YOU THINK THEY'RE AFTER *YOU?*

WHENEVER *GUN-SWORD-OR-AXE-WIELDING MANIACS* TURN UP WITH *MURDER* ON THEIR MINDS, IT'S A *SAFE BET* THEY'RE AFTER ME.

I TAKE IT YOU HAVE A LOT OF *ENEMIES,* THEN?

MA'AM, IF I HAVEN'T MADE *AT LEAST A DOZEN* ENEMIES BEFORE *BREAKFAST-TIME,* I FIGURE IT'S *A WASTED DAY.*

SUPERLATIVE!

I'M AN ADVOCATE OF THE PHILOSOPHY THAT A PERSON'S CHARACTER SHOULD BE JUDGED BY THE CALIBRE OF HIS, OR *HER,* ENEMIES.

WHO?

AS YOU'RE BOTH OF *ARISTOCRATIC BREEDING*, I WON'T INSIST UPON YOU *GENUFLECTING* IN MY *REGAL PRESENCE.*

I AM *SKUA-KHAN*, ONCE *BARBARIAN-KING* OF THE *MIGHTY MONGOL HORDE.*

YEAH? YOU DON'T SOUND VERY *BARBARIC.*

I PREFER TO THINK OF MYSELF AS A *NEO-BARBARIAN.*

A REPUTATION FOR *RAPE, PILLAGE* AND *MINDLESS SAVAGERY* DOES LITTLE TO PUT A NATION ON THE *POLITICAL* AND *CULTURAL MAP.*

WHEN I BECAME RULER OF MONGOLIA, I ENDEAVOURED TO EDUCATE THE POPULACE IN THE *NOBLER*, MORE *POLITICALLY CORRECT* ASPECTS OF OUR SOCIETY.

FEMINISM, *SEXUAL* AND *RACIAL EQUALITY*, *VEGETARIANISM...*

DID THEY *FALL* FOR IT?

SADLY, THE SCENARIO SEEMED *SOMEWHAT BEYOND* THE REACH OF THEIR INTELLECTUAL CAPACITY. THEY *EJECTED* ME FROM MY THRONE, *EXILED* ME FROM THE VERY LAND I WAS BORN TO RULE.

NO WONDER...

THEY PROBABLY FIGURED YOU SHOULD BE WEARING A *PINK FEATHER BOA* INSTEAD OF *ANIMAL-SKINS.*

YOU *SHORT-SIGHTED*, *PETTY-MINDED*, *INTELLECTUALLY-STUNTED IGNORAMUS!*

JUST BECAUSE I'M IN TOUCH WITH MY *FEMININE SIDE* DOESN'T MEAN MY *MASCULINITY* IS IN DOUBT!

WARRIORS OF THE MONGOL HORDE ARE FITTED WITH A *BERSERKER TRIGGER* WHICH UNLEASHES THE FULL POWERRR OF THE TERRRIFYING *BESTIALITY* THAT EXISTS AT THE HEARRRT OF MAN!

KLK

GGRRAAARR!!

FUOCO...

RR-UHHRRR!?

SHUPP

WHAM

HHKK!

PERSONALLY, I PREFER MEN TO BE *MEN* AND WOMEN TO BE *WOMEN*.

WE'RE ALL *HUMAN* AND ALL JUST AS *BAD* AS EACH OTHER, BUT AT LEAST THEN WE KNOW WHERE WE *STAND*.

NO ONE EVER ADMITTED IT, BUT *THE BATTLE OF THE SEXES* WAS NEVER ABOUT *EQUALITY*, IT WAS ABOUT *SUPERIORITY*.

BOTH SIDES WANTED TO *WIN*.

FOR ALL YOUR POLITICAL CORRECTNESS, YOU — LIKE *ALL* MALE SPECIES — RESORT TO *BRUTE STRENGTH* AND *AGGRESSION*, WHEN IT'S *FAR MORE* EFFECTIVE TO TURN YOUR OPPONENTS' STRENGTHS *AGAINST* THEM.

KRR-KRK-KRK!

WE, ON THE OTHER HAND, *CONFUSE* AND *INFURIATE*, OUTWIT AND MANIPULATE, MAKE SURE YOU *NEVER EVER* UNDERSTAND US.

THAT'S WHY *WOMEN* WILL ALWAYS BE *THE SUPERIOR SEX*.

CALL IT... THE FEMININE TOUCH.

KRAAAAN!

GOOD BOY, NIKOLAI! WELL DONE!

YOU DEFEATED HIM WHEN YOU WERE ONLY SEMI-CONSCIOUS. WHAT A *BRAVE WARRIOR* YOU ARE.

Uhhh... YEAH, RIGHT. BRAVE.

I THINK PERHAPS WE SHOULD GET MOVING, BEFORE WE BECOME *HUMAN TARGETS* AGAIN.

THAT'S IT, CHILD. ONE FOOT IN FRONT OF THE OTHER.

SURE AND THAT'S A *NASTY* WAY TO GO.

BARBARIC. BUT AT LEAST NOW WE DON'T HAVE TO WORRY 'BOUT THE COMPETITION.

SURE WOULD'VE BEEN A *SLUR* ON OUR REPUTATIONS IF WE'D BEEN BEATEN TO THE KILL BY A GUY IN *HAIRY UNDERPANTS.*

BOJEMOI, WHERE THE HELL ARE WE NOW?

THE ROMANOV NECROPOLIS. RESTING PLACE FOR GENERATIONS UPON GENERATIONS OF THE FAMILY ROMANOV.

CONGRATULATIONS, NIKOLAI, YOU'VE LED US TO OUR GRAVES.

SPAK

SPAK

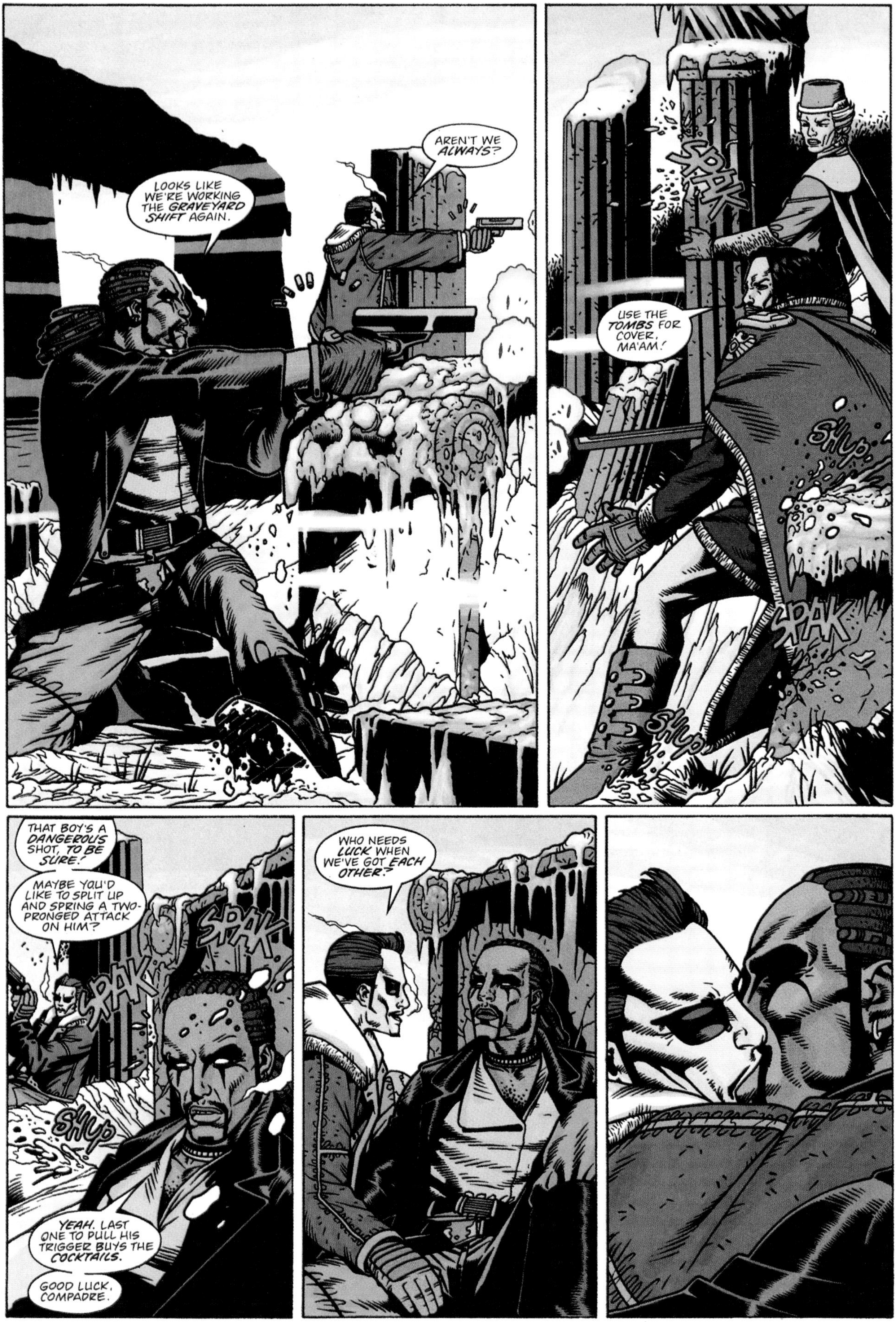

LOOKS LIKE WE'RE WORKING THE GRAVEYARD SHIFT AGAIN.
AREN'T WE ALWAYS?
SPAK
USE THE TOMBS FOR COVER, MA'AM!
SHUP
SPAK
SHUP
THAT BOY'S A DANGEROUS SHOT, TO BE SURE!
MAYBE YOU'D LIKE TO SPLIT UP AND SPRING A TWO-PRONGED ATTACK ON HIM?
SPAK
SPAK
SHUP
YEAH. LAST ONE TO PULL HIS TRIGGER BUYS THE COCKTAILS.
GOOD LUCK, COMPADRE.
WHO NEEDS LUCK WHEN WE'VE GOT EACH OTHER?

HEAD BACK INTO THE FOREST AND TRY TO REACH THE REST OF THE FAMILY.

I'LL HANG BACK AND HUNT THEM DOWN— OR *MORE LIKELY*, KNOWING MY *LUCK*, DRAW THEIR FIRE.

I'M TOO *TIRED*, NIKOLAI. YOU HAVE NO IDEA HOW TIRED OF IT ALL I AM.

AND YOU'RE TOO *YOUNG* TO DIE ALONE.

WITH RESPECT, MA'AM...

I'M NOT THE DYING TYPE.

FAMOUS LAST WORDS!

UNGHH!

QUIT REACHING FOR THE RIFLE— IT'S BAD ENOUGH THAT I'M GONNA SHOOT YOU IN THE *HEAD* WITHOUT BLOWING OFF YOUR *FINGERS* TOO.

Hack into his optical implants on my signal, Crest, and switch them from weapons-targeting to televisual reception.

NOW!

CHANNEL 55

CARAMBA! MARTIAN HARDCORE!

AND I DON'T EVEN SUBSCRIBE.

MARTIAN HARDCORE

AIN'T NO ALIEN ORGY GONNA PUT ME OFF MY AIM, COMPADRE!

SPAK

SHUP

HEY! WHOA! WHERE'S THE PICTURE GONE?

IT WAS JUST GETTING TO THE GOOD BIT...

ZZZK KZZZK

NO... THIS IS THE GOOD BIT.

UH-OH.

KA-CHOW!

AAAAGH-KK!!

MAN, AM I GLAD TO SEE YOU!

THAT WAS CLOSER THAN WE'VE COME IN A LONG WHILE.

HEY, COOL IT WITH THE INFECTIOUS AFFECTION. NOT WHILE WE'RE ON THE JOB.

I SAVED THE OLD DRAGON FOR YOU.

WON'T BE AS MUCH FUN AS SHOOTING THAT SPLINKY LITTLE BUGGER, BUT SURE AND IT WOULD BE SELFISH IF IT WAS ME WHO DID ALL THE KILLING.

PPT-CHPW!

Always knew if we were gonna go...we'd go together...

YOUR SHOT HIT MY WEAPONS CREST. THE BULLET WAS AUTOMATICALLY DEFLECTED BY CYBORGANIC SHIELDING.

I believe the operative phrase is 'OUCH'.

NOW, WHO HIRED YOU TO KILL ME?

YOU?

WE WEREN'T HIRED TO KILL YOU.

Who the hell are you anyway, man?

THE STALKING GROUNDS OF THE ROMANOV DYNASTY. THE VALLEY OF SOULS.

WE'VE GOT IT NOW. IT'LL NEVER MAKE THAT JUMP.

WE'LL MAKE IT A CLEAN KILL. THE BEAST GAVE GOOD SPORT, DESPITE ITS YOUTH.

WHO WISHES TO DO THE HONOURS?

PPTT-CHOW!

KRAK

WHO?!

THE CUB'S ESCAPING!

DANTE?

YOU MISSED, BOY.

NO.

YOU DID.

THE END

COVER GALLERY

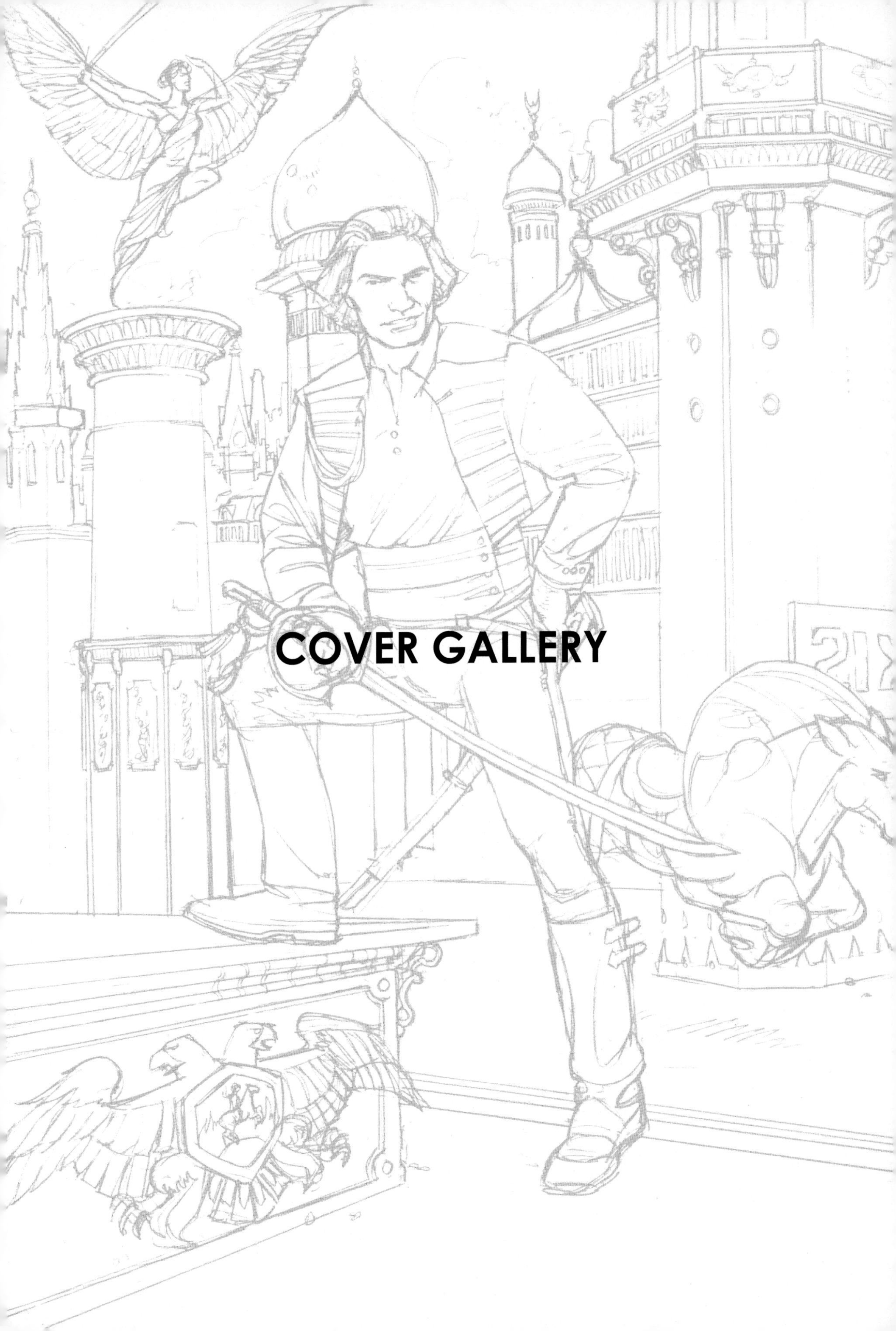

Nikolai Dante: Pin-up by **Simon Fraser**

Nikolai Dante: Pin-up by **Simon Fraser**

2000 AD Prog 1103: Cover by **Greg Staples**

2000 AD Prog 1110: Cover by **John Charles**

2000 AD Prog 1126: Cover by **Siku**

2000 AD Prog 1137: Cover by **Steve Cook**

2000 AD Prog 1116: Cover by **Simon Fraser**

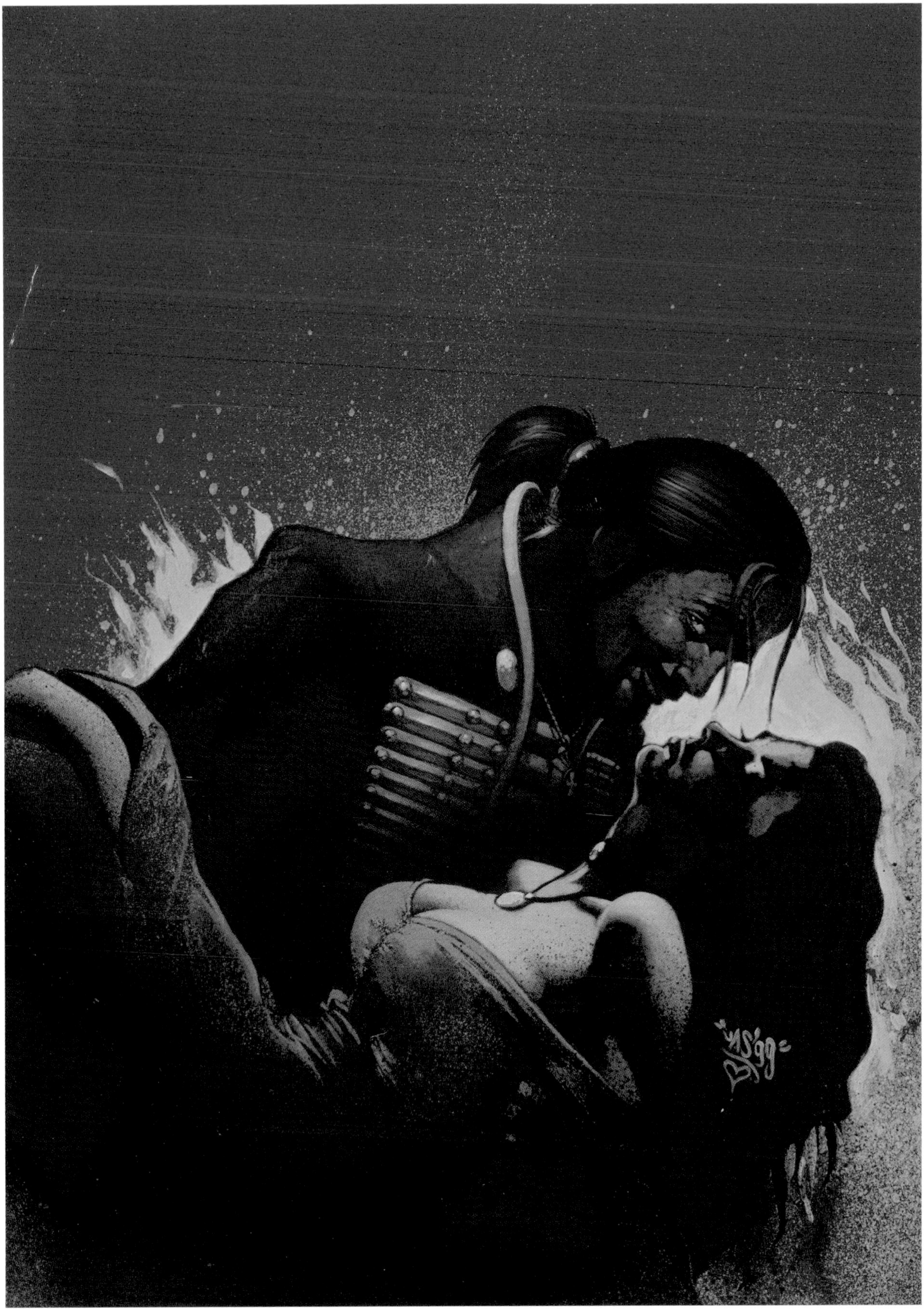

2000 AD Prog 1131: Cover by **Jason Brashill**

2000 AD Prog 1139: Cover by **Simon Fraser**

Nikolai Dante: The Great Game: Cover by **Simon Fraser**